A Charlie & Simm Mystery

SMOKE AND SECRETS

A.J. McCarthy

Black Rose Writing | Texas

ISBN: 978-1-68513-623-9
PUBLISHED BY BLACK ROSE WRITING
www.blackrosewriting.com

Printed in the United States of America
Suggested Retail Price (SRP) $21.95

Smoke and Secrets is printed in EB Garamond

*As a planet-friendly publisher, Black Rose Writing does its best to eliminate unnecessary waste to reduce paper usage and energy costs, while never compromising the reading experience. As a result, the final word count vs. page count may not meet common expectations.

PRAISE FOR
SMOKE AND SECRETS

"A dilapidated mansion full of secrets, a mysterious murder that hides multi-million dollar fraud; *Smoke and Secrets* taunts readers to solve the puzzle each step of the way."
–Timothy Gene Sojka, award-winning author of
Payback Jack, Politikill, and *Claws*

"...a suspenseful thriller worthy of the *Charlie & Simm* mystery legacy"
–Gail Ward Ormsted, bestselling author of
Katherine's Remarkable Roadtrip

"McCarthy creates a complex web of personalities, friendship, love, and intrigue that keeps readers guessing."
–Lena Gibson, award-winning author of the *Train Hoppers* series

"McCarthy's writing is vibrant, bringing the scenery to life and putting the reader in the middle of the action. The book moves at a perfect pace, with enough tension to keep the pages turning."
–Travis Tougaw, author of the *Marcotte & Collins* thriller series

"Those who have a nostalgia for classic mystery writing with a contemporary feel, this one is for you."
–Sandro Martini, author of *Ciao, Amore, Ciao*

"The plot is filled with twists, turns, and suspense. And the setting is super cool in a scary and mysterious way. Be prepared to read through the night, because you won't be able to put this book down."
–Karen Osborne, award-winning author of *True Grace*

In memory of Kelso, my inspiration for Harley.
Rest in peace, good boy.
And to Bosco, still a living legend.

SMOKE
AND
SECRETS

CHAPTER 1

A jolt of adrenaline shot through Charlie Butler as a stranger with piercing blue eyes and a cold, hard gaze entered the pub. He scanned the room with an unusual intensity, his eyes lingering on Charlie with a peculiar interest. A chill washed over her with a sense of déjà vu. This stranger wasn't a regular Friday night customer. This was something different. Something unexpected, perhaps dangerous.

Although busy, the evening began like most others, with no hint of an unexpected twist before the sun had set. Charlie weaved her way through the throng of people, avoiding elbows, feet, and swinging arms with practiced ease. She smiled at everyone, even the annoying drunks who thought she was fair game. She avoided their roaming hands while preserving her upbeat mood and not spilling a drop.

A sizeable crowd filled the pub. A sign of the season. As April nudged soggy March out of the way, the optimistic and warmth-loving Montreal residents inundated the downtown sidewalks. And that flood drove them back indoors for refreshments, either warm or cold.

Winter had struck hard this year. Bitter temperatures along with a greater than usual number of snowstorms battered the province of Quebec, and people welcomed with open arms the sunshine and dry, snow-free streets.

Charlie thrived on action, the type that involved full seats at the bar and the bustle of people, laughter, and cheerful voices. Whether friends reunited, girls had a night out, or guys cheered on favorite teams, it thrilled Charlie to be part of it.

Some action she could live without. This included murders, threats, chases, and anything involving physical harm. She and Simm had steered clear of those for several months, and Charlie was grateful for the break. They'd agreed upon a simple rule: if a case sounded dangerous, they'd refuse it, especially since a baby could soon be on the way.

"What's with the mysterious smile?"

Charlie glanced at Frank. "Caught me. Thinking about the baby."

Frank's eyes widened. "Are you...?"

"Not yet, but fingers crossed. I've waited so long to convince Simm to have a child. It needs to happen fast, before he changes his mind." She laughed. In truth, Charlie was certain her husband wouldn't go back on his word.

"I hope I'm one of the first you tell," Frank said.

Charlie covered his enormous hand with her much smaller one. "Of course. You're second on the list."

Their bond ran deep, forged in her early days as a pub owner, fresh out of university, and him, a bright-eyed student she'd taken a chance on hiring.

Charlie was the sole proprietor of Butler's Pub for several years before she retained Simm, a private investigator, to uncover the source of mysterious packages she'd received. That case led to them falling in love and getting married in a small civil ceremony, with Frank as their only witness.

Soon after, Simm left his private investigation business to partner with Charlie in the pub. As they expanded and acquired another bar close by, Frank joined them as an equal partner.

The trio had been together through thick and thin ever since. A lot of thick and thin. Mostly because, with Charlie's encouragement, Simm hadn't completely relinquished his past career. He'd investigated a few interesting cases, and Charlie, being her curious self, liked to ride shotgun.

Charlie smiled at a group of customers that Melissa, their hostess, ushered to a table. From her vantage point behind the counter, she allowed her gaze to roam the room. As it often did, a sense of pride bubbled in her chest. She'd preserved Jim O'Reilly's legacy, maintaining the Irish pub/sports bar style he'd created, although she'd changed the name from O'Reilly's to Butler's. The rich mahogany furnishings, the gleaming brass spigots lining the counter offering Guinness, Murphy's, and several domestic brands, the TVs mounted around the room in strategic spots. Very little had changed since Jim passed away and left the bar in Charlie's capable hands—hands he'd trained since she was in her mid-teens.

With most tables filled, only three seats remained at the counter. Frank worked at her side, pulling beer and mixing drinks. They made an odd-looking pair. Charlie, petite and slender with her long, brown hair pulled back into a ponytail, looked like a child beside Frank. He towered over her at six foot four, his ebony skin a sharp contrast to her fair Irish complexion. But his ready grin softened his intimidating, buff physique.

While Charlie mixed a gin and tonic, her gaze followed the stranger she'd spotted with an unfamiliar anxiety as he claimed one of the few barstools in front of her. His build rivaled Frank's. With broad shoulders, muscular arms revealed by his T-shirt, and a neck reminiscent of football players, he made an imposing sight.

Charlie handed a tray of drinks to a server before turning a guarded smile on the newcomer.

"Hi there. What can I get you?" Her gaze roamed over him, searching for the reason behind the effect he had on her.

His closely shaved hair hinted at a thick, perhaps undisciplined, mane underneath. A five o'clock shadow darkened his jawline, and those piercing blue eyes surveyed the line of bottles behind her with a mixture of curiosity and wariness.

That sharp gaze returned to hers, and a faint smile quirked one corner of his mouth. "Surprise me, Charlie."

CHAPTER 2

Charlie stifled a gasp. She'd worked in this pub for the last fourteen years, ever since she was sixteen. She may not remember the name of every customer, but their faces and their drink preferences were practically tattooed on the inside of her eyelids. Rarely did she forget one. But he stumped her.

Charlie narrowed her gaze and studied his face, up for the challenge. His eyes glimmered with amusement, his full lips suppressing a smile. The eyes meant something to her.

Like a smack on the side of her head, a memory flashed. Could it be? It wasn't possible, but...

"Noah?" The name floated on her breath, uncertain.

From the smile emerged a full-fledged grin, including white, even teeth. Charlie smothered her screech with her hands. Beside her, Frank stiffened and moved closer until his arm touched her shoulder.

Charlie laid a reassuring hand on her friend's forearm before she darted around the bar and launched herself at the burly stranger. The man's surprise at Charlie's enthusiastic welcome was only surpassed by Simm's, who materialized from the kitchen doorway to witness his wife in the arms of a strange, handsome man.

He approached them with a curious frown and cleared his throat. Charlie spun to face her husband.

"Look who's here. Do you believe it?" she said, breathless.

"I might if I knew him." Simm's thick, brown hair was mussed, probably from dealing with the plumbing problem in the kitchen. His chocolate brown eyes, usually warm, were red hot as he glowered at the stranger.

The man slid from the stool, standing taller than Simm's six foot three. Far from fat, his build was large and muscular. Her husband, far from skinny, was lean and strong. The newcomer reached out a hand to Simm as Charlie blurted, "It's Noah."

Simm's jaw dropped as he clasped the other man's hand. "You're kidding." He scrutinized Noah, much as his wife had. "It is!"

A smile broke out on Simm's face, and he pulled Noah in for a brief man hug. "What a surprise. Never thought I'd see you in downtown Montreal."

"Never thought I'd be here," Noah said in his low, rumbling voice.

Memories rushed through Charlie's mind of a cabin in the woods of Quebec's Gatineau area. Memories of suspicion, betrayal, and deep emotional pain. A man crushed by the loss of his wife and children. A man who'd locked himself away and lived in self-imposed torture.

Charlie often thought of Noah. And, like Simm, she never imagined him sitting in their pub in bustling Montreal. It was like finding a rhinoceros in a subway car.

A thought occurred to Charlie. "Where's Bosco?"

Noah waved his hand toward the door. "Outside. I hooked him on a pole."

Charlie's eyes widened. "Poor thing. You can't leave him there. Someone could take him."

Simm and Noah laughed in unison.

"He won't go anywhere without me," Noah said. "I promise."

"I'll get him. Harley'll be so happy." Charlie headed to the door, the two men trailing behind.

A small crowd had gathered, admiring the sleek, muscular, brown dog, who sat in a majestic pose, his eyes fixed on the pub entrance. Despite their fascination, no one drew closer than six feet to him, for obvious reasons.

He may have adopted a docile pose, but the Cane Corso mastiff outweighed more than a few of the observers. His massive head contained massive teeth. Even though he didn't display them, any idiot would take heed.

When he spotted Charlie, Noah, and Simm stepping out of the pub into the spring sunshine, Bosco's stubby tail began a rhythmic thump against the sidewalk.

"Bosco!" Charlie didn't rush at the dog. She gave him time to recognize her voice and her scent. The constant, happy movement of his hindquarters reassured her. So did Noah's presence at her side.

Once back inside, the crowd parted like the Red Sea to let Noah lead Bosco through on his leash. The man and his dog ascended the stairs behind Charlie and Simm to their home above the pub. Noah's expression revealed his surprise when his gaze swept the space. The airy apartment provided a sharp contrast to the low-lit, dark mahogany decor of the pub below. Instead of wooden chairs topped with black leather, the living area boasted plush white leather couches. Cream-colored cabinets lined the kitchen, and sunshine streamed through the south-facing windows.

Alerted by the visitors, a small, squat, beige blur emerged from the office. The pug skidded to a halt and froze upon spotting the much larger dog in his domain. Three excited yips from Harley and one booming bark from Bosco later, the two met midway and began the cycle of circling and sniffing before Harley led Bosco on an animated tour of the apartment.

"Nice set-up," Noah said as he took in their living quarters.

Charlie smiled. "Made it as homey as possible. Used to be rental units until Simm and I married. Converted them into one larger space. Two bedrooms, an office, and easy access to the pub downstairs. It works." She shrugged.

Charlie focused her attention on Noah. She couldn't believe this was the same man she'd met when she and Simm worked the case in Gatineau. A hermit with scraggly hair and a matted beard that touched his chest, his size and unkempt appearance at the time reminded Charlie of Hagrid from the Harry Potter movies. But those deep-set, piercing, blue eyes were unforgettable, as was his rough, gravelly voice. What a difference grooming and clothes made. Clad casually in a blue plaid shirt and clean jeans with a pair of hiking boots, Noah wasn't dressed to the nines, but he'd certainly turn women's heads, given his rugged handsomeness and strong, silent-type aura.

And here he was, on their couch on Drummond Street in downtown Montreal, hours and a lifetime away from a riverbank cabin in the woods. Rustic would be a generous description of Noah's home.

"Did you move to Montreal?" Charlie couldn't withhold her curiosity any longer.

A surprised laugh burst from him. "Can you picture me living here?"

Charlie grimaced. No, but she longed to discover the reason for his visit. Thankfully, he solved her dilemma.

"My sister-in-law, Sarah Heaton, lives in Westmount. I'm visiting her for a few days."

"Is she your...?" Charlie worried about triggering a sensitive memory. The tragedy that struck down Noah's wife and children led to his hermit's life. Now that he was inching out of his shell, Charlie didn't want to delve too deep and disturb that delicate migration.

"Yes, my wife's sister. She and Lyann were close. We kept in touch through the years."

"How long are you here for?" Simm asked.

Noah lowered his brows and leaned forward, resting his elbows on his knees, knitting his fingers together. Bosco and Harley chose that moment to reappear. The mastiff must have sensed distress in his master and laid his head on Noah's forearm. Noah released his hands and used them to massage the dog's ears, but his gaze turned inward.

"Something's wrong," Charlie said. It wasn't a question.

"I think so. No, I know so." He lifted his head and moved his gaze from Charlie to Simm. "I need your help."

CHAPTER 3

Over the next hour, Noah's story mesmerized them. Charlie and Simm were already aware of the tragedy that ripped his family from him years ago—a car accident involving a drunken driver. It seemed an unbearable weight for one person to carry. But apparently, the universe wasn't done dealing Noah a cruel hand.

"I had a brother, Ethan. He was two years younger than me." Noah gazed at his calloused hands as Charlie noted he spoke of his brother in the past tense. A chilling premonition crept up her spine.

Noah reached into his shirt pocket and pulled out a photograph, the edges softened with wear, a testament to the countless times he took it out and examined it. She reached for it and leaned toward her husband, offering him a view.

Noah and another man stood together; their arms slung around each other's shoulders. Identical grins stretched across their faces. Ethan was a couple of inches shorter than his brother and not as muscular, but he was lean and handsome, his hair just as dark and thick. A scruff of beard covered his jawline. Charlie guessed someone snapped the photo in happier days, before the terrible events in Noah's life.

"As kids, we were close," Noah said, a note of wistfulness seeping into his voice. "As adults, we grew apart, although we still cared for each other. That picture dates back about five years," he said, confirming Charlie's suspicions. "We didn't work hard enough to keep in touch. I guess we were too different and too busy."

"Different how?" Simm asked.

Noah sighed, a deep rumble that seemed to come from his core. "I wanted a stable life, a career, a family. Ethan was the wild child. He traveled, explored the world, moved from job to job, woman to woman. Stability didn't exist in his dictionary." A crooked grin appeared on his face. "At times, I felt envious, maybe downright jealous. Ethan was a charmer, carefree, living the life. But that wasn't my style. I was behind the door when they handed out the charm gene."

Charlie smiled. Noah may not be a lively charmer, but he possessed an appeal that could draw people like a magnet if he let them.

"Anyway, like I said, we lost track of each other, especially after... well, you know."

Charlie knew the rest—after he shut himself away from the world.

"I have a post office box in Wakefield. I check on it every few months. No reason to go more often. I live off the grid and don't have many bills to pay. Most of my mail goes straight into the trash. But last month, a lawyer's letter said my brother was dead."

The stark pronouncement hung in the air, heavy with sorrow. Even though Charlie expected the news, hearing it spoken aloud jolted her.

"I'm sorry," Simm said. "How did he die?"

"In a fire. He was puttering on a car in his workshop." Noah shook his head. "He lit a fire in a wood stove and didn't close the stove door. Apparently, with the built-up gas fumes, the place exploded. He didn't make it out."

"How horrible," Charlie said, her hand on her throat. She couldn't imagine a worse way to perish.

"They used dental records to identify him," Noah said, adding to the horrific images marching through Charlie's mind. "Nothing I could've done. He was dead two weeks before I found out."

"You suspect foul play?" Simm said. "Is that why you want our help?"

"No, nothing like that. The investigators ruled it an accident. I believe them. Ethan wasn't the most cautious person." Noah hesitated, seeming to weigh his thoughts. "I'm aware you checked out my background last year, but I don't know how deep you dug or what you discovered. So, I'll fill you in."

Charlie, intrigued, edged forward a few inches.

"I'm from a well-off family," Noah said. He lowered his gaze, as if the words embarrassed him.

Charlie's eyebrows lifted, and she shot a glance at Simm. There'd been no sign of wealth when they searched for information on Noah last year, and his living conditions didn't shout "millionaire."

"It's old money, ancient money," Noah said. "Passed down from one generation to another. I wanted no part of it. I chose independence, without a great-great-grandfather's influence."

Charlie sat back and turned her attention to her husband. His gaze slid to hers, and his mouth twitched into a slight smile. Their thoughts aligned. Simm also came from wealth, perhaps not as old as Noah's, but plenty of it. And, like Noah, he didn't want it, needing to live on his own terms.

Noah tilted his head as his eyes narrowed. "Am I missing something?"

Charlie waved a hand. "We'll explain later. Continue your story. Please."

After an uncertain nod, Noah took up his narrative. "I told Ethan he could keep it all. Nothing in writing, but he knew me. I wouldn't go back on my word."

Charlie grasped this as well. Noah had the vibe of someone who stuck to his commitments, no matter what.

"As the executor of his estate, I got a copy of his will, and as I suspected, it was clear-cut. Whatever he had was now mine. Ethan never settled down. No family besides me. I knew he'd invested the money in simple, straightforward certificates. I thought I'd give it to a charity." He shrugged. "There was no rush. I'd take my time choosing which one. Or maybe pick a few. I figured I had plenty to go around." His gaze shuttled back and forth between them, and he spread his hands. "It's gone."

"What's gone?" Charlie asked, her voice laced with concern.

"The money. It's not there."

Simm frowned. "Ethan spent it all?"

"Doesn't look like it. I called the bank where he had his investments. They'd been transferred out a few days before his death."

"Transferred? He moved them to another institution?" Charlie said.

"I don't think so. The bank couldn't trace the transaction. We assume someone stole the money. That was the only explanation."

"You went to the police?" Simm asked.

"Yep. They're baffled. Can't trace it either. They say they're pursuing it, but I suspect they're spinning their wheels."

It also baffled Charlie. "You want us to find the money?" she said.

A flicker of hope ignited in his eyes. "I have more faith in you than the police."

Charlie understood Noah's feelings. He'd lost confidence in justice when that accident took his family. However, law enforcement had more tools for a financial crime than Simm did.

"What you need is a forensic accountant," Simm said. Charlie nodded. That was exactly what Noah needed.

"I want the two of you. If you decide you want a forensic accountant to help, or anyone else, then we'll do it. But I want you to lead the investigation." Noah's tone was firm.

Charlie and Simm glanced at each other before Simm responded. "Let us look at it, and we'll get back to you."

"Fair enough," Noah said as he rose to his feet. Bosco followed suit and waited for a command from his master. "I need to get back. Sarah's waiting for me."

•   •   •

"I'm surprised you didn't say yes right away," Charlie said when she was alone with her husband.

"Bit surprised myself," Simm said. "I'll check things out. We shouldn't take the case if we can't handle it."

The next day, Simm isolated himself from the pub, glued to his laptop. Whenever Charlie checked on him, she received a curt response that he'd found some interesting stuff but wasn't ready to share. Accustomed to

Simm's intensity when he sank deep into research, Charlie concentrated on the pub and left him to his devices.

After a couple of hours, Charlie carried a plate of food up to the apartment, thinking a full stomach might render him more amenable to talking. Curiosity ate at her like a dog gnawing on a bone.

Judging by his smile, Simm appreciated the delivery, so Charlie settled into the chair beside him. His thick hair was in disarray, and fatigue lined his face.

"And?" she asked.

Simm swallowed a bite of his burger. "There's a lot about Noah we weren't aware of. He hid his past well."

Charlie straightened. "Like what? Something bad?"

"No. Only the fact he's from a very wealthy family."

"That's what he told us. Wealthier than yours?"

Simm pursed his lips. "I think so."

This surprised Charlie. When she'd first met Simm, he'd been a self-employed private investigator with little money to his name, and she'd assumed that was the story of his life. Later, she discovered he was the son of Winston Simmons, the real estate and publishing magnate, and the name on Simm's birth certificate was Winston Simmons Junior. But, in disdain, her husband had walked away from his father, the money, and the name. He insisted on being called Simm and nothing else.

Loaded with money, anyone richer than his family was very rich indeed.

"His wealth goes back several generations," Simm said. "And his roots are in Ontario. Niagara-on-the-Lake, to be specific."

"Isn't that wine country?"

"It is. And it's filled with history, dating back to the late 1700s. The home of the famous Shaw Festival."

"Theater?"

"Have you been studying?" Simm shot her a wink and a teasing grin.

Charlie swatted his arm. "Just because I'm a homebody doesn't mean I'm ignorant about the world."

Simm's arm snaked around her waist as he pulled her close and planted a kiss on her forehead. "It sounds like a nice place."

Charlie rested her head on Simm's shoulder. "Okay, so Noah hid his roots. People do that."

Simm smiled. "Touché."

Her husband never advertised his family's wealth. Revealing his real name was torturous for him.

"What else?" Charlie asked.

He sighed and shook his head. "As for the disappearing money, we have three explanations. One, Ethan moved it himself so no one would find it; two, someone close to him knew his passwords and accessed his accounts; or three, a pro hacked him."

"Makes sense."

"What I can't figure out is how that money shifted from his accounts to somewhere else, and nobody can trace it. How can that happen?"

Simm ran his fingers through his hair, explaining its current state. Charlie stood and circled behind his chair. Her hands massaged his shoulders for a minute before she leaned over and kissed his cheek.

"You'll figure it out. I have faith."

His hand wrapped around one of hers. "Thanks for the vote of confidence, but I'm gonna need help. I have trouble with the tech stuff."

"We'll get it."

"Something else bothers me."

Charlie didn't like his ominous tone. She straightened and moved to face him. "What is it?"

"I suspect Ethan's death wasn't accidental."

CHAPTER 4

Simm disconnected the call and met Charlie's gaze. "It's all set. We'll meet him at his sister-in-law's house tomorrow morning and go over the details."

"Do you plan to share your suspicions about his brother's death?" Curiosity nibbled at Charlie.

Simm considered the question. "I don't know. They're more hunches than concrete suspicions at this point. Nothing to go on, other than a solid distrust in coincidences. If it turns out the case involves murder, we'll reevaluate whether we take it further."

That was good enough for Charlie. She trusted Simm's judgment.

The unassuming bungalow was in Montreal's Verdun borough, nestled amongst mature trees budding with tiny green leaves. The well-maintained yard and flower gardens surrounding the red brick house teamed perfectly with the understated but neat exterior. It suggested meticulous owners.

A pretty woman of Charlie's age answered their knock. Her mid-length, natural blonde hair, hazel eyes, and delicate features gave her a pixie-like appearance. Charlie searched for a resemblance between her and her sister Lyann, Noah's deceased wife, but it wasn't obvious. Of course, Charlie had never met Lyann, only seeing her in photographs. Their mannerisms could hold similarities.

A warm smile lit the woman's face. "You must be Charlie and Simm. Noah told me so much about you. I'm Sarah."

The foyer provided a clear view of the dining and living rooms. It reinforced Charlie's impression of order and attention. Without clutter, everything, from furniture to knick-knacks, was symmetrical and almost military in their alignment. She didn't need to ask if children lived in the house. She pictured her own living space in a few years. It would likely be chaotic and devoid of anything breakable or dangerous to a toddler on the loose.

Noah emerged from the kitchen, balancing a tray precariously laden with delicate china cups and a cream and sugar set. His large hands dwarfed the dainty tea service, and he walked with care, not glancing upward, clearly worried about upsetting the perfectly arranged display.

With the platter settled on the coffee table, Noah and Sarah sat side by side, their shoulders almost touching, on the floral-patterned couch while Charlie and Simm lowered themselves onto matching Victorian-style armchairs opposite them.

Aiming for discretion, Charlie said, "Your husband won't be joining us?"

Sarah's smile hinted that she picked up on Charlie's clumsy pretense. "I live alone. That's why Noah's visit gives me a welcome reprieve. Someone to talk to."

Charlie caught the affectionate glance Sarah sent Noah and wondered if Noah's presence was more than simply a convenient place to stay while in Montreal. Was a romance brewing? If so, it would prove the adage that opposites attract. Charlie couldn't imagine two people being more different. Noah lived in a bush shack. He was big and gruff, while Sarah, small and delicate, looked like she wouldn't survive five minutes in a backwoods environment.

"Sarah's a professor at McGill University," Noah said, obvious pride in his voice.

"What do you teach?" Simm asked.

"Molecular biology for the undergraduate neuroscience program, and I consult for the Montreal Science Centre," Sarah said matter-of-factly. "I understand you own two pubs."

"We do." Simm wasn't the least bit intimidated by Sarah's impressive credentials.

Charlie and Simm took turns filling her in on how they formed a partnership with Frank to become owners of two downtown pubs.

"And you met Noah last year in Gatineau?" Sarah sent a side glance to her brother-in-law.

"I've taken cases in the past few years, and one of them took us to Wakefield." Simm didn't go into details or describe their initial rocky relationship with Noah.

He chuckled. "Noah surprised us yesterday, turning up at the pub."

"It took me a while," Charlie said. "But the eyes gave him away. You clean up nice, Noah."

The big man flushed before directing the conversation to his predicament. "I'm glad you decided to help me."

"So am I," Sarah said, moving to the edge of her seat. "This is distressing for Noah. It's difficult losing a sibling." She blinked several times. Her sibling had been Noah's wife. She waved her hand as if to wipe away her faux pas.

"I can't guarantee I'll find the money," Simm said. "But I'll do my best, and if I need other resources, I'll get them."

"That's all I ask," Noah said.

"Let's start with the basics." Simm held his notepad and pen. "Fill us in on your family as far back as you remember."

"My roots are in Niagara-on-the-Lake in southern Ontario," Noah said, leaning back on the sofa. "My ancestors emigrated from England to Ontario in the mid-1800s. They farmed but soon got into the wine business. That became their mainstay, but each generation branched out into other related businesses. Hotels, restaurants, casinos, any place that served wine or alcohol. During Prohibition, creativity was the key, and our family grew adept at bypassing the laws and lawmakers."

"Illegal money?" Simm asked.

"No doubt," Noah said, seemingly unbothered. "They set up speakeasies with hidden passageways and secret rooms where the rich and famous paid for bootlegged alcohol, along with a woman or two."

"They got away with it?"

"No arrests, as far as I know. I suspect they gave the police free passes for turning the other way."

The story resonated with Charlie. Growing up alongside her father's best friend and original owner of the pub, Jim O'Reilly, she heard countless tales passed down from the previous generations who lived through the 1920s and 30s. Booze had been a source of addiction and income for centuries, and prohibition bred organized crime.

"Fast forward to your life growing up," Simm suggested.

"My father, David, was a businessman. He owned a slew of hotels and restaurants in the Niagara area, many of them handed down from his father. Some he acquired on his own," Noah said. Something about his tone led Charlie to believe he wasn't enamored with his father. It was the same tone Simm used when discussing his parent.

"My uncle Eli owns extensive wineries and was a major supplier of my father's businesses. I was nine when Dad went into politics. He ran for the Federal Conservative Party and won a seat. We moved to Ottawa and spent most of our time there, visiting Niagara during the summer break. My father kept the old homestead."

"And his businesses?" Simm asked.

"Yes. Set it up so there'd be no worries about conflicts of interest, but he still raked in plenty of profits."

"You didn't want it," Simm said.

"I went to Queen's University in Kingston to get my business degree and to keep my father off my back. It didn't interest me, but I had no actual interest in anything else."

Charlie's eyes widened. It was as if Noah was telling Simm's life story, except Simm went to McGill University. In one way, she envied these men. She'd worked at the pub as a teenager and saved every dime she had to pay for her business degree from Concordia University, an education that now served her well.

"I met Lyann at Queen's, and we settled in Montreal," Noah said. "I took up photography as a career." He snorted a laugh. "You can guess how that went. My father's first major disappointment."

"What about Ethan? You said he was younger than you?" Simm asked.

"Two years. Like I told you, a wild child. Tried university for a few months, decided it wasn't for him, backpacked across Europe for six months, came back to Canada, and made money from odd jobs. Dad tried everything to bring him around and teach him responsibility, but that wasn't Ethan's style. He rejected desk imprisonment. I understood." Noah shrugged. "Our parents passed away nine months apart a few years ago. According to the stipulations of the family trust, the bulk of the fortune was handed down to me. I let Ethan have it. He lived an expensive lifestyle, but a lot remained in the coffers before he died. Now it's gone."

"No wife, significant other?"

"No wife. Had plenty of girlfriends along the way. He wasn't a monk, but he never spoke to me of anyone serious."

"What was his last job?"

"I don't think he held any once he got hold of the purse strings. Work wasn't his favorite pastime. He did it to survive when he had to."

"And his home base was Niagara-on-the-Lake? That's where he died?"

"Yes and yes."

Simm's glance asked Charlie if she had other questions. She shook her head. Simm turned back to Noah.

"I'll need all you have relating to the investments, the financial advisor's contact info, and if you have it, the names of the detectives that investigated both the fire and the fraud."

Noah's eyes narrowed. "Why the fire? It was an accident."

"I need to know everything that happened when the money disappeared, including the fire. You never know what may turn up."

Charlie caught the doubtful expression on Noah's face, but he didn't argue with Simm.

Sarah reached for a folder that sat on a side table. "I compiled everything I could find—bank statements, investment records, even the police reports. It's all there," she said. "If not, call us."

Charlie took the folder and flipped through it. As expected, everything appeared perfectly documented. Despite having just met her, Charlie had absolute faith in Sarah's efficiency.

"I may need to visit the family place in Niagara-on-the-Lake, see it, talk to people. You still own it?" Simm asked.

"Yes, of course. No problem," Noah said.

"Good." Simm nodded. "I'll set up appointments with the authorities and whoever took care of the investments."

"We should go with them, Noah," Sarah said, turning toward him and clasping his arm. Excitement filled her expression. "The semester's over. If I'm called for consultation, I can do it remotely. I'm free to go." She smiled brightly.

Surprise flashed across Noah's face, as if uncertain about the conversation's direction. Obviously, if Sarah had her way, he wouldn't just hand things over to Simm and wait for results. He'd be involved. Charlie didn't want to add more pressure, but she thought Noah's presence could speed up the investigation.

"I...I guess we could. What's your opinion?" he asked them with a frown.

"If you have no other obligations, I think it'd help," Simm said, echoing Charlie's thoughts.

Over the next half hour, they hammered out the details. They'd leave in three days. That'd give Charlie and Simm time to organize Frank and the staff for their departure. Simm would rent an SUV big enough for four people and two canines. Noah would contact both the caretaker in Niagara and his uncle to inform them about their arrival.

As they drove home, Charlie couldn't suppress her excitement. Despite the morbid circumstances, she looked forward to her southern Ontario visit. Although she lived only a seven-hour drive away, she'd never gone to the area. As a matter of fact, until she met Simm, she'd never traveled outside of Montreal. As an only child who led a somewhat sheltered upbringing, she grew up without a need to travel. But now, she welcomed an occasional excursion outside her bubble.

And it sounded like an idyllic location. Maybe they'd have time for rest and relaxation. She smiled as a pleasant thought occurred to her. Perhaps they'd conceive their baby in a beautiful mansion in wine country.

CHAPTER 5

The pub's early closing on Mondays offered a rare chance for Charlie and Simm to unwind. Sprawled on the couch, they usually enjoyed the mindless distraction of a home improvement show. But tonight, despite her earlier excitement, Charlie felt a knot of unease tighten in her stomach. The upcoming case wasn't the only thing eating at her. It was the tangled mess of emotions it unearthed. And she needed to discuss those emotions with Simm.

But any such discussion threatened to ruin their peaceful interlude.

Charlie sighed. "Simm?"

"Mmm?" he said as he flipped channels with the remote. Her usual pet peeve, it barely registered on Charlie's radar this time.

"I've been thinking," she began, bracing for his playful jab.

"Oh no. Not again." A smile tugged at his lips.

She swatted playfully at the hand that snaked around her shoulders. "The only way to clear out bad thoughts is to talk about them, remember?"

Simm groaned theatrically. "Now?"

"We leave in two days. Who knows when we'll get another quiet night like this?"

Simm laid his head against the couch and closed his eyes. "Okay. Let me guess. Noah comes from a rich family, isn't enthused with his father, and left behind the business and the cash. On top of that, the way he and his brother grew apart over the years reminded you of my relationship with Walt." He swiveled his head to stare at her with raised brows.

"Wow. You really know me." Her smile dazzled as she twisted her head to peer at her husband. "We're in sync."

"I know you like to bang that drum." Simm's tone was sardonic.

Charlie scooted onto her knees and faced Simm. His arm dropped to his side. "Let's admit it's an important topic. If I didn't bang that drum, you'd ignore it and regret it later."

Simm gave her a dubious look. "No regrets here."

Charlie's brows lowered and so did her voice. "You agreed we'd start a family."

Simm pressed his lips together before letting one word escape their confines. "Yes."

After finally reaching the decision a few months ago, Simm's enthusiasm for the idea had spiked, catching everyone, even Charlie, off guard.

In his free time, he jotted down ideas for renovations to accommodate a nursery. Several times, Charlie caught him searching online for a family-sized car, safety seats, and even baby names.

"I don't want a child while a dark cloud hovers above me. I want clear skies."

"Hon, my relationship with Walt is not connected to our child or our relationship. It's just an unfortunate circumstance."

"You need to resolve it. It's on your mind, and seeing Noah resurrected your feelings. You think I didn't notice you tossing and turning last night?"

"I'll resolve it later. I promise. There's no time now."

"Tomorrow evening. We'll invite them over for dinner."

Simm stared at her, disbelieving, as if she'd told him she was a mermaid. "What?"

"Nothing fancy. We'll get something from the pub kitchen and bring it here to talk in private."

"What do you want us to talk about?" Simm spread his arms. "You want us to fight it out? Here?"

"No fighting. Talking, casual socializing. We don't even have to mention what happened in Gatineau. I'd prefer it if we didn't. We can save that for another time. For now, we'll simply reconnect."

Simm shook his head in wonder. "This is too last minute. They won't be available. Walter is probably in the middle of a hostile takeover of a small country."

Charlie swung her legs off the couch and grabbed her phone. "We won't know unless we ask."

Fifteen minutes later, the invitation was delivered and accepted. Walter Simmons and his wife, Clarisse, would join them for dinner the next evening.

.   .   .

Charlie felt Simm's gaze on her as she darted around the apartment, tidying and rearranging furniture.

"I thought you said casual," Simm said, his voice laced with a teasing lilt. "Why the sudden interior design frenzy?"

"Just making things presentable," she said, dodging his gaze. His skepticism was as clear as a glacial lake.

Simm's doubt morphed to confusion when she pulled out an iron and ironing board.

"I didn't know we had an iron," he said.

"Everyone has one." Charlie maintained an even tone.

"What'll you do with it?"

"Iron the tablecloth."

"We have a tablecloth?"

Charlie sent him a frustrated glance.

Simm laughed. "Next, you'll tell me we have a secret stash of china somewhere."

It took all of Charlie's willpower not to glance at the box that sat in the corner. It contained her mother's fine china and silver cutlery. She remained silent. Chances were good Simm wouldn't notice.

Hoping to distract him, Charlie huffed and planted her hands on her hips. "If you'd like to help, there's plenty to do."

Simm held up his hands in mock surrender. "Orders, ma'am?"

Charlie gazed around the apartment and couldn't think of one thing she'd trust him with that wouldn't elicit another sarcastic remark. "Why don't you give Frank a hand in the pub?"

"That, I can handle." With a look of relief, Simm grabbed his coffee mug and left the apartment, descending the stairs to the pub.

A slow time of day, Charlie imagined her husband sliding onto a barstool to seek commiseration from Frank. Her friend would listen, nod, grumble in agreement, but he'd have her back, like he always did.

From the first time they met, Charlie and Frank clicked. He listened to Charlie's stories of happiness or woes, and she returned the favor. They shared tales of family struggles and past relationships that went downhill. Their ties remained strong, and now those ties included Simm. Knowing Frank, he'd smooth Simm's feathers without ruffling hers, his specialty.

Charlie consulted her list. She didn't admit it to Simm, but tightly strung nerves hummed through her body. She'd visited Walter's home once, and it was the epitome of wealth and elegance. Albert, a proper butler, had answered the door and granted them entrance.

Simm grew up with the same level of opulence, even the same butler, something far outside Charlie's experience. Despite his assurances of being content with their simple life above the pub, she couldn't shake a sliver of self-doubt.

Apart from the impossible feat of struggling to make an apartment look like an upscale penthouse condo, Charlie faced the challenge of preparing an acceptable meal for people accustomed to the best.

She was a people person, someone comfortable greeting customers, chatting them up, serving them drinks, engaging them in conversations. Her two least favorite activities were sitting behind a desk taking care of paperwork and cooking. Simm took over the former. The latter was a work in progress aided by the pub's cook, Dave.

Tonight, she craved a home-cooked feel, but edible was the key word— a challenge when Charlie held the spatula. She'd sent Dave a desperate text first thing in the morning, asking for his advice, hoping he'd volunteer to prepare the entire meal for them.

Her wish came true. The table settings and the wine were among her only worries. Yet, the biggest hurdle remained—navigating a potentially volatile evening. What had she been thinking?

CHAPTER 6

Charlie curbed the compulsion to wring her hands. She wanted to appear calm and confident about the evening ahead. Judging by Simm's doubtful expression, she hadn't convinced him. When the intercom buzzed, she visibly jumped.

Frank's message that their guests were there sent her scurrying to the door of the apartment. "I'll bring them up."

Charlie descended the stairs with care. She'd gone the extra mile by putting on a skirt, blouse, and heels. Accustomed to jeans, T-shirts, and sneakers, this was out of the ordinary for her, and although not overly high heels, she worried she'd take a tumble. She caught the encouraging wink and smile Frank sent her as he came into view.

Walter and Clarisse were predictably prompt but appeared uneasy as they stood by the bar. Walter wore a dark suit with shiny black shoes but had ditched the tie and left the top shirt button undone. Clarisse's slender frame displayed an expensive dress in a shade of blue that matched her eyes and highlighted her long, blonde hair. She appeared entirely comfortable in heels a couple of inches higher than Charlie's.

Charlie gave them a warm smile, but only Clarisse returned it.

Walter nodded and said, "Hello, Charlene." Very few people called her by her given name. Most were unaware of the name on her birth certificate or understood how much she disliked it. She'd overlook Walter's blunder this evening to keep everything friendly.

Charlie took a moment to study her brother-in-law. His frown and stiff posture didn't bode well for the evening, mostly because Simm's demeanor mirrored it perfectly. The similarities between Simm and his brother ended there. Apart from their wildly distinct characters, Walter clocked in at a little under six feet, and his build grew more rotund as time passed, making his resemblance to his father striking. Simm inherited his lean physique from his mother.

"I'm so happy you could make it with such a last-minute invitation," Charlie said, giving them each an awkward hug.

"It was a wonderful surprise. We wouldn't miss it for the world," Clarisse said, sounding sincere.

Judging from the expression on Walter's face, he would've gone to great lengths to miss it. Why didn't he? Did his wife hold that much influence over him? She never seemed to in the past. Was Clarisse as intent on re-establishing the brothers' relationship as Charlie was? Having someone on her side would be a plus.

Charlie led them through the pub and up the stairs to their apartment.

"Oh, this is lovely," Clarisse said as she stepped over the threshold. Charlie, viewing it through an outsider's eyes, felt a flicker of pride. White linen, freshly ironed, covered the table. Her mother's china and silverware adorned it, along with a vase of fresh flowers and long, white, tapered candles.

Simm came out of the office dressed in dark gray slacks and a blue button-up shirt. He took the hint when Charlie laid them on the bed. Politely greeting Clarisse, he gave Walter only a grim nod, making Charlie worry about the evening's prospects. Harley hastened to greet their guests, evoking another gasp of delight from Clarisse.

"You still have that ugly dog?" Walter asked.

Charlie struggled to keep a light tone. "First, he's not ugly, and second, of course we still have him. Why wouldn't we?"

"He's adorable," Clarisse said as Harley responded to her petting with violent tail wags. "I've always wanted a dog, but Walt is against the idea."

"It's an animal. It belongs outside, not in a house," he grumbled.

Charlie sent a warning glance to her husband, hoping to deflect an argument within the first few minutes of his brother's arrival. They needed to overlook Walter's rudeness.

"I love your china," Clarisse said, her gaze sweeping over the table. "It's so elegant."

Charlie smiled and thanked her, ignoring Simm's bewildered expression as she urged their visitors to make themselves comfortable and, with Simm's help, prepared drinks for everyone.

Charlie and Clarisse kept an awkward conversation rolling with discussions about the pub, Walter and Clarisse's children, and mundane topics like the weather and the Canadiens' chances of winning the Stanley Cup.

The chirp of Charlie's phone signaled a text, Dave alerting her to the upcoming arrival of the meal. A knock on the door followed, and Charlie rushed to answer, welcoming Melissa and Cathy carrying large trays brimming with dishes. They placed bowls of soup on the table, while they laid appetizers on the counter beside the main course, each covered with stainless steel domes. Desserts waited in the fridge. The aroma of savory food wafted through the apartment.

As the two women left, Charlie ushered their guests to the table. Pre-planned, she sat Simm and Walter across from each other.

Cream of leek soup followed by individual shrimp cocktails garnered appreciative remarks, while the women carried the stilted conversation. The men remained silent, except for the occasional grunt of agreement.

By the time she served the mouth-watering and aromatic Beef Wellington, Charlie witnessed a slight thaw in Walter's icy demeanor. A genuine smile appeared on his lips as he complimented the food. The wine paired with each course might have encouraged his good behavior, but it didn't have the same effect on Simm, who remained tight-lipped.

"This meal is absolutely delicious," Clarisse said, rubbing her flat stomach. "I've eaten so much; I'll need to walk home to work it off."

Charlie laughed. "Thank you. As you know, I can't take credit for it. Dave, the pub's cook, prepared everything. Simm often cooks for us,"

Charlie said, with a smile in her husband's direction, hoping to have it returned. Her remark landed with a thud.

Walter snorted. "A hot-shot PI, a pub owner, and a cook. Plenty of hidden talents." His tone was laced with a mockery that grated on Charlie's nerves. At only thirty-two years of age, Walter oversaw a business empire. Granted, he wasn't self-made—his father handed him the company—but it didn't flounder in his hands.

Charlie knew Walter's arrogance fueled the fire that smoldered within her husband. As a young man, when Simm became a police officer, his father reacted with fury. Winston Senior couldn't understand why his eldest son didn't want the enterprise he'd built. That Simm relinquished it in exchange for a career as a cop infuriated him even more. When Simm moved from the force to embark on his own business as a private investigator, his father's demeanor didn't improve. And Simm didn't care.

"Hidden talents?" Simm shrugged. "I like doing for myself. I don't need servants to do everything."

"You don't need anyone, do you? Not even your family. It must kill you to let your wife take care of anything." Walter's words dripped with venom.

Anger radiated from Simm, and Charlie needed to defuse the situation. "Simm and I planned this evening together," she interjected. "We wanted to spend time with you and clear up misconceptions."

Over the years, Simm's distrust of his brother had grown. They were close as children, with Simm fulfilling his role as big brother to Walter and their younger sibling Susan. But after cancer struck down their mother and Simm moved into his teen years, he tossed aside his rose-colored glasses and realized how ruthless, narcissistic, and self-centered his father was. Walter, three years younger, idolized Winston Simmons Senior and emulated him as he aged, until Simm saw nothing but his father's reflection in Walter.

A year ago, in Gatineau, their relationship reached an all-time low when Simm and Charlie stumbled across a seemingly unrelated drunk driving case that killed Noah's family. When Simm discovered a connection between his brother, another man charged with the crime, and that man's employer, Marcus Vaughn, he thought Walter was involved in a cover-up and vowed to prove it. So far, his search only drove a deeper wedge between the siblings.

"All the misconceptions are in his mind." Walter pointed a furious finger at Simm.

"We don't need anger, and we don't need finger pointing," Charlie said in her most patient tone, like a mother who wanted to send her children to their rooms as punishment. "You're brothers. You were close when you were young. What happened?"

"He decided I was evil." Despite Charlie's request, Walter pointed another finger in Simm's direction.

"You're a carbon copy of our father. That says it all," Simm shot back.

"Stop," Charlie said. "I won't allow you two to turn this evening into a circus. You're both grown men. I suggest you act like it."

Walter's sheepish expression surprised Charlie, and Simm huffed out a breath before reaching over to take her hand and give it a contrite squeeze.

"I'm sorry, Charlie," Walter said, surprising her again. "I didn't want to come tonight. I knew how it'd turn out, but Clarisse convinced me. I promised her I'd behave and let Simm's comments slide off my back. I didn't keep my promise." Walter sent an apologetic glance at his wife.

Clarisse smiled at him with pride. "It's not too late," she said, turning to Charlie. "I looked forward to this evening. We've never spent much time together, and I think we're long past due. Aren't we?"

Charlie was happy to find an ally. In the past, Clarisse struck her as meek and mild. The few times they'd been together, Clarisse agreed to everything her husband said, a silent shadow by his side. It worried Charlie. Was Clarisse an abused wife? She didn't show outward signs of physical abuse, but that didn't negate its existence. Verbal abuse remained a high possibility.

She couldn't imagine anyone who shared Simm's blood as an abuser, but Charlie wasn't naïve. It happened.

Now, an independent Clarisse faced her. Her husband almost deferred to her, which floored Charlie. Perhaps they'd struck a new bargain. If their marriage underwent a shake-up that changed Walter, maybe there was hope for him.

Intrigued, Charlie couldn't help but size Walter up again. If both she and Clarisse could navigate the choppy waters between their husbands, maybe, just maybe, they could bridge the gap between the estranged brothers. And, Charlie reasoned, if it didn't happen, fine. At the very least, she'd spend time with her in-laws and judge for herself if Walter deserved his brother's animosity.

Charlie sent Simm a beseeching gaze.

He forced a smile. "Why don't we change the subject?"

Clarisse clapped her hands in delight at her minor victory. "I'm curious to find out if you're working on any interesting cases," she asked. "Or are you too busy with the pubs?"

"Actually, we've just taken on a fresh case," Charlie said, sending Clarisse a thankful smile as Simm cleared his throat beside her. "We're leaving tomorrow for Niagara-on-the-Lake. I'm looking forward to it."

"Really?" Clarisse's eyes widened. "That's out of your territory, isn't it?"

"Simm doesn't have a territory," Charlie said. "The case came to him from a connection of ours."

"I understand it's lovely there," Clarisse said. She crossed her arms on the table as she leaned forward, her gaze intense. "Tell me about the case. How were you drawn into it?"

"Maybe we should have dessert instead," Simm said. He stood and started gathering plates. "Help me with this please, hon?"

Charlie stood but remained beside the table. "A friend of ours, Noah Wolfe, his brother died, and he's asked us to..." Too late, Charlie realized her mistake. In her urgent quest to change the subject, she'd circled around to the principal source of animosity between Simm and his brother—the events that ripped Noah's family from him.

CHAPTER 7

The shocked expression on Clarisse's face confirmed Charlie's faux pas, followed by Walter's angry flush that quickly turned into confusion.

"Noah Wolfe? He's part of the Wolfe family from Niagara-on-the-Lake?" Walter said.

It was Charlie's turn to be confused. Glancing at her husband, she watched his brows lower into a question mark.

Simm, after a long uncomfortable pause, spoke in a low voice. "Yes, he is. What of it?"

"I know them," Walter said, before he shook his head. "Or at least I've heard of the family. I didn't know…" He trailed off, gesturing vaguely with his hand, his gaze flickering away from them.

Walter's revelation didn't surprise Charlie. Canada's wealthy were a tangled web, even those from different industries. Their paths crossed at galas, board meetings, and exclusive golf courses. They married into each other's dynasty.

"Noah and his brother lived most of their lives in Ottawa. Their father was a politician," Charlie said, hoping to wrap up the uncomfortable conversation.

But Walter didn't get the hint. He swung toward his wife. "You're from Ottawa. Your father was in politics. Had you met them?"

Clarisse seemed taken aback by the sudden shift of focus. "Just because I lived in Ottawa doesn't mean I knew everyone there. It's a big enough city."

Walter pivoted his attention back to Simm, his voice with a warning edge. "I'd be careful if I were you. That family's known for some shady deals."

Simm coughed to cover up a laugh, but he didn't succeed.

Walter's face reddened. "I'm serious. Restaurants and casinos. Perfect fronts for organized crime. I heard the rumors, but someone covered everything up."

"You'd know about cover-ups, wouldn't you?" Simm said.

Charlie wheeled on her husband, but before she said a word, he raised his hands in defense then let them fall. "I'm sorry," he mumbled.

Walter stood and tossed his napkin on the table. "We should go. Come on, Clarisse."

His wife got to her feet and sent Charlie an apologetic smile, a tiny flicker of defiance in her usually timid eyes. "Thank you so much for the lovely meal," she said. Her cold and clammy hand grasped Charlie's.

Walter huffed, grabbed Clarisse's elbow, and steered her toward the door. He swung back to Simm one last time, his expression outraged.

"You hate me. You love to sneer at me and my lifestyle, act like I'm a clone of our father, the monster you've convinced yourself he was. You forget the start he gave you, and he got you out of a bind as a teenager. You were happy to have his money then."

Simm met his gaze head-on, his jaw clenched tight. "He made me pay too high a price for everything he did. I can't live that way."

"Nobody said you had to. Believe what you want, but you're my brother, and when I say to be careful, I say it because I don't want anything to happen to you."

As the door closed behind them, Charlie shot a searing glare at Simm through narrowed eyes.

He plunged his hands into his pant pockets and studied his feet.

Charlie put her fists on her hips. "Was it too much to ask to have a nice evening?"

"I'm sorry," he said, lifting his head. "I have flashes of my father every time I'm with him."

"A physical resemblance doesn't mean he has the same character."

Simm gestured toward the door. "You saw what he's like."

"He's rude and abrasive, that I've seen. Many people are. But, by coming here, he offered an olive branch. And I suspect he did it to please his wife, which is worth something."

A slight flush climbed Simm's cheeks. "It is." He put his arms around Charlie and pulled her close. "I'm sorry. I'll do better next time. I promise."

Charlie leaned into his embrace, the anger melting away. She couldn't stay mad at him. He was right; this fractured relationship with Walter was a raw nerve, easily exposed. Besides, they had bigger things to worry about now.

"There's a bright side," Simm said, pulling away slightly.

Charlie couldn't imagine what that might be, considering the disastrous evening they'd just endured. "What's that?"

"More dessert for us." His grin was sheepish as he turned toward the kitchen.

·   ·   ·

Charlie stood beside her bed and frowned. Four people and two dogs, one of them huge. She and Simm could only take one bag between them. Charlie ruthlessly edited her clothing choices, shoving the rejects into a growing pile.

An hour later, with a triumphant grunt, she slammed the suitcase shut and packed a small container of food and treats for Harley. Hearing the apartment door close, she knew Simm had arrived with the rental vehicle.

Charlie was excited about the trip, despite the flurry of last-minute arrangements and logistics. She'd googled Niagara-on-the-Lake and looked forward to seeing it in person. Pictures of charming streets, historical landmarks, and sprawling vineyards danced in her head, and she hoped to convince Simm to take a break from the case to explore. She imagined a view overlooking the lake, with a bottle of wine and a platter of hors d'oeuvres between them.

It would also be fun and interesting to spend time with Noah and Sarah. Charlie thought they made a delightful couple and held hope for a relationship.

"You won't meddle, will you?" Simm said. He latched his gaze onto hers when Charlie mentioned her hopes.

"Of course not. When do I stick my nose into things?"

Simm rolled his eyes. "You ask me that with a straight face? You always try to fix people up or become involved in their relationships."

Charlie ground her protest to a halt. Her husband had a point. "I want everyone to be as happy as I am," she said in a sugary tone.

That earned another eye roll.

By eleven o'clock that morning, they were on the road. Simm drove with Noah acting as co-pilot, while Sarah and Charlie sat in the back seat. Despite the spacious SUV, the luggage required the women to share their seat with the dogs. Bosco planted his bottom between the two women and lay sprawled across Sarah, as Harley snuggled on Charlie's lap. Within fifteen minutes, once the initial excitement died down, both dogs snored, setting the pace for most of the trip.

To Charlie's surprise, the seven-hour drive passed quickly. Conversation flowed between the women, and Charlie extracted more information about Noah's sister-in-law. Apart from being highly intelligent and organized, she had a surprisingly adventurous side. Sarah indulged in hiking and rock climbing, but the real rock climbing, not the kind in a gym with thick mats for protection. She rappelled up mountains. And it seemed, no matter what she did, it was with a fierce intensity.

With two stops to let everyone stretch their legs, especially the dogs, and one lunch break, they arrived in Niagara-on-the-Lake before dusk. Noah directed them to the northern edge of town where large estates boasted towering trees that cast long shadows on the mansions built during another era. Black wrought iron fences or high hedges shrouded some properties, and hasty glimpses afforded them views of stately manors in red brick or gray stone.

Charlie imagined the estates in years gone by with horse-drawn carriages transporting the residents to and from their grand soirees. Maids in starched black uniforms and white aprons served the families, and dignified butlers answered the doors and managed the households. The idea of sleeping in a former residence of the rich and privileged, maybe in a celebrity's bed, sent a shiver of excitement down her spine.

"Turn right at the next street," Noah instructed, "Left, first driveway." His memory proved reliable despite the years since his last visit.

Under a canopy of elm branches, Simm steered into the driveway. The dogs, alert to the change in atmosphere, pressed their damp noses against the windows.

Charlie frowned in confusion when she had her first clear view of the Wolfe mansion. There had to be a mistake. Two stories tall, with a central turret dividing the upper floor and another on the left. A spacious lawn surrounded it, dotted with flower beds and magnificent trees. A grand, covered porch stretched across the house's width, meant to add to its stately charm.

But the charm and beauty of the home were barely visible beneath the vines that overran the structure. Chipped paint and rotten wood marred the once-white façade. Black asphalt tiles curled on the roof. Broken and dilapidated steps led to a set of double doors badly needing a fresh coat of paint.

Noah's usual stoic expression morphed into shock. Clearly, he hadn't expected to find the house in such a state.

"I don't understand," he said. "How did this happen?"

"Isn't there a caretaker?" Simm asked.

"Yes. Mike's taken care of the place for as long as I remember."

Noah couldn't pull his gaze from the house. Simm parked the car and stepped out, the signal for everyone to break from their trance and follow. Dogs, uncaring of humans' disappointment or shock, frolicked on the grass, finally free from the vehicle.

Noah approached the steps and stood at the bottom, his shoulders slumped. "Ethan told me he took care of it."

Charlie felt a surge of sympathy for Noah. This was his family's homestead. Happy childhood memories resided here. When he gave Ethan free rein of their inheritance, he entrusted him with the house's safekeeping. Now it lay in shambles, and the money was gone. Did Ethan squander the money, leaving nothing for maintaining the estate?

Noah turned left and followed the walkway along the expanse of the house. The three others trailed behind like guests in a funeral procession. Moss and weeds escaped between the pavers beneath their feet. Circling the house, the charred remains of a building came into view—the converted workshop where Ethan died a horrible and tragic death.

All were quiet, eyes fixed on the building's remnants. Even the dogs stopped their scurrying and settled on the ground beside their masters, their tongues lolling. Ashes carpeted the cement floor and the surrounding area. A car's skeleton sat in the center like a morbid tribute to a man's demise. The only items to survive the inferno were those made of metal: the car's frame, the cast-iron stove, various tools, and metal containers. Everything was cauterized and blackened, and the heavy smell of smoke and fire invaded their nostrils, even weeks after the event.

It reminded Charlie of the fire damage in their pub a year earlier. The same smell, but with less extensive damage. A neighbor noticed the flames, and the rapid response saved their livelihood, but the arsonist remained free. Was this shell a result of an accident or arson? Would they ever know?

No one dared advance closer to the ruins, feeling respect for a life lost.

Bosco broke the silence as he alerted them to another presence, springing to his feet, a low growl in his throat, his attention directed behind them.

CHAPTER 8

They turned in unison. A rail-thin man stopped in mid-stride. Understandable, considering the size of the beast that faced him. The breeze ruffled his few strands of gray hair that surrounded a large bald patch. Dirty jeans and a checkered jacket hung loosely on his gaunt frame, with dark eyes projecting his fear. He clenched his fists, and his feet danced from side to side, as if ready to take on a group attack.

Noah restrained Bosco with a simple hand signal, but the dog followed beside him as he approached the stranger.

"Mike."

Relief washed over the older man's face, a nervous chuckle escaping his lips. "Noah? Is that you? Thank heavens. I thought I was a goner."

Noah didn't return Mike's smile. The solemn and daunting man from Gatineau had returned. "What happened here?"

Confusion shadowed Mike's features. "You mean...?" He stammered as he pointed at the workshop's remains.

"The house, the grounds, all of this." Noah waved his arm to encompass the weed-choked gardens, the once-stately house fallen into disrepair, the cracked and undulating pavement of the driveway. "Aren't you the caretaker? This didn't happen in the past few weeks."

Mike stared at the house, dawning comprehension flickering in his eyes. "No, you're right. It's been a while."

Dumbfounded, everyone gawked at him. Charlie felt like she'd stumbled into a surreal comedy skit. When would it make sense?

"Explain yourself." Noah's growl was more ominous than Bosco's.

Mike's gaze darted between them, landing anywhere but on their faces. His hands twisted together then flapped at his sides in a display of nervous energy. "Ethan wouldn't let me do anything. Only do a minimum of stuff and monitor the place when he was gone, you know, for vandalism and the like. I talked to him about it—the roof, the steps, the windows—but he refused to listen."

"Why?" Simm asked, stepping forward.

Thin shoulders lifted and dropped as his gaze bounced off Simm and shifted to the side. "I don't know. He wasn't here much. Didn't seem to take any interest in the place. Too preoccupied, I think. I figured he had no money."

Charlie and Simm shared a meaningful glance.

"He didn't explain anything? He told you not to fix the place?" Noah's voice softened as he clearly realized who was to blame for the estate's poor condition. It was also obvious to Charlie that Mike was likely neurodiverse. The flinching, twitching, and lack of eye contact pointed to something other than simple nervousness.

"Yep. Basically," Mike said. He punctuated each syllable with a shrug of his bony shoulders. "And he refused to hire a housekeeper. So, things kinda got out of hand."

"We have questions," Simm said. "Do you have a minute? Could we go inside and get comfortable?"

The man sent a confused glance toward Noah.

"Sorry," Noah said. "This is Simm and his wife Charlie, friends of mine. They're here to help me sort out the estate. And this is my sister-in-law, Sarah." He gently tugged on her arm to pull her next to him. His words introduced her as a relative, but his actions appeared more possessive.

Mike shook their hands with a tight-lipped smile that didn't reach his eyes before gesturing for them to follow him.

Treading on the least damaged steps with care, they went inside. Each creaking footfall on the uneven floor mirrored the growing unease in

Charlie's stomach. The thick, stale air radiated a musty odor that clung to everything. Cobwebs draped the corners like ghostly remnants, and dust particles floated in the dim light filtering through the grime-coated windows. Dark wood furniture crowded the hallways and rooms. Despite the high ceilings and immense windows, the thick curtains and weak lighting created a dungeon-like effect. The place resembled a forgotten tomb.

It struck Charlie that her idyllic getaway lay shredded into tiny pieces. The likelihood of sleeping in a beautiful four-poster bed with a picturesque view disappeared like smoke in the wind. Instead, a sinister chill tickled her spine. Maybe a hotel search wasn't a bad idea.

Mike led them into the front living room. Plenty of room to sit, but the dust-coated chairs appeared flimsy and unsafe. The caretaker swatted at the seats, creating a cloud that threatened to send them into coughing fits.

After the trouble Mike went to, nobody wanted to insult him, so they cautiously lowered themselves onto the ancient furniture, leaving the more robust for Noah and Simm.

The dogs curled up together on the tattered rug.

"I'm sorry, Noah. I should've warned you, but I thought Ethan kept you informed," Mike said, wringing his hands.

Noah's somber gaze roamed the neglected room. "We didn't talk often. My fault, not his."

"Truth is," Mike said, "your brother shut himself off. He'd come and go without a word. And he seemed tired, worried about something."

Mike never stood still as he spoke. In perpetual motion, he bounced on his feet and constantly tugged on his shirt and pants.

"That wasn't like him," Noah said, wiping his confused face. "Ethan was the most carefree guy ever."

"He was a rabble-rouser in the old days." Mike grinned. "Always into mischief. Nothing mean, but he enjoyed living on the edge. Parties, lots of girlfriends, drinking. He drove your parents nuts." His shoulders jittered. "But he changed lately. Got quiet. When he was here, he'd poke at his cars. Did little else."

"This change, when did it start? Do you remember?" Simm asked.

Mike furrowed his brow, concentrating as if searching for the answer in the cob-webbed corners of the room. "Roughly a year ago, I'd say."

"Anything else unusual?" Simm said.

"Not that I noticed. I'm not here often. He said to do the basics. I dropped by on occasion. I didn't see anybody, but I suspect he had visitors." A twinkle appeared in Mike's eyes. "Things tidied up a bit, and extra dishes in the sink. Little clues pointed to a girlfriend. But I don't know who."

Charlie felt a jolt of curiosity. A girlfriend? Could this woman be connected to Ethan's death? Or could she at least offer some clues?

"What about the day he died? Tell us about that," Simm said.

Charlie braced herself. How much detail were they prepared to hear? Thinking about dying in a fire created a cold dread in the pit of her stomach.

Sorrow settled on Mike's face, and his shoulders slumped. His vision focused on the rug's faded pattern. "It was terrible. Worst thing I ever experienced. The investigator said the wood stove exploded. I spotted the flames when I drove by. Thought it was at the neighbor's place at first. I guess I hoped it was. When I saw the workshop, I called the fire department. Ran into the house to get Ethan, but he didn't answer. I couldn't find him." Tears welled in the man's eyes. "I prayed he wasn't in that workshop, but he was. They found his body after." He lifted his gaze to Noah. "I still have nightmares about it."

Simm gave Mike a moment to compose himself before asking another question.

"When did you pass by?"

"Just after midnight," he said, his voice thick with emotion. "I remember thinking it was late when I left Rob's place."

"Who's Rob? Where does he live?" Noah said.

"Rob Parker," Mike said, wiping his eyes with a shaky hand. "Birch Street, about four blocks over."

"How long were you there?" Simm asked.

Mike raised his hands against the barrage of questions. "I know what you're doing. Cops grilled me too. I was at Rob's place all evening, but he can't confirm it because he was drunk when I left. Remembers nothing from eleven o'clock on. But I was there." The man seemed more annoyed than angry. "And it was an accident. Ethan left the woodstove door open. Wasn't the first time, and I warned him about it." Mike shook his head, sadness clear on his face. "He was reckless once too often."

Charlie witnessed the genuine grief on the older man's face. He'd known Ethan forever and considered him a friend as well as an employer.

Simm glanced at Noah, raising his brows as if to confirm if Noah had more questions. Noah shook his head. Charlie felt sorry for him. His despair and grief broke her heart. Gruesome images of a man suffering and dying in a fire rolled through her brain. How much worse were those images when the victim was your brother?

Mike waited with his hands in his pockets, a forlorn look on his face. "Anything I can do? Help you clean up here?"

"Can you recommend a decent hotel nearby?" Charlie asked.

CHAPTER 9

Prepared for battle, the four of them returned to the old mansion the next morning.

To her surprise, Charlie had slept well. The long drive, the previous day's tension, and the search for pet-friendly accommodation took its toll. By the time they booked three rooms at a local boutique hotel and polished off dinner in the hotel's restaurant, Charlie was ready to call it a night. She sank into the soft bed and fell asleep instantly.

But sunrise, peeking through the window overlooking the quiet main street, brought a fresh wave of anxieties. The charming shops and cafés that lined the street seemed a world away from the looming shadows of the Wolfe mansion. In the distance, she spotted the vineyards that graced the rolling hills and wondered if they'd ever visit them.

Fueled by a desperate need for caffeine, Charlie fumbled with the tiny coffee machine and sent a silent apology to Simm who stirred on the bed. A groan confirmed his awareness.

"Sorry." She grimaced. "I tried to be quiet."

Simm glanced at his watch with heavy-lidded eyes. "We need to go, anyway. There's a lot to do."

Their game plan, hatched over dinner the previous night, was ready to be executed.

Charlie and Simm dressed and descended to the restaurant for breakfast, accepting another cup of coffee with eager smiles. First Noah then Sarah joined them. Charlie didn't ask if Noah felt rested. The dark circles under his eyes spoke volumes about his lack of sleep. Sarah, on the other hand, seemed energized and ready to tackle the day. Despite their vastly different backgrounds, Charlie felt a kinship with Noah's sister-in-law. Both possessed a shared energy and a "get-it-done" attitude.

After their meal, the hardware store and supermarket filled their needs. Now, armed with basic tools, cleaning supplies, and enough snacks to feed an army, or at least a platoon, they ventured into the neglected house. After a quick huddle, they delegated tasks.

Charlie flung open the drapes, bathing the sitting room in a shaft of warm sunlight. Turning her back to the window, she realized the light magnified the room's neglect. A simple scrubbing wouldn't restore its former glory, but it was a start. Making it habitable was their first step; grandeur could wait.

After an hour of dusting, sweeping, and mopping, Charlie stretched her aching back. In search of a change of scenery, she checked on Sarah's progress. The kitchen, Sarah's chosen domain, presented a much more daunting task. Time melted away as they emptied and cleaned cupboards, tossed expired dried goods, disinfected surfaces, and scrubbed floors. The layers of grime suggested Ethan had neglected this area entirely.

As they worked shoulder-to-shoulder, Charlie couldn't resist steering the conversation in a direction that piqued her curiosity.

"So, you and Noah keep in touch?"

"Yes," Sarah said after a slight hesitation. "Although, it's difficult when he's sequestered in a cabin with no electricity, no internet, and no cell phone. When he goes into town for supplies, he contacts me with the library computer."

"Kind of him to update you," Charlie commented, rearranging clean dishes while her mind searched for a path to the crux of the matter.

"He's nice, even though he tries to hide it," Sarah said.

"He's not hiding it these days. You've brought him out of his shell," Charlie said. Noah, despite the hardship with his brother and the estate, was a different man from the one they met a year ago. Although Charlie liked to think she saw through his façade in Gatineau, she'd never seen him like he was now. Here, with Sarah by his side, he had genuine conversations, smiling more often. A remarkable change. What Charlie didn't mention was the warmth that flickered in his eyes whenever he looked at his sister-in-law.

Pink crept into Sarah's cheeks, and she turned back to the almost empty fridge. A garbage bin stood beside her and was filling up with decomposing provisions. "I had nothing to do with that."

The pungent smell of rotting food wafted throughout the kitchen, driving Charlie to help Sarah with the fridge clean-up. The sooner it went outside the better.

"I believe you're one of the few he trusts," Charlie said, averting her gaze from the foodstuffs. "You persuaded him to come."

A shy smile appeared on Sarah's face, hinting at the soft spot she had for Noah.

"His presence here is crucial for his mental health. He needs to reconnect with his roots, and being here will make him feel closer to the brother he lost." Sarah's smile morphed into a frown. "But I'm worried about him. Losing Lyann and the kids was horrible. And now with Ethan... what if someone murdered him? How would Noah react? I don't want him to bury himself in the woods again."

Sarah's words surprised Charlie. Simm hadn't discussed his concerns with anyone besides her. "What makes you think someone murdered Ethan?" she asked.

"It's possible, isn't it? Or what if somebody close to Noah stole the money?" Sarah wrung a rag in her hand. "It'd crush him."

"We can't jump to conclusions." Charlie read the distress on Sarah's face. With a smile, she said, "Let's change the subject. Why don't you tell me something about yourself? Where are you from?"

Sarah smiled and returned to her mission, pulling items from the fridge with her latex-covered hands. "I was born and raised in Ottawa with Lyann and a younger brother, Mark."

"Another one from Ottawa." Charlie chuckled.

Sarah drew back and stared at her. "What do you mean?"

"Noah and Ethan lived there, and I just discovered my sister-in-law is also from Ottawa. Did you know the brothers then?"

"Not growing up, no. My sister met Noah at the university in Kingston. From there, they moved to Montreal. So did I, after I married."

Charlie's eyes widened. "You're married?" She remembered Sarah declaring she lived alone.

"I was." Sarah grimaced. "Divorced now. It's been five years. I reverted to my maiden name."

"I'm sorry."

"Don't worry." Sarah shrugged. "In hindsight, it was for the best."

"Messy?"

"Somewhat. However, no children were involved, so I'm thankful for that." She opened a mustard jar and sniffed it before tossing it in the bin. "We were young and immature. Not meant to be."

"High school sweethearts?" Charlie asked.

"Not quite," Sarah said, her face averted.

"How'd you meet?"

"It doesn't matter."

Charlie's head snapped up in surprise. Sarah's harsh tone felt like a door slamming in her face, so unlike the woman she'd spent the last two days with.

Sarah wanted to keep her personal life private, that much was obvious. Upon reflection, Charlie understood. She reacted the same way when she first met Simm and he asked questions about her connection to Jim O'Reilly. Sometimes, you didn't want to share everything with strangers, whether it was your own life or that of someone close to you.

Charlie tackled another cupboard, hauling platters and porcelain dishes out onto the counter so she could wipe the grime off the shelves.

"I should tell you how Simm and I got together," she said, trying to lighten the mood. She related the story about the strange packages she received a few years back and how she hired Simm to help her.

"We fell in love, got married, became partners in the pub, and the rest is history," Charlie said. Sarah's smile encouraged her. Maybe her earlier intrusion was forgotten.

"You left something out," Sarah said. "If he gave up the PI business, why is he still in it? As are you."

Charlie chuckled. "The truth is, I worried our simple life bored him. He disagrees with me, yet when presented with a problem, he takes charge and embraces it." She shrugged. "As for my implication in the cases... it's just my meddling nature, as Simm would say."

. . .

Three hours later, the kitchen was halfway decent. It might not pass a food inspector's test, but the rotten smell had vanished, masked by lemon-scented cleansers. The walls needed a full wash-down, and Charlie and Sarah agreed the gray, torn linoleum had to be ripped out. They hoped lovely hardwood floors hid underneath.

As they worked in that room, other noises reverberated throughout the house. The men moved from place to place, grumbling, planning, and shifting furniture.

Noah and Simm trudged into the room and sank onto chairs.

"Bad?" Charlie asked.

"Dirty," Noah said. "I swear, Ethan did nothing here. So much dust and cobwebs. Bugs, dead and alive." He shook his head, despondent.

"The good news is most repairs seem minor," Simm said. "Structure appears sound, but I think it'd be worthwhile to have an expert inspect it. The roof needs replacing, that's for sure. If we're lucky, the plywood underneath the tiles didn't rot."

"That's doable," Charlie said, grasping for the positive. She studied Noah's face to gauge his thoughts, but despair clouded his expression.

"How about lunch?" Sarah said, her upbeat tone in full force.

The men reacted as expected, straightening and displaying an avid interest in the idea. They washed up and prepared to leave in search of food when a knock set off the dogs. Harley's sharp bark complemented Bosco's deep, throaty growl. Noah's command silenced his pet, but Harley ignored Charlie's efforts. When Simm eased the door open, the pug launched himself at the new arrival, who obliged him with petting and ear scratches, while the man eyed Bosco with trepidation.

CHAPTER 10

"Uncle Eli?" Noah said.

The man opened his arms and wrapped Noah in a tight hug. Elijah Wolfe pounded his nephew's back as his delighted laugh echoed through the cavernous entranceway.

For no apparent reason, Charlie had formed an impression of a frail, elderly man. Yet, almost as tall as Noah, with a lean, wiry build, Eli projected a boundless energy that belied his years. A thick mane of gray hair touched his shoulders and surrounded his tanned and lined face. He rubbed his hands together with glee.

"I'm so happy to see you. Introduce me to your friends," he said, his sharp blue eyes gleaming as his gaze slid over the intrigued and bewildered group.

Noah did the honors, keeping details brief. He commanded Bosco to behave himself as Eli ran his hand over the dog's head.

Relieved the kitchen appeared clean, Charlie instructed everyone to settle around the contemporary and functional table she'd filled with fresh coffee and store-bought cookies, lunch temporarily forgotten.

"Were you shocked when you arrived?" Eli said to Noah, his smile faltering slightly as their gazes met.

"That's putting it mildly," Noah said. "It bowled me over. Why didn't anyone tell me?"

The older man shrugged. "I thought you knew. Ethan said you were up to date."

"I wasn't. What got into him?"

"He changed," Eli said with a troubled shake of his head, echoing Mike's comments. "He didn't act like himself anymore. No more carefree, fun-loving guy. I tried talking to him, but he brushed me off, insisting everything was fine. Claimed he'd matured. Nothing to worry about. The more I pestered him, the testier he got. I finally backed off."

Simm leaned forward. "How often did you see him?"

"Often enough a few years ago," Eli said, reaching for another cookie. "We'd get together for meals or sometimes just a drink. He was away a lot, and so was I. But my visits grew fewer about a year ago. To be honest, I didn't feel welcome anymore."

Noah's jaw clenched. "Mike mentioned a change too," he said. "Any idea what triggered it?"

Eli's gaze clouded with a hint of sadness. "Not a clue."

"Did you catch sight of any visitors or strangers hanging around?" Sarah asked.

Eli shook his head. "Never when I was here."

A frustrated sigh escaped Noah's lips. "I don't get it. I didn't speak to him often, but when I did, he sounded fine. It must've been an act."

"What about money?" Charlie asked Eli. "Did he mention anything about it? Did he spend a lot? Complain about not having enough?"

The older man stiffened, his thick, gray brows lowered into a frown, and he spoke in a clipped tone. "We didn't talk money. My brother and the boys got it all. I made my way. Nothing to discuss." He slammed his palm on the table with surprising force, the rattle of the cups making everyone jump. "And now it's gone. It would've been safer with me."

Charlie flinched, regretting her question. She'd hoped to pry loose some information about the missing funds, but instead, she hit a nerve.

Noah cleared his throat and steered the conversation back to the renovation efforts, but the damage was done. Eli's earlier cheerfulness vanished, replaced by an angry silence. He finished his coffee in a single gulp, pushed back his chair, and stood abruptly.

"Well, it was a pleasure meeting all of you," he said, his voice devoid of warmth. "If you need anything, Noah, you know where to find me."

Without another word, Eli strode out the front door, leaving the group stunned.

Charlie gave Noah an apologetic smile.

"Don't worry about it," he said. "Uncle Eli was always bitter about the inheritance. Percy Wolfe, the original millionaire, created a trust for his fortune and set the rules. The eldest son of each generation would inherit it. That included my father, and then me."

"What if there were no boys? Only girls? Or the girl was the eldest?" Charlie asked, feeling affronted on behalf of the female gender.

Noah chuckled. "In Percy's mind, the Wolfe genes would always produce what he considered the superior sex. And mostly, they did." When Charlie's eyes widened, Noah hurried to qualify his statement. "I mean, every generation had boys. There were also girls, but they were pushed aside in favor of the males." He lifted his hands in defense. "Don't shoot the messenger. I'm just relaying the facts."

"I understand," Charlie said. "But that doesn't mean I agree with his principles."

"Neither do I. Eli tried to negotiate with my father to split up the money, but Dad refused. He argued he needed to respect the wishes of our ancestors. A fair share of jealousy and bad blood existed between the brothers ever since. We saw little of Uncle Eli until my father died. Then he became part of our lives, but I questioned his intentions. Love or money?"

"Does he need it?" Charlie asked, confused. She'd spotted the Mercedes in the driveway when he arrived. His clothing, though casual, was top of the line.

"Not at all. He established his own vineyards, from scratch and from buying out others. He's not hurting, but probably pays a fortune in alimony payments to his two ex-wives." Noah's mouth twitched into a smile. "Ethan inherited his fun-loving ways from Uncle Eli."

•   •   •

They returned to their chores with Sarah putting finishing touches on the kitchen while Charlie headed for the library. It drew her in as the most fascinating place in the house, a haven for bookworms.

A desk and two chairs sat dwarfed by towering bookshelves that lined two walls. Dusty volumes filled the shelves, many in perfect condition, but the majority suffered tattered spines or missing covers. An enormous window took up a large portion of one wall, and a cluster of portraits occupied the remaining one.

Charlie studied the subjects of the paintings as she carefully ran the duster over them. The haunting gazes of four men and two women stared back. The women's portraits were smaller, hung on each side, with the men in the center forming a square. Although no expert, their clothing suggested late 1800s or early 1900s. Sarah might have more insight. With no plaques or anything to hint at their identity, Charlie assumed the Wolfe ancestors lined the wall.

She wondered why no one smiled. They wore grim expressions. You'd think they'd want their memory preserved differently.

One portrait depicted a man with dark eyes and thin, almost cruel lips. Sharp angles and deep lines defined his face. The only physical resemblance he had to Noah was his thick dark hair, but his glare pierced her soul, much like Noah's had when they first met.

Shaking off the unsettling feeling, Charlie turned to face the desk. She presumed Ethan had used it for personal matters. The enormous leather chair engulfed her when she lowered herself into it, and she struggled to position it within reach of the immense, solid wood desk. Her gaze swept over the intricate carvings, and her eyes narrowed as she leaned closer. Snakes with their tongues lashing out curled around the legs and across the drawer fronts. Charlie's lips twisted into a grimace at the original owner's choice of decor.

Two drawers lined each side with one long narrow one in the middle. It slid open with ease as if used often. Randomly strewn in the drawer were pens, pencils, and pads, many of them from ritzy hotels in various cities around the world. No doubt Ethan had collected them on his travels. She ran her hand along the inside of the drawer, searching with no luck for something that might reveal information about Noah's brother and his fate.

Charlie tugged open the top drawer on the left and discovered a folder containing bills for electricity and property taxes. Other mundane invoices filled another one.

She grabbed the handle of the next drawer down and found it locked. Searching the other drawers for a key, she came up empty-handed. An examination of the lock revealed it required an old-fashioned key, and she wondered if it was easy to pick. This was Simm's area of expertise. She'd enlist his help.

The locked drawer intrigued her. What secrets did it hold? Financial records? Incriminating evidence? Or perhaps just personal mementos? Charlie knew they needed to access its contents. With a renewed sense of purpose, she rejoined the others to share her news.

CHAPTER 11

"Nothing I do works. We'll have to break or dismantle it." Simm glanced at Noah. Technically, the desk belonged to him, making it his call.

Noah didn't hesitate. "We'll dismantle it. It might be empty, or it could hold the answers to our questions. We won't know until we look."

"What about his computer?" Charlie asked. "Ethan must've had one."

Simm nodded. "The cops'll have it. Probably the fraud investigator. I'll ask when I meet them."

As the men took apart the antique desk while inflicting the least damage possible, Charlie and Sarah set out to find food for dinner. Grateful to escape the musty house, Charlie looked forward to wandering the downtown streets for an hour. Moving from shop to shop, they soaked up the warm, spring sun.

"This is a lovely city," Charlie said, taking in the area's quaintness, with the historic buildings converted to boutiques, shops, and restaurants. Flowering window boxes added a kaleidoscope of colors to the scene. Inviting outdoor patios lined the roadways. "I'd love a full day to explore, but we probably won't have time."

"There's plenty to do here. So many historical sites, and the lake is beautiful."

With surprise, Charlie stared at the woman. "You've been here before?"

Sarah's gaze fastened on a store across the street. "Twice. It's a major tourist region." She shrugged a shoulder.

Charlie didn't argue the point but wondered why Sarah had never mentioned it. There'd been plenty of opportunities during their long drive from Montreal.

After making a few stops, they returned with steaks, vegetables, and a bakery fresh apple pie.

Sarah offered to prepare the meal, an offer Charlie eagerly accepted.

With perfect timing, she arrived in the library as Simm removed the last screw and gently set the paper-filled drawer on the floor. Uncertain of its worth but excited to find out, Charlie took over the task to delve into the contents.

She sat cross-legged beside it and sorted through the documents as the men hammered, swore, and reconstructed the desk. Three piles took shape before her. The first held unremarkable bills and random items. The second contained important-looking papers that warranted closer scrutiny. But it was the third pile that truly captivated her—a worn journal bursting with notes, facts, and cryptic dates scrawled in a slanted, difficult-to-read cursive. After a few minutes of struggling with the notebook, Charlie's head ached from trying to decipher words. Maybe paperwork-delving wasn't that exciting after all.

"Oh, what's that?" Sarah's voice held a heavy layer of awe.

A genuine smile broke across Charlie's face, relieved to find an enthusiast. "This, my friend, is what you'll find fascinating. An old journal filled with notes, dates, and who knows what secrets."

Sarah's eyes widened. She looked like a kid who'd received the new bike she'd dreamed about. She sank onto the floor beside Charlie and picked up the notebook with care, as if it might disintegrate in her hands.

"This is amazing," she said. "Exactly what I was looking for."

Charlie stared at her. "What do you mean? Did you know it was here?"

"Of course not," Sarah said, her tone defensive. "How would I know that? I meant I love this kind of thing, and it's what I'd expect to find in a house like this. Do you know whose it is?"

"Not yet. Have at it," Charlie said. "I'll sift through this pile of legal stuff. Perhaps I'll find detailed instructions for finding the money." Simm's amused glance told her he picked up on her sarcasm.

"We're finished here." Noah straightened and stretched his back. "I'll help with dinner."

"Everything's on the counter. I'll finish it," Sarah said, rising to her feet.

"Don't worry. It'll be a pleasant change to cook for others instead of just myself," Noah said.

Charlie silently agreed. Cooking could be therapy, a way for Noah to process his grief. A smile returned to her lips as she watched Sarah settle in with the journal, her avid gaze glued to the faded pages.

Simm bowed and held out his hand to Charlie. "A stroll in the gardens, my dear?" He spoke in his best upper-class British accent.

"I'd be delighted, sir," Charlie mimicked as she allowed him to pull her to her feet. They exited through the kitchen where Noah chopped onions with a heavy hand and a focus as sharp as the knife.

The vast backyard stretched several hundred feet toward the back of the property. Immense trees, fences, and vines obscured the neighbors' houses, further reinforcing the sense of isolation. The lawn resembled a hayfield with the grass swaying in the breeze. Clover and various weeds Charlie couldn't name fought for supremacy. As she and Simm strolled, arm in arm, heading to the back fence, they left a trail of flattened greenery behind them.

Fountains, devoid of water, stood guard on either side of the lawn, the ceramic nymphs facing each other. Moss and algae carpeted the once-white sculptures. Neglected hydrangea and azalea bushes battled a tall yellow weed for sunlight. An expansive rock garden held a promise of beauty but needed hours of maintenance to return it to its former glory.

"It's so sad," Charlie said. "Imagine the loveliness here in the past, perhaps a century ago."

"According to Noah, it was beautiful the last time he was here. Mike did the upkeep. He must know what he's doing." Simm sounded doubtful, and after witnessing Mike's attitude, Charlie didn't blame him.

She stopped and faced her husband. "I don't understand. How could Mike let this fall to ruin, even obeying Ethan's orders? In his place, it would've broken my heart."

"I sense he doesn't see it the way we do. But I'll check him out," Simm said. "And Eli."

Charlie's eyes widened. "You think one of them stole the money?"

"My thoughts aren't worth mentioning without more to go on. It's hard to picture either of them masterminding a fraud, but they may not have worked alone." He hesitated. "My instincts tell me this is more than a financial crime. I don't think someone just hacked into Ethan's account and took the money. It'll probably be more complicated than we expected."

"Want to back out?"

"No," Simm said, his voice firm. "Like I told Noah, I'll do as much as I can. If there's something I can't handle, I'll find somebody to help."

"What's the next step?"

"Tomorrow, I'll schedule meetings with the detectives assigned to Ethan's case—the one handling the death investigation and the one on the fraud side. The fire investigator and Ethan's financial advisor are also on my list." He turned and gazed back at the house. "But for now, let's pick our bedroom and clean it up."

"Sleep here?" Charlie's voice held a note of surprise. The thought hadn't even crossed her mind.

A hint of a smile played on Simm's lips. "Why not? We've made progress today, and frankly, I'm exhausted."

"Sounds like a plan," Charlie conceded.

. . .

Simm lowered himself onto the worn sofa, leaned his head back, and closed his eyes. "I'm beat."

Charlie snuggled in close and rested her head on his chest. Noah occupied an armchair, his long legs stretched out with Bosco by his side. Sarah settled on a matching chair, still clutching the journal. Harley completed the group, snoring softly on the rug.

"At least we don't need a hotel tonight," Sarah said. "Not luxurious, but we made progress, and we'll be comfortable."

While Noah had prepared dinner, the three others tackled the bedrooms. Dust bunnies danced in the light as they swept and vacuumed. With beds stripped, linens washed and dried, and windows flung open to air out the stale smell of neglect, they transformed three bedrooms into habitable spaces.

Finally, bone-tired, Charlie burrowed under the freshly washed sheets beside her husband and expelled a long breath. Although accustomed to working physically, she'd discovered muscles she didn't realize existed.

Beside her, Simm chuckled softly. "You sound wiped out."

"Just a tad," Charlie said, a smile tugging at the corners of her lips. "This old bed is surprisingly comfortable."

"Probably hasn't been slept in for years," Simm said.

"Maybe not." Charlie's gaze drifted to the window. The moon cast a glow on the treetops, their branches swaying in the blustery wind. The house's old timbers creaked around them.

She turned her head until she met Simm's gaze. "Do you think this place is haunted?"

Simm's eyes widened. "You believe in ghosts?"

"I don't not believe in ghosts. I keep an open mind. You don't think they exist?"

"No. My feet remain firmly on the ground. Nothing floating around, no white sheets, no mumbo jumbo."

"C'mon. How can you say that? There's scientific evidence that backs it up."

"Really? How scientific do you think it is?"

"Cameras and thermometers. You can't argue with those."

Simm chuckled. "I'm sure someone could. Ask Sarah. She's the scientist." He seemed to register Charlie's dismay. "I appreciate your open mind, and I hope you appreciate my right to an opinion. To answer your question, no, I don't think anything haunts this place." He raised a finger. "But if you see a ghost sitting on the end of our bed tonight, wake me up, and I'll be your personal ghostbuster."

CHAPTER 12

Despite their difference in viewpoints, Charlie slept undisturbed by humans or phantoms and woke up nestled in Simm's arms. Bright sunshine pushed past the frilled curtains that were probably green in a previous life. Her gaze skimmed across the room, taking in the peeling floral wallpaper, yellowed in spots, and faded almost to invisibility in others. Four dark wooden posts, dulled and scratched with age, rose from each corner of the bed. A threadbare canopy stretched limply overhead, attempting to spare them a view of the chipped ceiling. A matching high-boy dresser stood in the corner with a single chair beside it, its padded needlepoint seat pale and tattered.

After their work the day before, the place showed a glimmer of the charm Charlie expected, if she overlooked its shabby condition. It made it hard to believe anything illegal or sinister happened here. And maybe it hadn't, she reminded herself.

Charlie slithered out of bed without waking Simm. Grabbing a robe, she went downstairs and entered the kitchen. Noah stirred something in a bowl, his back to her. She relished the moment, thinking about the big, bearded hermit they'd met last year who terrified people with a single glance. She never imagined she'd see that man as a gentle, domesticated giant.

Noah had shopped for provisions. Bacon sizzled and popped on the stove, and coffee gurgled in the coffeemaker, the welcoming scent filling the room, as he prepared what appeared to be blueberry pancakes.

"I'm impressed," Charlie said, catching his attention. "Always been a cook?"

A hint of sadness appeared in Noah's eyes. "Only since I had no choice. I helped in the kitchen, but Lyann did the bulk of the cooking."

Charlie snuck a glance at him as she poured a coffee. "Either she taught you well, or you're a great learner." A teasing smile accompanied her words.

"She taught me many things." The wistfulness in his voice deepened.

"You miss her," Charlie said. "I couldn't even contemplate losing Simm." A pain formed in her chest at the thought.

"I didn't want to go on," Noah said. "But you know that. You saw how I lived."

"What changed?" she asked.

His hands stilled, and his gaze lifted to stare out the window. "Plenty, I guess. You and Simm had something to do with it," he said, smiling in her direction. "You jolted me out of my self-pity and made me realize the world kept spinning even after Lyann was gone." His concentration shifted to the bowl again, although Charlie doubted he noticed the mixture. "Then there was Sarah. She needled me to visit her in Montreal and threatened to come to the cabin if I didn't. I couldn't let her do that."

"So, you went to visit her?"

"I did. It was awkward at first. I hadn't seen much of her since Lyann died." A big shoulder lifted and dropped. "But she made me feel comfortable, and the next time, it was easier."

"She's a nice person," Charlie said, watching him closely.

Noah smiled and nodded.

"Are you done with it? Will you leave your cabin?" Charlie thought of the crude shack in the woods. She wouldn't spend a night in it, let alone years of Canada's diverse seasons.

"I may keep it as a getaway, but I don't think I'll live in it full time."

Charlie detected a trace of melancholy in his words and wondered at the source. If he loved the cabin, why move? Did Sarah factor into the equation?

"Would you come here?" she asked. "It's yours now."

"It always was. I told Ethan he could have it, but we never completed the paperwork." Noah's reflective gaze roamed around the kitchen. "Needs upkeep. Expensive renovations. Property taxes are outside my range. I can't afford it, not if we don't find the money. I'd have to sell."

It's a shame, Charlie thought with a heavy heart. The home, although in disrepair, had remained in the Wolfe family for several generations. A stranger would buy it, and Noah would lose his legacy.

"Could you go back to photography? That could help with the finances."

"It's possible. I'd have to do something," he said, his expression pained. "I lived cheap, but my savings are pretty much depleted. On top of that, I'm out of practice. I've spent so much time wrapped in grief and bitterness; I've forgotten how to do anything else."

Charlie laid her hand on his arm, his agony touching her. "It'll come back to you. You'll make it work."

Noah snorted. "Really? On both a social and professional scale, I'm inept. It'd be like learning to walk again."

"And learning to love again," Charlie added. She focused on the coffee in her mug, but she felt Noah's gaze on her.

"What smells so good?"

Charlie and Noah turned as Simm strode into the kitchen.

"Noah, are you teaching my wife how to cook?" he asked.

"I'm taking notes for you, hon. I'd love to eat like this every morning," Charlie said.

Simm sent Noah a mock frown.

Charlie settled at the table with her coffee mug cradled in her hands. "Sarah's not up yet?"

"I'm here." The sleepy voice answered Charlie's question. Sarah, clasping the worn journal to her chest, shuffled in, with dark circles under her eyes, her hair in a messy bun.

"Are you okay?" Noah asked, his expression concerned.

"I'm fine. Didn't sleep much." She turned to Charlie, holding up the notebook. "This is so fascinating. I'm addicted."

"Anything interesting?" Charlie asked with raised brows.

"Everything's interesting, but does it solve the mystery of the missing money? Probably not." She sat down and set the journal on the table. Simm joined them as Noah arranged platters heaped with food before them.

"I can't stand the suspense," Charlie said, helping herself to pancakes and bacon. "What's it about? Who wrote it?"

"Daphne Wolfe. It's dated from 1875 to late 1876. The wife of Percival Wolfe, founder of the family empire. Not happily married. The way she tells it, Old Percy was a tyrant and considered her only valuable for her looks and producing children. But she only gave him two, a girl and a boy. Of course, he considered girls of no use, and the boy was God's gift."

"Was the girl the firstborn?" Charlie asked, leaning forward in her chair.

"Yes. And that's when Percival decreed only firstborn boys stood to inherit whatever assets remained in his estate."

"That poor little girl," Charlie said, shaking her head.

"She was a child when Daphne wrote the journal, but I imagine she married an ugly old rich man who needed someone to breed children, as her mother had." Sarah didn't hide her disgust.

"So, the diary is about Daphne's unhappy marriage?" Simm asked, spearing a piece of bacon.

"In a way. She despised Percy and wanted revenge. I think she tried to reveal his secrets, but she wrote in code."

"Code?" Simm said, his tone disbelieving. "Like a secret language or something?"

"Poetry. I'll give you an example," Sarah said. She opened the journal where a napkin stood in as a bookmark. She cleared her throat. "Listen to this."

Overcome by the depths of deception
Crushed by betrayal and unkindness
I searched for answers from the inception
With your disregard so cheap and mindless
If not love, was it my name?
I have the key to win this game
You think your secrets are hidden
But you will fall unbidden.

Sarah waited, a faint smile on her lips.

Charlie glanced at Simm and Noah, wondering if they caught the poem's message, but baffled expressions confirmed her fears.

Simm cleared his throat. "I have a limited knowledge of poetry, but I doubt that's award-winning."

Sarah shook her head. "Don't worry about the form. Did you hear the content?"

"She sounds bitter," Charlie ventured. "Her husband may have cheated on her. Or betrayed her in some other way."

Sarah regarded her as if she were a child on the brink of solving a complicated math problem. "And?"

"And...she's planning her revenge?" Charlie said, her tone uncertain. She wished Sarah would blurt out the answer and save them the suspense.

"Yes. Obviously. But she's discovered his secret." A triumphant smile lit Sarah's face.

"Okay, so he may have had an affair," Noah said. "His wife found out, and she's pissed enough to write bad poetry about it. How does that help us?"

Sarah's shoulders slumped. "It may not, but she located the key."

"A key? You mean a physical key? For what?" Charlie asked.

Sarah waved her hand around the room. "This house is a hundred and fifty years old. It probably has secret rooms or passageways or little nooks to hide things. We need the key to find what's hidden."

"What if it's a metaphorical key? Like a key to his heart or a key to happiness?" Charlie said.

"It could be, but I have a feeling it's not. She talks about hidden secrets. It makes sense that the evidence of his secrets and the key are in physical form."

Noah ran his hands through his hair, looking unconvinced. "Something may be hidden, but how's it related to Ethan and the money? What's the connection between Daphne in 1875 and Ethan now?"

Simm's expression betrayed his skepticism. "Finding a key in this labyrinth of a house could take weeks."

Sarah's eyes gleamed with unwavering determination. "Exploring this place might reveal other clues. Hidden compartments, secret passages—the possibilities are endless. Ask yourself why the journal was in a locked drawer. There has to be a reason."

A tense silence descended upon the group. Charlie wasn't sure whose side to take. Simm always applied a methodical approach, while Sarah's enthusiasm offered a tantalizing glimpse into the Wolfe family's hidden past.

"Fine," Simm finally relented, a hint of resignation in his voice. "We'll work on both fronts. But let me know if you find anything remotely suspicious, Sarah."

A delighted grin stretched across Sarah's face. "Consider it done."

Charlie's mind raced. The Wolfe home, once a symbol of grandeur and power, now held a deeper secret, a secret that whispered of hidden rooms, coded messages, and a wife's thirst for revenge. The mystery had taken a fascinating, and slightly unsettling, turn.

She wondered what Sarah thought about ghosts.

CHAPTER 13

Simm left the trio to their devices and headed downtown to the Ontario Provincial Police station. He'd set up an early meeting with Detective Baxter, the cop who handled the investigation into Ethan's death. As an ex-cop, Simm realized police officers hated having private investigators interrogate them. It was about avoiding scrutiny, along with the alpha male syndrome. Simm required tact to keep things smooth.

The OPP building, which also housed the fire department, was modern and a decent size by small-town standards. He'd probably meet the fire investigator here when the time came. Inside, he stepped up to the plexiglass reception booth where a stern-faced, middle-aged woman greeted him. She examined him with a gaze as sharp as a hawk's when he explained he had a meeting with Detective Baxter. She instructed him to wait a moment while she called the detective.

Shortly, a weary-looking man in his fifties emerged from the end of the hallway. Tall and heavyset, he paired his snug gray suit with a white shirt and no tie. Simm was sure the rumpled suit jacket spent its time on a chair and the cop grabbed it as he left his office. Baxter's salt-and-pepper hair was full but trimmed, as was the gray mustache that sat above stern, unsmiling lips. Displeasure and resignation hung over him like a fog.

Shaking Simm's hand, the man muttered, "Come on."

Simm followed him down the corridor and wrinkled his nose as a whiff of stale cigarette smoke drifted back. They entered a tidy office via another corridor and doorway. It contained a desk, two chairs, a computer, scanner, and printer. A few family pictures decorated the walls, offering a glimpse of his life outside the sterile precinct.

"I'm impressed," Simm said, adopting a light tone. "When I was a cop, my space was a mess. Files and papers everywhere."

"Welcome to the digital age. If we waste a piece of paper, we hear about it. Doris gives us the speech. Believe me, you don't want to hear the speech."

Simm assumed Doris was the friendly receptionist.

Baxter waved to the chair opposite his desk. As Simm sat, the cop leaned back and threaded his fingers together over his stomach.

"Ethan Wolfe. The brother hired you to investigate his death?" From the detective's tone, he could've been discussing an outbreak of leprosy.

"Not exactly." Simm leaned back in his seat and crossed his left foot over his right knee, going for a casual, "let's chat" look. "He hired me to find the missing money, but it's a coincidence that Ethan died two days after the fortune disappeared. I have a few questions about his death. Just to satisfy my curiosity."

"The fire investigator ruled it an accident."

A rapid-fire delivery, Baxter obviously wanted the words out and over with.

Simm nodded, already planning his next move. "I'll talk to him, but I wanted your perspective. I understand Mike Wade called in the fire."

"He called 9-1-1. Then they informed us," the detective said.

"Who arrived first?"

"The fire department... by a few seconds."

"Where was Mike when everyone got there?"

"In front, standing by his truck."

"Did you question him?"

"I did."

"And? Did he seem all right? Was he inebriated? Did he smell like gasoline? Any signs of injury?" Simm had hoped for a more talkative cop, but Baxter was naturally concise, or he wanted to reveal as little as possible. Simm's suspicions leaned toward the latter.

"He was fine. At a friend's house, drove by, saw the fire, and called it in." Baxter related the facts like he'd describe a fender bender, not a deadly fire.

"The friend can't vouch for him."

"That's correct. No reason to believe Mike would harm Ethan."

Simm tried to hide his surprise at such a blanket statement. Did the detective serve as judge and jury for the town? "How well do you know Mike? Or Ethan?" he asked.

The cop's voice hardened. "Everyone around here knows the Wolfe family. I'd never met Mike."

Simm locked eyes with the man until Baxter averted his gaze.

"Anything else?" the detective said. "I've got work to do."

"Yeah, one other thing. Who has Ethan's computer? You or the financial guy?"

Baxter's response was a curt shake of his head. "Neither. Didn't find one."

Simm's eyes widened. "You're kidding."

Baxter shook his head, his gaze hard.

Disbelief coursed through Simm. Ethan's laptop gone. Not a good sign.

Recovering, Simm stood and shook the detective's hand. "Thanks for your help. I'll find my way out."

CHAPTER 14

"Did it go well?" Charlie asked.

She'd stepped outside to let Harley do his business and watched Simm pull into the driveway. Her husband scratched the pug behind his ears and straightened to give Charlie a quick kiss. His dismayed expression concerned her.

He sighed, the sound heavy in the muggy afternoon air. "In the sense that I talked to Detective Baxter, yes. Informative? Not so much."

Charlie's stomach tightened. "What did he say?"

"The usual," Simm muttered, his jaw clenching. "Confirmed everything we already knew. An accident. Case closed."

Disappointment tinged Charlie's voice. "Nothing more?"

"There was something," Simm said, his gaze hardening. "He lied to me."

Adrenaline jolted through Charlie. "About what?"

Simm hesitated then met her gaze head-on. "It's hard to pinpoint exactly, but his body language, his eyes... they told a different story. My gut feeling is he's holding something back. And he wasn't happy about it. Deep down, he's not a liar."

"You think Ethan's death wasn't accidental, and the cop's covering it up?" It chilled Charlie to say the words aloud.

"That's what I suspect, but I don't want to mention it to Noah yet. There's no need to upset him unless we're sure."

Charlie nodded. She'd hoped the meeting would produce a more positive result. Although Sarah's quest for a key intrigued her, Charlie also had difficulty linking it to financial fraud and murder.

"There's something else," Simm said.

"Really? What?"

"According to the detective, they didn't find Ethan's computer."

This information stunned Charlie. They'd assumed the OPP confiscated the laptop as standard procedure. If that wasn't the case, it meant someone stole it. Probably the same person who'd come across a windfall.

A movement caught Charlie's eye. She turned as Bosco loped toward them, looking for attention. Noah stood on the porch, beside the newly repaired steps, and observed Charlie and Simm.

"Any news?" he asked.

Even from this distance, Charlie saw the tension in Noah's stance. During Simm's absence, as Charlie continued her quest for cleanliness, Noah pounded nails into the wood as if he could beat information out of them. If only it was so easy.

"Nothing new," Simm said, keeping his tone neutral. "Anything here?"

"Actually, yes. Sarah thinks she's found something."

Charlie hurried into the house with Simm. The dogs trailed close behind. Eager for good news, she followed Noah to the kitchen where the open journal rested on the table among notes and diagrams, all written in Sarah's orderly script. The scientist bristled with excitement, her eyes bright and a smile on her face.

"I discovered something," she said, her voice brimming with enthusiasm. "As you know, Daphne was an amateur poet and loved to sprinkle poems throughout her diaries. Since the first one hinted at a key, I studied the rest. Listen to this."

Shambles is my heart
And we cannot part
Our love is no more
But I've found the door
Freedom will be mine
All in good time
Regrets I will not keep
As you reach eternal sleep

The three of them stared at her in expectation.

"Don't you get it?" Sarah asked, a touch of exasperation creeping into her voice. "It jumped out at me."

The only thing jumping out at Charlie was that she didn't comprehend poetry, but she understood Daphne's talent was only a tiny step above "Roses are Red, Violets are Blue."

"The key, once we find it, will unlock a hidden door," Sarah said. "To be honest, I'd started doubting whether a physical key existed, but I'm sure now. There's a door, and it needs a key."

Charlie suspected Sarah pounced on one word in the poem and used it as a springboard to a wild conclusion. But, with no other conclusions, why not? "What about no regrets and eternal sleep? Does that mean she wanted to murder him?"

"It's possible," Sarah said. She turned to Noah. "Any rumors of past murders?"

"Not that I know of," he said, bewilderment reflected in his tone.

"Maybe she killed him, and now he's haunting the place," Charlie said, ignoring Simm's glare.

Sarah and Noah shifted their attention to Charlie.

"Ghosts?" Noah asked, his expression stunned.

"I said maybe."

"Let's not worry about who may or may not have been murdered and whether we're rooming with ghosts. We need to stay focused on why we're here," Simm said. "I like your theory, Sarah, but we don't know where to find a key or hidden doors."

Sarah's shoulders slumped. "Neither do I. This place is so big."

"Let's think," Charlie proposed, pacing the kitchen, deep in thought. "If Daphne filled the journal with negative comments about her husband, she wouldn't have left it in full view. She would've hidden it. But it was in the desk drawer, and I presume the desk originally belonged to Percy." She recalled the snake-decorated desk and thought it was an apt pairing with the despot in the portrait.

"You think he found it?" Noah said.

"Anyone could have, over the years," Simm said.

"Exactly. Whoever found it locked it in the desk," Charlie said. "Probably because they knew it was special or contained damaging information." She stopped her pacing and held up a finger. "What if it led them to the key? And the door that it unlocked?"

The three others stared at her in anticipation.

Charlie continued. "What if the person was Ethan?"

"Playing devil's advocate here, but why Ethan?" Simm asked. "Like I said, it could've been anyone."

"You're right," Charlie said. "We don't know what happened in this house. Unless that journal or others reveal more, we can only work with what we have. Something bothered Ethan. He was preoccupied, perhaps distressed. Let's assume Ethan found the key. What if he used it to hide something pertaining to the money or a crime of some sort? Let's see if we can find it and learn where it leads."

She saw nods of approval, more hesitant from the men.

"Where would he keep it?" Charlie said.

"In his room?" Noah suggested.

Sarah spoke up, her expression doubtful. "We went through it. We didn't find anything."

"Noah, you knew him best," Charlie said. "Can you think of something?"

Sorrow loomed in Noah's eyes. "I didn't know him well, not in the past years. I'm kicking myself now."

Charlie winced, regretting her words. "Can Mike help?"

"Good idea," Simm said. "Let's call him. At least he's familiar with the place."

Noah looked uncertain. "I wouldn't count on Mike too much. You saw what he's like. He has trouble focusing on one thing at a time. He's been working here since he was a kid. No one ever had the heart to replace him because he's so loyal."

Despite his doubts, Noah made the call, and within half an hour, Mike Wade's pickup pulled into the driveway and parked behind the rented SUV. He'd already passed the sniff test with the dogs, so they gave him a brief greeting before assuming their positions on the floor.

Mike's wide-eyed and wary expression signaled his nervousness as he entered the library. He'd received no explanation, only a request to see them as soon as possible.

"What's up?" he asked Noah, his gaze moving from person to person. "Something wrong?"

"Nothing's wrong, but we need your help." Noah sent an uncertain glance toward Sarah before returning his gaze to Mike. "We're searching for a key. One that may open a door...possibly a hidden door."

With each word, Noah's discomfort clearly increased. The poems and Sarah's suppositions didn't convince him. He looked at his sister-in-law for help.

"Let me explain," Sarah said, taking center stage. "I studied a journal that we found. I think there's a key that unlocks a concealed room or passageway."

"Okay," Mike said, appearing unfazed by the bizarre story. "My keys are only for doors and buildings. Nothing for a hidden room." His gaze swiveled from side to side as if he'd suddenly discover a secret door.

"No, we didn't expect you to. But maybe Ethan found the key, and he hid it somewhere. Did he ever mention it to you?"

"No," Mike said, pursing his lips.

"Any ideas where he'd hide one?" Sarah asked.

Mike squinted and contemplated the question. "I'd guess his bedroom, the kitchen, or the workshop."

"Are you aware of any hidden rooms?" Simm asked. A muscle spasmed in his jawline, and Charlie could tell her husband's patience was running out.

"I don't know of any, but it's an old house, so it wouldn't surprise me. They did things like that back then." He jiggled his legs and tugged his shirt.

"I'm going to the workshop," Simm said. Everyone trailed behind as he spun on his heel and stalked outside. They halted at the outskirts of the building's remains. Hundreds of footprints disturbed the ashes, no doubt left by firefighters, cops, paramedics, and investigators.

Charlie snuck a glance at Noah. He hadn't ventured near the workshop since their initial arrival, and the sight of it clearly brought back painful memories. Since then, everybody gave it a wide berth, mostly because cleaning the house took priority, but also it was a stark and eerie reminder of how Ethan died. Now, like birds on a wire, they formed a line in front of it.

Did Ethan hide a key there? Possibly, but finding it amongst the rubble and dirt would be challenging.

"No one step in, please," Simm said. He took out his cell phone and snapped pictures from every angle, walking around the structure's perimeter, zooming in and out, until he lowered the phone with a satisfied nod.

"Do we clean it up and search?" Noah asked.

"I don't think we have a choice. But we can work on several fronts." Simm turned to the caretaker. "I was going to search out the blueprints from the city, but I never thought to ask you. Do you know of any blueprints or schematics of the property floating around?"

Charlie interrupted before Mike responded. "I think I spotted some amongst the stuff from the drawers."

"Good," Simm said. "Can you and Sarah examine those with Mike to search for a hiding spot? You can also check out Ethan's room and the kitchen again, more in depth. Noah and I will tackle this."

Charlie glanced at Noah, her brow wrinkled with worry. Would it be too difficult to scour the place where his brother died such a horrible death?

Noah caught her look and gave her a slight smile. "It's okay. I got this."

Charlie squeezed his forearm before she followed Sarah and Mike into the house.

CHAPTER 15

Charlie led them to the piles of papers on the desk. From one of them, she pulled a worn and yellowed sheath of documents rolled and tied with a frayed string. She spread them on the desk's surface, the edges curling like ancient scrolls. Mike leaned in, and his brow furrowed as he squinted at the faded ink.

"Yep, it's this property." A thin, twitchy finger moved across the brittle paper. "Here's the house, exactly as we see it. And that's the little storage shed tucked away in the corner."

"Where's the building that burned?" Charlie asked.

"Not on here. It was only built fifty years ago."

Charlie peered closer, the spidery cursive writing blurring before her eyes. The faded ink offered no clues except the year 1875, no hidden chambers marked with bold lettering. Disappointment nibbled at her.

"What do you think?" Charlie asked Mike. "Are these the correct measurements? Is there space for a passageway or room?"

He pressed his lips together and shook his head. "Maybe. I can measure it."

"Could you do that, please? Sarah and I will search Ethan's room again, but we'll purge it this time."

They left Mike with his assignment and traipsed up the stairs to one of the largest bedrooms, decorated with the same faded and peeling wallpaper and dark, heavy furniture. Apart from dusting, washing the bedding, and sweeping the floor, they'd disturbed nothing else. His clothes remained in the closet, and his belongings filled the roomy dresser drawers. A bookcase lined with old books, an armchair, and a floor lamp sat in one corner. Paintings dated from the early 1900s adorned the walls. The room was bare of anything that hinted at Ethan's interests, friends, or immediate family. It was simply where he laid his head.

They flipped the room upside down, scrutinized every book on the shelf, even wrestled the heavy dresser away from the wall, hoping to find a hidden key, a secret passage—anything to explain the cryptic messages in the journal.

Charlie heaved a sigh and regarded Sarah's concentrated look as she ran her fingers underneath the bedframe. Her curiosity overcame her. "Were you and your sister a lot alike?"

Sarah's face registered surprise at the unexpected question. "No, not at all." She chuckled. "You know how it is with siblings. They're often opposites."

"Actually, I don't. I'm an only child."

"Sorry to hear that. Although I'm sure you were happy, I wouldn't have traded my sister for anything." Melancholy filled her voice. "She was so pretty and smart."

Charlie didn't interrupt Sarah, but she could easily argue pretty and smart ran in the family.

"Lyann was very calm and serene. You may think Noah is reserved, but that wasn't always the case. With Lyann, he was cheerful and almost gregarious. A wonderful father. He loved his family so much. It was awful. He suffered alone, and so did I. I wanted to help him, and I wanted his help. But, apart from a couple of get-togethers over the years, we didn't really connect until recently." She swiped at her cheeks and gazed around the room. "God knows I'd wish nothing bad on Ethan, but his death drew Noah out of his self-imposed confinement. That's what it took."

Yes, Charlie thought, Sarah was right. Without this tragedy, Noah would still live in the bush, mourning his family. Instead, he mourned his brother. Would it ever end?

"I'm sorry," Charlie said. "I shouldn't have brought it up. Sometimes, my curiosity overtakes my common sense."

Sarah gave her a watery smile. "It's okay. Despite the tears, it helps to talk about it. Eventually, I'll discuss it without crying."

"We'd better finish our search, or the guys will give us something to cry about." Charlie laughed, hoping to lighten the mood.

They removed and examined each piece of clothing from the wardrobe. With the help of a flashlight, they searched every inch of the musty closet for a hidden key. They stripped the bedding again, lifted the mattress, and inspected the springs and headboard of the antique bed. Nothing.

Huffing out a breath, Sarah looked at Charlie. "The kitchen's next."

As they trekked down the stairs, a wave of futility swept over Charlie. Why were they doing this? Would a key give them answers about the missing fortune? Or a potential murder?

Yet, besides cleaning the house, how else would she fill her time? This way, she cleaned while hunting for a mysterious key that may or may not exist.

At the bottom of the steps, they met Mike, tape measure in hand. "So far, the sitting room and main living room fit the plans. Same for the entranceway." Several times, he pulled out the tape measure and let it snap back into place as he hopped from foot to foot. "Library next."

A sudden thought occurred to Charlie. "Is there an attic in this house?"

"Sure is," Mike said. "There's a drop-down ladder in one of the bedroom closets. I forget which one."

Sarah and Charlie exchanged a look.

Their search for access ended in a south-facing room decorated with washed-out sunflower wallpaper. Two sharp tugs on the rope released a ladder and a cascade of dust.

Charlie followed Sarah up the ladder while Mike took the rear. A gasp from ahead made Charlie tighten her hands on the rung and lift a fearful gaze upward.

"What's wrong?" she said, as her stomach clenched.

"So much stuff." Sarah's voice was filled with wonder, and Charlie released a breath of relief.

As her head cleared the opening, Charlie understood. Dust motes danced in the slivers of sunlight that pierced through the attic window. Following Sarah, Charlie navigated the labyrinth of cobweb-draped furniture, her flashlight beam revealing more clutter than treasure.

Mike remained by the entrance, a nervous, shadowy figure. He muttered something about ghosts and cobwebs, earning a glare from Sarah.

They rifled through boxes and trunks, bags and packages, the palms of their hands black with dirt.

"Anything?" Charlie called out, her voice echoing in the stale air.

"Not yet," Sarah replied, her voice muffled as she sifted through a trunk. "Just stinky moth-eaten shawls and enough porcelain dolls to populate a horror movie."

Charlie resolved to end her search after one last box. Inside, she discovered a collection of photo albums. Opening the first one, she recognized Noah as a young boy, his features evident. Her laugh of pleasure drew Sarah to her side. Flipping through the pages, they witnessed a colorful portrayal of joyful times among family and friends. Unsure if anything would come of it, they repatriated the box to the main floor.

With the box tucked away in a corner, Sarah and Charlie, once again, tackled the kitchen. They took up positions at opposite ends of the cupboards and started a methodical search. They'd barely begun when Simm and Noah entered by the back door. One glimpse of Simm's face told Charlie the news wasn't good.

"What's wrong?" she said, pushing herself to her feet. She saw Noah's thunderstruck expression, and her throat clogged with dread. She watched as he lowered himself onto a chair and stared at the table, his gaze unfocused.

"We found something strange." Simm shot a concerned glance in Noah's direction. "Of course, I'll check with the cops and the fire investigator, but I don't understand how they could've deemed the fire accidental."

"What is it?" Sarah, unable to disguise the tremor in her voice, took the seat next to Noah and laid her hand upon his. He didn't react to her touch.

"Not the key, if that's what you think," Simm said. "But we found a scratch on the car's underside, near the gas tank. It happened after the fire. It was clean, no soot or fire damage."

"I don't understand," Charlie said. "What does that mean?"

"Someone removed something from the vehicle after the fact. They didn't want the investigator to find it. I suspected a remote-controlled device that created a spark and set the car on fire."

Charlie's heartbeat increased as she absorbed this information.

"We searched the entire grounds," Simm said. He held up his gloved hand. In it, was a small black square gadget with a button in the middle. "Found this in the hedge."

CHAPTER 16

Sarah chirped in distress, but Charlie's attention focused on Noah. A fresh layer of grief etched his face, and he seemed to shrink further into himself. This wasn't accidental. Ethan hadn't died in a tragic, accidental fire—he'd been murdered.

Silence reigned for several long minutes, everyone's thoughts freezing them in place, until Sarah stood and slid her arm across Noah's shoulders.

A fist slammed onto the table, the sudden noise making Sarah jump and Charlie flinch. "Damn it!" Noah roared, his voice raw with a mixture of grief and fury. "Why? Why would anyone kill him?"

"We don't understand the whys yet, but we will," Simm said in his usual calm manner. "At least we know the how."

Simm sent a meaningful glance toward Charlie. She got the message. Another safe assignment, one involving a white-collar, financial crime, turned into a murder case, and the killer was at large.

"We'll give that to the police," she said, gesturing at the remote control. "Let them take it from there."

Noah's eyes narrowed into a fierce glare. "A lot of good that'll do. Simm told me about his meeting with the detective. It's a cover-up."

Anger rolled off him in waves, but Charlie knew he didn't direct it at her. Noah's mistrust of the police fueled his rage. He didn't have wonderful memories of the authorities in Gatineau. They'd suspected him of mysterious deaths in the area, and Noah didn't appreciate it.

However, Charlie speculated his mistrust was justified this time.

"What do we do?" Sarah asked, her voice trembling. "This is serious. We're talking murder."

Noah shifted his intense, blue eyes to Simm. "I want you to work the case." His words left no room for argument. "I trust you and Charlie."

"It's a criminal act. The police should handle it," Simm said.

"We're not sure it's murder," Noah said. "So far, it's a suspicion. If you discover it is, we'll tell the cops. Right now, I have no confidence in them." Noah clearly sought to rationalize his opinion.

Simm held his gaze for a moment before turning to Charlie. She understood her husband was torn. He wanted to help Noah, but not if she wasn't comfortable. It was her call.

Charlie hesitated. The key they'd been searching for, the hidden fortune—it all felt insignificant now. A life had been taken, and justice demanded to be served.

"Look," she finally said, "let's give it a shot. We'll attempt to gather more evidence, get to the bottom of it. If we hit a dead end, we hand everything to the OPP."

Simm nodded. "Agreed. We'll give it five more days, a week in all."

"Sounds like a good plan. Ethan died, and the money disappeared weeks ago," Sarah said, her brow creased. "A delay of another week won't make a difference."

"Noah, are you okay with that?" Simm asked.

He nodded, a steely determination in his eyes.

"What's next?" Charlie asked no one in particular. "Do we keep looking for the key? Will that lead us anywhere?" She put into words her doubts about the key, despite knowing it'd disappoint Sarah if they abandoned the search.

"I haven't lined up any more meetings today," Simm said. "I suggest we look. Stay open to everything. Something else might tell us what happened in Ethan's life. I'm talking documents, letters, USBs, backup drives, passwords, anything." He glanced at Noah. "The detective said they didn't find Ethan's laptop. Either someone stole it, or it's hidden. We'd strike gold if we found it."

"Chances are somebody took it," Sarah said, despair in her tone. "Whoever did this." She waved her hand in disgust toward the deadly black object that rested in the middle of the table.

A shuffling sound caught their attention. Mike stood in the doorway, wringing his hands.

"I did the ground floor, and everything checks out, but I gotta run. I can come back later."

"Thanks, Mike," Simm said. "We'll be in touch."

No one spoke until the door closed behind the caretaker.

"I'm not sure what he heard," Simm said, "but I'd like to keep this to ourselves."

Noah frowned. "You think Mike is wrapped up in this?" He sounded dubious.

"It's possible. He has access to the house and grounds." Simm shrugged. "If not, he might reveal something to someone else without meaning to. Just being cautious."

With a newfound sense of urgency, they split the house search into two groups. The men took the dining room, moving heavy buffets and cabinets, while Charlie and Sarah focused on the kitchen.

After another hour of emptying and examining cupboards, Charlie stood and stretched, feeling the ache in her back. An easier route had to exist.

She put herself in Ethan's shoes. Anyone searching for the key would follow the path they themselves took. Where's the weirdest hiding spot? Somewhere not so accessible, a place no one happened upon in their daily life.

Charlie's gaze wandered the room. The antique cupboards, clearly original to the house, bore the marks of countless repairs and renovations over the years. At some point, an owner substituted the sink and taps with an antique style that fit the decor. They added modern appliances: the refrigerator, stove, and dishwasher. She assumed an ice box had stood where the fridge was now. The stainless-steel stove replaced the ancient wood-burning model and oven she pictured in her mind. For the dishwasher, they would have removed a section of cupboards, added plumbing, and slid it into place.

Charlie studied the appliance. The workmanship wasn't top notch. It had space on each side and wobbled. Bending over to examine it, she realized it was a portable version on wheels, shoved under the counter. Peering at the cracked and aged linoleum, she ran a finger over the dirty wheel tracks imbedded in it.

A surge of energy shot through her as she grasped the sides of the dishwasher. With surprising ease, the rusty wheels moved, and the appliance rolled out, revealing a tangle of hoses and wires behind it. Sarah, drawn by the commotion, stood beside her, eyebrows raised.

"What are you doing?" Sarah asked.

"There might be something back here," Charlie replied, her voice tight with anticipation.

Together, they maneuvered the dishwasher until it rested at an angle, and Charlie had a clear view of the appliance's back.

Taped at eye-level, was an antique key.

CHAPTER 17

"It was Ethan, after all." A hush fell over the room at Noah's words.

Charlie agreed with him. The dishwasher was a recent model. It may have replaced an older one, but Ethan installed it during his time.

Simm raised an eyebrow. "What tipped you off, Charlie?"

A wry chuckle escaped Charlie's lips. "The wheels. They scratched tracks on the linoleum. When I wiped those tracks, rust came off—a dead giveaway that Ethan moved the appliance recently."

Simm flashed her a proud smile.

Sarah paced the room, her brows lowered in concentration. "Ethan read the journal and found the key," she said. "Did he find something the key opened?"

"Could it be for the desk?" Charlie said. "For the drawer we tried to open?"

Her words elicited a scramble to the library. Charlie strived to ignore the snake carvings as she watched Simm insert the key into the lock. After several futile attempts, they eliminated the desk as a match for the key.

"So, it's definitely for something else, but what?" Simm said.

"We'll only know once we locate it." Charlie was determined to do so. Especially if Ethan hid his computer somewhere. "We haven't come across a box or chest that requires a key, so do we agree it's a door?" Charlie asked, moving her glance from person to person. If nothing else, the discovery lifted everyone's spirits, adding a gleam of determination to their expressions.

"Look for a door, and we may stumble across something. Keep your eyes open," Simm said.

They split up, each taking a room. They knocked on walls, checked for hollow spaces, and peeked behind furniture, searching for anything unusual.

Again, Charlie found herself in the library. She stood with her hands on her hips, surveying the vast collection of books lining two walls. Visions of movie scenes flashed through her mind—a strategically placed book triggering a cascade of movement that revealed a hidden passage.

She hoped that wasn't the case here. Testing every book would take an eternity. A better scenario was a concealed button or lever, but where?

Charlie shifted her attention to another wall. Portraits, hiding a vault, also a movie standard. She couldn't ignore them. Carefully, she peeked behind the framed faces, climbing on a chair for the higher ones. Nothing but blank walls greeted her.

Pushing the chair back into place, she studied the creepiest portrait. The man appeared angry and unpleasant. Charlie pegged his age at about fifty with hair more pepper than salt and a well-trimmed mustache. The pose included only his head and shoulders, showing a white shirt, black jacket, and black cravat, but it suggested a trim build. His eyes drew her attention. Darker than Noah's but hard and cruel. This man brooked no argument and fewer fools.

Charlie took a step back and compared his portrait to the others. Instead of facing forward, his gaze focused to the side. She followed it and put herself in his line of vision.

Charlie swiveled so his eyes burned into her back, and she slowly placed one foot in front of the other, trying not to deviate from her path. Harley padded beside her, curious about his mistress' doings. Reaching the wall of books, Charlie glanced over her shoulder to confirm she was on the right track.

Facing them, she studied the titles, but nothing stood out. She pulled her cell phone from her back pocket and sent out a quick text. Within minutes, Sarah entered the room, Simm and Noah close behind.

"What happened?" Sarah asked, her concerned gaze searching the surroundings.

Charlie swept her arms toward the books she faced. "Look at these. Anything strike you as familiar? Something in the journal?"

Sarah peered over her right shoulder as Simm moved to Charlie's other side. "Why are you standing here?" he asked.

Charlie explained her theory about the man's stare. "It sounds farfetched, but it's worth a try."

"A brilliant try," Sarah said. She frowned in concentration as she squinted at each book. "I'm trying to remember things Daphne wrote in her poems that might connect to a novel, but I'm drawing a blank." She pointed to a black, leather-bound book entitled *Uncle Tom's Cabin*. "That's a classic. Try it."

Charlie removed the volume from its spot and held her breath. No creaking of gears. No swinging shelves. Disappointment settled heavily in Charlie's gut as she flipped through the pages, the musty scent of aged paper filling her nostrils. With a sigh, she slammed the book shut and stepped back, ready to abandon the theory.

"Hold on." Simm took her place and ran his gaze over the books.

"It was a stupid idea," Charlie said. "Let's move on."

"Sarah, try again," Simm said. "Anything else strike you?"

Sarah leaned forward to peek around him, her eyes narrowed. "I don't know. There're so many. I'll crosscheck the poems and journal for something that stands out." Her shoulders slumped. "It may all be for nothing."

The fading of Sarah's eternal optimism distressed Charlie.

Noah's long arm reached over Sarah's shoulder and pointed at a book covered in red leather directly in line with Simm's nose.

CHAPTER 18

Diana of the Crossways by George Meredith.

Simm removed it and slowly flipped through the pages with Charlie peeking around his arm. She gave a startled yelp when she spotted a few words scribbled in the right-hand margin. Further on, several more pages with notes. Simm relinquished the novel to an eager Sarah, who practically snatched it from his grasp. With a determined glint in her eyes, Sarah rushed to the desk and grabbed a pen and paper, ready to transcribe what they hoped was a message.

Simm turned to Noah. "Lucky guess, wouldn't you say?" he asked, a grin spreading across his face.

Noah shrugged, a hint of amusement dancing in his eyes. "Just a hunch based on two things," he said. "Daphne and Percy's eldest daughter was named Diana. And, from the time he was a kid, Ethan had a fascination with puzzles, codes, and mysteries, kind of like Sarah and Charlie." He grinned. "It doesn't surprise me he got wrapped up in this. He might've used Daphne's journals to either find something or hide it. Maybe both."

Charlie peered over Sarah's shoulder. "Can you read it?" The faded and smudged cursive writing convinced Charlie that Sarah was better equipped to handle the job.

"Most of it, yes." Sarah pulled open the desk drawer and removed a magnifying glass. As she studied the book and scribbled notes, the others took chairs and made themselves comfortable, the dogs settling at their feet.

Charlie, her gaze darting between the book and Sarah's focused expression, couldn't help but feel a pang of doubt. The odds seemed impossibly stacked against them. In a vast library filled with thousands of volumes, how could they have stumbled upon a book containing instructions for the key? And even if they had, what were the chances the key led anywhere significant? Or were they so in tune with Ethan's thoughts they inadvertently followed in his footsteps?

Her attention drifted across the room, landing on the stern portrait that led to the discovery. She leaned back in her chair.

"Is that Percy Wolfe?" she asked, directing the question at Noah.

Noah's gaze followed hers, settling on the imposing figure in the painting. "Yes." His voice was laced with a hint of bitterness. "The original tyrant."

"Did many follow in his footsteps?" Simm asked.

Noah snorted. "Every generation had one, at least until ours." His eyes narrowed in thought. "I don't consider myself a tyrant, although I can be difficult. Ethan was anything but."

"Do you have cousins?" Charlie asked.

"No. It was just Eli and my father. We're the last of this generation." A pained expression crossed his face as his words sunk in. "It's only me now. Once I'm gone, that'll be it."

As an only child of only children, Charlie understood the concept of being a family's lone survivor. Taking on that role because of a murder was heartrending.

"Is Eli the tyrant, or was it your father?" Simm asked, determined to steer the conversation back on track.

"My father. No doubt there. Eli is stubborn and prickly at times, but he's a pussycat compared to good old dad." Noah's bitter tone was familiar to Charlie. It echoed Simm's when he discussed his father and brother.

"Tell us about him," Charlie asked. She didn't miss the interested glance Sarah sent toward Noah. The other woman lowered her head and continued with her task, yet Charlie was certain she listened intently.

A hardness descended over Noah's features. "He was all business, not caring about anything besides money and power. Restaurants, hotels, and casinos made up the bulk of his holdings, most of them in Ontario."

"A smart man," Charlie said. She poked the bear, but she expected to reap some revelations.

"Yes," Noah admitted with a sneer. "Also ruthless, overbearing, demanding, and absent. Plus, suspicions of fraud and ties to organized crime drove him from his political life. All in all, a well-rounded person."

Simm nodded his head in understanding. Apart from the political career, Noah's father was a replica of Simm's.

"How did he die?" Simm asked.

"He abused his liver. It gave up."

"And Eli leads a straight and narrow life but inherits nothing," Simm said.

"Nothing from the family trust. Unless something happens to me. Since I have no children."

Noah's voice lowered as he uttered those last five words, a stark reminder of his grief. Charlie's fierce desire for a child made the agony of Noah's loss even more piercing.

"But there's no need to feel sorry for Uncle Eli," Noah continued. "He bought the original vineyards from my grandfather for a song and amassed a fortune with them. At one point, he was the biggest supplier of wine to my father's businesses. That eventually soured. Some sort of disagreement. No surprise." Noah rolled his eyes. "But Eli's not as pure as the driven snow either. He's hard-hearted when negotiating a deal. Just not nearly as cutthroat as my father."

This description didn't shock Charlie. She found Eli pleasant and affable, but she'd spotted a harsh glint in his eyes and suspected he'd be a tough man to do business with.

The sound of Sarah clearing her throat startled everyone from their thoughts. Charlie had almost forgotten about the woman decoding the book's scribbles.

"I copied the notes in sequence," she said, her voice trembling with excitement. "I guessed a few words too difficult to make out, but it hangs together."

She had Charlie's full attention. "What does it say?"

"Don't get too excited. I said it hung together, but it might not tell us a lot. It's a story. Fact or fiction, I don't know."

Sarah cleared her throat again.

The woman needed to change her fortune. She had to escape the confines. As had he. He'd provided his own escape. Why not she? If he only knew she'd hidden her escape within his. He's single-minded. He doesn't see. He believes her without a brain, without a thought. She will protect what is hers, within his. Steps are taken, down they will go, once left, to make it right.

Sarah raised her uncertain gaze to the others. "Ideas? Impressions?"

"Confusing," Charlie said. "Read it again, please."

Sarah obliged, enunciating each word as everyone listened, their expressions focused. "Some things caught my attention," she remarked.

"Go ahead," Noah said. "I didn't grasp much."

"As we already knew, Daphne was in an unhappy marriage," Sarah said. "If this story reflects reality, she planned an escape."

"It's written in the third person," Charlie said. "How are we sure Daphne wrote it, or that it refers to her?"

"We don't. It resembles her handwriting, but without an expert opinion, I can't guarantee she composed it," Sarah said. "Let's assume she wanted deniability. Writing in the first person, Percy could point the finger directly at her. Instead, she could claim she invented a story or interpreted a text. Perhaps, Percy wasn't a reader. Maybe these were Daphne's books and reading was her passion."

Sarah turned her attention to Noah. "Do you remember any stories about Percy and Daphne? Did they remain together? Die of old age?"

"Percy died in his eighties. Daphne fell down a flight of stairs many years earlier and broke her neck. Apparently, an accident. I'm not sure how old she was."

Charlie's gaze darted to Percival Wolfe's portrait. His firmly set mouth, his face's sharp angles, and his almost black eyes exuded evil.

Sarah raised her brows and nodded. "Sounds suspicious."

"Agreed," Charlie said. "And it's obvious her attempt at freedom failed. But what did she mean by his escape? What was he running from?"

"Twice she mentioned 'within his.' What's that about?" Simm asked.

Noah sat with his elbows on his knees and his gaze fixed on the hardwood floor. "Read the last line again."

"Steps are taken, down they will go, once left, to make it right."

Charlie looked at Noah, wondering what he interpreted other than gibberish. "Are you sure you didn't miss a section there?" she asked Sarah. "It makes no sense."

"Exactly what I thought, but I checked it several times. I looked for missing pages. That's the sequence."

Noah straightened. "Directions," he said, his voice filled with newfound conviction.

"What?" Simm said.

"She's giving directions. Down the stairs, turn left, then go right."

"Of course," Charlie said with a gasp. She sprang to her feet and hurried to the entranceway. The others followed and gathered at the foot of the spiral staircase.

Simm directed. "Stairs, left, you're in the hallway. A right leads to the sitting room."

Charlie groaned. "We went through it with a fine-toothed comb. There's nothing there."

"Maybe underneath the stairway?" Sarah said.

Noah shook his head. "No way in."

Several minutes of tapping on walls, feeling for latches or levers, and examining with a flashlight gave no results.

"It's a dead end," Noah said.

Charlie thought about the notes. "Wait a second. Who said these stairs?"

"Basement stairs?" Sarah asked.

"There's no real basement," Noah said. "Just a crawl space under the house, but I remember three or four steps leading into it."

"Show us," Simm said.

Charlie shuddered when Noah led them outside and pushed aside a curtain of ivy to reveal a small door set at an angle against the foundation, its paint peeling like a snake shedding its skin. She'd always hated basements and dark spaces, and incidents during Simm's past cases increased her distaste for them a hundredfold. The heavy clouds blocking the sun and the cool wind that lifted the hair from the back of her neck didn't improve her composure.

Simm struggled to pull free the door, hampered by rusty hinges. Noah grasped it and, with a loud grunt, yanked it open. The door protested with a piercing screech that made Harley press against Charlie's leg. A stale, earthy smell floated out, thick with the mustiness of age. Cobwebs, like tattered shrouds, hung from the doorway. Goosebumps erupted on Charlie's skin as her imagination conjured up crawling creatures lurking within the darkness. Or perhaps those with tiny feet and long, skinny tails.

A narrow opening led downwards with four steps, rough-hewn and dirty. Noah descended until he reached hard-packed earth. Turning in a circle, his brows lowered in perplexity. "There's nothing here, either left or right."

He kneeled and peered into the inky blackness under the house. "It's a tight fit."

"Any volunteers to go under there? Charlie?" Simm asked.

Charlie's eyes widened, and she glared at her husband. He was fully aware of her fears.

"Just kidding." He chuckled and pulled her close.

"Flashlight?" Noah asked, extending a hand.

Charlie fumbled in her pocket for her phone, her fingers trembling as she leaned over and handed it to Noah.

He dropped to his knees and aimed the beam under the house. After several long seconds, he shook his head. "Don't see anything under there but dirt." Noah turned and examined the steps, knocking on each one and running his hands along the sides. Charlie grimaced at the thought of the spiderwebs he encountered.

"What are you looking for?" Simm said.

"I don't know, but there's nothing else down here to look at." Noah's voice was muffled as he crouched beside the steps. "Can't write it off until I look. Wait. What's this?"

He grunted, holding the light in one hand and probing underneath the steps with the other. Nothing happened. Until another louder grunt produced a result.

CHAPTER 19

The steps folded in against a wall. The onlookers gasped. Everyone stepped forward at once, curious to see the revealed space. A deep abyss greeted them. A rickety wooden ladder, barely wider than a shoulder, snaked down into the pitch-black darkness. Charlie's stomach lurched. The mere thought of descending into that claustrophobic unknown created a knot of fear in her chest.

Simm read her mind. "We won't all go." He looked at Noah. "No offense, buddy, but I'm not sure you'll fit, and I don't feel like pulling you out if you get wedged in."

"I'll go," Sarah said.

Charlie stared in astonishment. "What? You'd go in there?"

"Of course." Sarah gave a nonchalant shrug. "As a student, I worked on archaeological digs in Egypt. I squeezed into smaller places than that."

"I'll go with you," Simm said.

Panic clawed at Charlie's throat. "What if you get stuck? What if the ladder breaks? What's even down there?"

Simm gave her a reassuring smile. "It'll be okay. If something happens, you guys'll be here to help."

His decision made, Charlie's chest tightened, and she wouldn't draw a steady breath until her husband returned unharmed.

Noah said, "Hold on," before rushing away, returning minutes later with another flashlight and two lengths of sturdy rope.

"Good thinking," Simm said. Noah tied one rope around Sarah's waist and the other around Simm.

"I'll go first," Simm said. "It'll be a test for the ladder. I wouldn't want to fall on top of you." He grinned, and Sarah laughed, but Charlie didn't appreciate their humor.

Simm gingerly stepped onto the ladder and lowered himself into the hole, testing each rung along the way.

"Take pictures," Noah reminded them as he held the end of Simm's rope in his hand while Charlie clutched Sarah's.

"Don't worry." Simm's muffled voice rose from the darkness. Charlie suspected he meant his words for her alone.

Next, Sarah descended into the pit. Charlie sat on her knees and peered downward, the rope wrapped around her arm and gripped in her fist. Sarah blocked her view of Simm, but the lack of crashing noises and screams of terror comforted her somewhat.

Charlie's tension grew as each minute passed. Simm's cell phone wouldn't work underground, so all she could do was wait, but the waiting killed her. What if the ground collapsed on top of them? What if there was a booby-trap? So many things could go wrong.

The next fifteen minutes were agonizing, but the rope had its constraints. Charlie heard Noah's grunt.

"What happened?" she snapped, her heart in her throat.

"Resistance," Noah said.

Charlie felt a tug. "Here too."

"They've reached the end of their rope." Noah smiled.

"They'll come back now?" Charlie said, ignoring his pun. The thought of Simm trapped underground rattled her nerves.

"It's the safer option."

Charlie prayed Simm and Sarah would choose safety over curiosity.

"There's slack. They must've turned back," Noah said.

Charlie released a shaky breath, the tension draining from her body. The rope relaxed in her hand, and minutes later, Sarah emerged, a triumphant grin plastered on her face. With deep breaths, she dragged in fresh air.

Noah grabbed her hand and guided her out of the hole. The hug he gave her convinced Charlie he worried about Sarah more than he revealed. Charlie stared into the opening and saw the top of Simm's head rising toward the surface. A mischievous glint danced in his eyes.

"See? Nothing to worry about."

If he only knew, she thought. She walked into his arms and held him close.

"Find anything?" Noah asked.

"Not sure," Simm said. "But I filmed a lot. There's a tunnel down there. Let's look."

A quick glance overhead told Charlie they were in for a downpour. Noah slid the steps back into place and closed the door, securing it tightly.

Once inside, Simm propped his phone on the kitchen table and activated the video. No one spoke as they focused on the footage.

The first part was a grainy view of Simm's legs descending the rickety ladder, followed by a dark, narrow tunnel, barely visible in the flashlight beam. His voice narrated the descent, calm and collected despite the close quarters.

"As you see, it's a tunnel. My guess is we went down about ten feet. There are wooden beams above and on the sides to support it. Makes me feel better." Their shoes shuffled on the dirt floor. "Headroom's decent too, no need to hunch over. Probably seven feet high by four feet wide."

The camera panned along the rough wooden beams lining the tunnel. Charlie noticed cobwebs clinging to the edges in some areas, but the tunnel itself seemed relatively clean.

"We need to keep an eye out for any openings or doors," Sarah's voice said from off-screen.

"Right," Simm replied. "So far, nothing but dirt walls." The video continued, capturing the slow, methodical exploration. A ninety-degree turn appeared, followed by a long, blurry stretch of tunnel.

"This must be the left turn mentioned in the message," Simm said. The flashlight beam danced ahead, revealing little. Just as the tension built,

Simm's voice cut in. "Oh, looks like we've reached the end of the rope. Press on or head back?"

Watching the video, Charlie cast a wide-eyed stare at Simm. He considered going with no rope?

"I would've made Sarah go back," he said with a sheepish grin.

Charlie's eyes narrowed. She didn't believe him.

"Let's turn back," Sarah's voice said on the video. "We'll get a longer rope next time."

The lens panned over the length of the tunnel. "There's a turn ahead, about twenty feet on," Simm said.

"A really long rope next time," Sarah added.

At that point, Simm shut off his camera and concentrated on returning to daylight.

Now, he turned to face Noah. "That's it. We don't know where it leads, but we've got info to work with. We definitely had a left turn followed by a right, if we'd continued on."

"I'll go to a hardware store and get us better equipped," Noah said, his enthusiasm for the project clear. "And next time, I can go down. I'll fit."

Simm chuckled. "Whether it's connected to Ethan's death is anyone's guess, but you're right—we can't ignore it. Especially with a detail Sarah noticed."

All eyes turned toward Sarah, who sat perched on the edge of her seat, a thoughtful expression on her face. "The cobwebs," she said. "We ran into cobwebs on the access door but hardly any in the tunnel itself. I think someone's been down there recently."

A shiver ran down Charlie's spine. This wasn't just a dusty old passage forgotten by time. Someone, it seemed, actively used the tunnel. The question was, who? And what secrets did it hold?

CHAPTER 20

With a firm handshake and a warm smile, Rick Clarke, the fire investigator, greeted Simm. Stepping into Clarke's office felt like entering a cluttered filing cabinet come to life. Manuals and reports lined the shelves, while documents overflowed his desk like a paper tsunami. Photos of Clarke with various dignitaries adorned the walls, testaments to a long career.

Simm settled into the chair opposite Rick's desk. The man's return call at the end of the previous afternoon with the promise of an early morning meeting brightened Simm's day.

"Montreal PI, eh?" Clarke said, leaning back, a smile creasing his weathered face. "I visited the city many times in my younger days. Stayed out late partying with friends. Of course, we're talking over thirty-five years ago. I'm a wise, old man of sixty-five now," Rick said, chuckling. He ran his right hand over his short graying hair and patted his rounded belly with his left, emphasizing the changes in his appearance over the past few decades.

"How long have you been an investigator?" Simm asked, speaking over the noise filtering into the office. Firefighters washed a truck in the bay, and their light-hearted banter bounced off the cement walls.

"I started as a firefighter. A knee injury forced me from the direct action into a peripheral role. Fire investigations always fascinated me, and I've put in thirty years now."

"Was the Ethan Wolfe fire typical?"

The smile faded from Clarke's face. "The family hired you?" Unlike Detective Baxter, Simm didn't detect animosity.

"Yes. Not to investigate Ethan's death, but it could affect the other case."

Clarke's troubled gaze focused on his folded hands. "It was a bad one. Always is when someone dies. But it wasn't unusual. People often learn the hard way that gas and fire don't mix."

"I'm a neophyte." Simm smiled slightly. "How do you know gas caused the fire?"

"Evidence he was working on his car. Tools and a metal creeper were beside it, and we determined the starting point was directly under the gas tank. The lowest point of carbonization. Forensics found fuel soaked into the cement floor, so he probably was fixing a leak. It was a pretty chilly night, and he lit the fire in the woodstove. Left the door open." The investigator's expression revealed how little he approved of that oversight.

"Is it really that dangerous? It's not like he poured gas on the fire, is it?"

"No ventilation. Shut the doors. Fumes built up, nasty business. But that wasn't the direct cause. Fire originated at the gas tank. My guess is a stray spark from the dry wood did the trick. Burning embers travel a surprising distance. All it took was one to land six feet away and ignite the leak under the car. Unfortunate. A cracked-open window and a closed woodstove door could've saved his life."

"Any possibility someone could've rigged it to appear like an accident?" Simm asked, leaning forward.

"Finding that is always my focus. Arson and murder. I don't handle this alone, not when a person dies or is seriously injured. The medical examiner determined Ethan Wolfe died from asphyxiation. Smoke overwhelmed him, trapping him inside. It happens. His clothing could have caught fire. He panicked, couldn't get the door open. No evidence of him being overpowered. No blunt force trauma. Fire department found the doors locked from the inside. Why he locked them, who knows. But if someone was in there with him and started the fire, how'd they escape?"

Simm paused, feigning deep thought. "What if someone set it by remote control?"

"It's possible, but we would've uncovered the device. Believe me, I looked. There was nothing. I'm sorry, but his own negligence killed Mr. Wolfe."

Simm nodded, appreciating the sincerity in the other man's tone. He was tempted to tell him about their find, but he'd promised Noah a few more days. "One last question. The fire happened on a Saturday night around midnight. When did you start your investigation?"

"Sunday, late morning. We let the site cool down." The investigator held up his hands. "I know where you're going. To prevent tampering with the scene, we posted cops to guard it." He waited for a beat. "I'm sorry about Mr. Wolfe's death. Seen my share of people who perished in fires, and it's not pleasant. I'm sure his brother is heartbroken, but he doesn't have to worry about it being deliberate."

"I'll pass that along. Thanks." Simm stood and shook the man's hand. "I'll see myself out."

The building housed the fire department and the police station, but separate entrances served the public. Simm circled around, entered through another door, and arrived at the police reception area. The same woman, Doris, manned the desk, and judging by her suspicious expression, she recognized him.

"Do you have another appointment with Detective Baxter?" she asked with raised brows. Her tone said she was aware he didn't.

"No. I was in the area and hoped to catch him. Have a few questions. It shouldn't take long."

"I'll check," she said, her lips pursed with displeasure. The detective would likely ask her to send him away.

Doris surprised him when she said, "He'll be right out."

Baxter left the jacket behind and appeared in a pale blue shirt and dress pants. A grim expression matched his hard handshake.

He nodded at the door. "C'mon. I was about to take a walk."

Simm followed him outside and gazed around the parking lot. Baxter headed toward the side of the building, and Simm stayed beside him.

"What do you want?" Baxter asked, without glancing his way.

"I just met with Rick Clarke. Thought I'd drop by to see if you have anything new."

"Nothing new will come up. They ruled the death an accident, and they closed the case."

"You told me the cops showed up seconds after the firefighters."

"That hasn't changed."

"Were you there?"

"Not at first. Once they discovered a dead body, they called me."

"When was that?"

They reached the corner of the building, and Baxter stopped, pulling a pack of cigarettes and a lighter from his pants pocket. "Around two a.m.," he said, lighting up and taking a long drag.

Simm took an instinctive step back as he faced the man, avoiding the smoke. "Sunday morning. A couple of hours after the fire."

"That's right."

"What did you do?"

Baxter shrugged, his eyes glued to a distant spot. "Opened an investigation. Questioned the neighbors, Mike Wade, the firefighters, that kind of thing."

The cop's lack of eye contact intrigued Simm.

"Did you walk the scene?"

"Yeah," Baxter said, exhaling a plume of smoke. "The next day."

"See anything suspicious?"

Another long drag on the cigarette, a beat of silence. "Nothing," Baxter finally said.

"Who determined it was an accident?" Simm asked.

The detective finally met Simm's gaze, his eyes narrowed. "I did, in collaboration with the fire investigator. We reviewed the evidence, interviewed witnesses—a clear-cut case."

"You're comfortable with that call?"

The cop's expression tightened in displeasure. It surprised Simm to make it this far before the man lost his cool.

Baxter gave him a glacier-melting glare. He spoke through gritted teeth. "I know all about you, Winston Simmons. Rejected daddy's money, became a cop, then a hotshot PI. But I've got plenty of extra years on you, and I worked hard for everything I have. I didn't have a trust fund to fall back on. That man died because of a preventable accident, and you can try to twist it into a pretzel, but nothing'll change. And if I were you, I'd let it go. You're wasting everybody's time."

The detective spun on his heel and strode back to headquarters, leaving Simm to wonder what upset him so much.

CHAPTER 21

Simm sat at the reconstructed desk in the library, his cell phone in his hand. His mind replayed his meeting with Detective Baxter. Simm knew cops. He'd been one. As with any profession, good ones and bad ones walked the streets. His instincts recognized Detective Baxter as a good cop but one with a dilemma.

He consulted his notepad and dialed the number. A woman's voice answered.

"Wendy Nolan here."

Simm hesitated for a beat. "Hello, Wendy. I'm sorry. I expected to speak to Brent Holmes."

"Brent doesn't work here anymore. Can I help you?"

Her tone held something that Simm couldn't put his finger on. Wariness? Sadness?

"I'm surprised. Is he with another firm now?"

"No. Brent passed away recently." Definitely sorrow.

Simm's eyebrows shot up. "I'm sorry to hear that. I wasn't aware he was sick."

"He died accidentally while on vacation in the Caribbean. The firm divided his clients amongst us. If you tell me your name, I'll find your new advisor."

"Actually, I'm a private investigator working on behalf of Ethan Wolfe's estate. I understand Mr. Holmes was Ethan's financial advisor, and I wanted to meet with him to discuss certain aspects of the estate."

The dead silence made Simm wonder if he'd lost the connection. "Are you there?" he said.

"Yes. Sorry. I'm aware of Mr. Wolfe's case. I'll speak to my supervisor, and someone will get back to you."

Simm shared his phone number with Wendy, wondering if he'd receive an answer. As he disconnected the call, he booted up his laptop. It took him a few minutes to find the news reports.

He recalled hearing about a Canadian's death in Jamaica, but the name didn't connect in his brain. Now, he read the brief article.

Brent Holmes, on vacation on the island in March, signed up for deep-sea fishing. A private tour with only him and three crewmembers. Holmes imbibed too much Jamaican rum and fell overboard. The crew did everything possible to save him. Despite a call for help to nearby vessels, they never recovered his body.

The report cited statistics on the number of alcohol-related deaths in Jamaica every year. The authorities suspected nothing unusual.

Simm didn't hold the same opinion.

Holmes' death occurred a week to the day after Ethan's. Did Holmes die a rich man? Had he stolen Ethan's money and traveled to Jamaica to put it to good use? If Simm was the cop investigating the financial crime, Holmes would make the list of primary suspects. Any sudden good fortune for the advisor raised a red flag.

Simm grabbed his phone again and dialed the number of the detective assigned to the fraud case. He'd already tried twice to reach him, leaving a voicemail with no response. This time, urgency colored his voice as he left a message demanding a call back.

.   .   .

Simm's head lifted at the sound of a loud knock. Barking creatures rushed to the front door. Simm hurried into the entranceway, almost colliding with Charlie as they both scrambled to restrain the animals.

Charlie swooped Harley into her arms while Simm took a firm grasp of Bosco's collar. He tried issuing commands, but the animal only responded to Noah's voice. The mastiff strained and pulled as his bark echoed through the vast entranceway, taking all Simm's strength to hold him back.

Charlie's hand rested on the doorknob as she glanced at Simm. Heavy footsteps and a deep voice behind them had the desired effect. Bosco sat on his haunches as Noah reached his side, but his body vibrated with excitement.

Simm glanced at the doorway, picturing a terrified mailman fleeing for his life. A wry smile played on his lips, but it vanished instantly when he saw who stood on the porch.

Walter and Clarisse. On anyone else, their frightened expressions would've appeared comical, but the fact his brother and sister-in-law suddenly showed up in Niagara-on-the-Lake eradicated all traces of humor.

"What are you doing here?" Simm said, with no word of greeting.

He met Charlie's disapproving glance before she set down her pug and stepped in front of him. "What a surprise," she said. "Come on in. Don't worry about the dogs. You already know Harley, and Bosco will get used to you."

The couple slid over the threshold, avoiding the large dog. Walter's suit and dress shirt looked out of place, although he'd removed his tie, probably as a concession to the rising humidity outside. Clarisse's bright summer dress and sandals were a splash of color against the old wood paneling.

His lips tight, his posture rigid and tense, Walter shooed an excited Harley away with a polished shoe.

"Sorry for the unexpected drop-in." Clarisse's smile was hesitant. "Walter had business in Toronto, and I joined him... since it was a short drive..."

"That's perfect," Charlie said. "Plenty of room here for you."

"Wonderful!" Excitement lit Clarisse's face. "We'd love to stay for a visit."

Simm's brows drew together, and he touched Charlie's elbow, hoping to catch her attention, although he couldn't retract her invitation without appearing rude.

"Oh no, we can't impose," Walter said, looking eager to leave. "We saw a decent hotel on our way."

His brother's attempt to backpedal on his wife's hasty acceptance amused Simm, though he forced himself to hide it.

"Not at all," Charlie declared. "See the size of this place? And we've cleaned most of the rooms."

"Honey, it's a little rundown," Simm said, taking a stab at salvaging his sanity. "They might not find it comfortable."

"It's very comfortable. Isn't it Sarah?"

Sarah's eyes widened into a deer-in-the-headlights look, obviously unsure how to handle this new family dynamic. "Yes. Yes, of course," she stammered.

"That's perfect then," Clarisse said, ignoring her husband's stern glare. "Thank you so much. It'll be fun spending time together."

Clarisse's behavior stunned Simm. His sister-in-law always seemed timid, never arguing with her husband. From what he witnessed now, Clarisse had yanked a page from Charlie's playbook. Although he disliked the idea of passing an extended amount of time with his brother, watching the women outmaneuver Walter amused him.

Yet, Simm felt a headache blooming behind his eyes as Charlie took care of the introductions. Walter and Clarisse's unexpected arrival threw a wrench into his already complex investigation. He couldn't focus on Ethan Wolfe's case with his uptight brother and his seemingly possessed sister-in-law underfoot.

"I'll need help with the bags," Walter stated, as if not having a bellboy at his disposal was the perfect argument for staying at a full-service hotel.

"I'll give you a hand," Noah said. If he noticed the tension between the brothers, he gave no sign.

Walter backed away as Bosco followed Noah onto the porch. With a resigned expression, Walter trudged after the larger man.

"What a lovely home," Clarisse said. Her gaze moved over the high ceilings, the chandelier, and the ornate staircase. "This belongs to Noah?"

"It does now," Charlie said.

"Beautiful. I'm sure it holds a lot of history."

"Yes," Charlie said. "Maybe a bit more than we expected."

Clarisse's delicate laugh tinkled. "What does that mean?"

"It's an ancient house built by an interesting family. I'm certain it hides plenty of secrets," Charlie said, her answer vague.

"Really? Are there ghosts?"

Charlie's head swiveled in her sister-in-law's direction, but Clarisse's smile was more enthusiastic than mocking. Simm suppressed an eye roll. Was everyone obsessed with the paranormal these days?

"We found copious amounts of dust and cobwebs," Charlie said. "And a mysterious journal," she added with raised brows.

Clarisse's head drew back. "It sounds like something from a movie," she said, blinking rapidly.

A spark of hope ignited in Simm's chest. Would the prospect of cobwebs, ghosts, and cryptic messages discourage Walter and Clarisse from staying? "Creepy-crawlies and things that go bump in the night are everywhere in this old house," he said.

The three women laughed, enjoying his joke.

Walter huffed as he dragged an oversized piece of luggage over the threshold. Annoyance and overexertion contorted his face. Noah followed him with a bag hanging from his shoulder and a large suitcase in each hand. Bosco took up the rear.

"Which room?" Noah asked.

Without an opinion, Simm deferred to Charlie.

"I think the sunflower room is ideal," Charlie said. "Sarah?"

"Agreed. The second door on the right."

"Follow me," Noah said as he stepped around Walter and started up the stairs.

Walter's expression morphed from annoyance to horror as he realized he had to carry his own bag up the winding staircase. Simm coughed to cover his laugh. His brother's concept of exercise was waving his arm to signal an underling for help.

He glanced at Clarisse and thought he detected an amused twinkle in her eye. Despite his annoyance at the idea of spending time with his brother, Simm enjoyed seeing this side of his sister-in-law.

CHAPTER 22

Simm's cell phone vibrated in his pocket. He checked the display and excused himself. Seeing Charlie's concerned look, he sent her a reassuring smile. Shutting the library door behind him, he answered the call.

"Detective Webber? I'm glad you got back to me." Simm withheld the word "finally."

"Sorry it took so long. I was out of town and swamped with work," the financial fraud detective said. "How can I help you? Your message said it was about Ethan Wolfe."

Simm explained his connection to the case, including the fact Noah hired him. He expected the usual friction from a cop who didn't appreciate a private investigator's involvement, but the detective surprised him.

"Listen, I'm glad you're on this. I've hit a brick wall—several, in fact."

"I presume you know about Brent Holmes."

"I do. That was the first wall."

"And the next?"

"Ethan Wolfe's files vanished. Poof."

"What files?" Simm said, his brows lowered.

"Everything pertaining to his investments."

"Everything? Gone?"

"Yep. Like a digital ghost."

Simm lurched back in his chair as if someone slapped him. "How? Didn't the investment company have backups?"

"I'm telling you, it's a mystery. And get this. Only Wolfe's vanished. Everyone else's is intact. The techies are baffled."

Simm struggled to process this information. "You've thrown me for a loop. What now? How do you move forward?"

"We've got our best guys on it, but so far, zilch. I'm not giving up hope, though."

Simm wouldn't describe himself as a tech expert, but it seemed impossible to lose a digital trail. Despite Noah's claim that the money vanished, Simm's faith in modern technology made him harbor the belief they'd find it. His hope now hung by a thread.

"What about Holmes' death?" Simm asked, grasping at the other straw. "It sounds suspicious."

"I agree, but we've been back and forth with the authorities in Jamaica, and they insist it was accidental." The detective paused for a moment. "I'd appreciate any ideas you have."

"You've caught me off guard," Simm said. "I'll let it sink in. The boss at the investment firm hasn't called me back yet, but I can guess what he'll tell me."

"Don't expect miracles. They're scrambling to cover their asses. Amazing the media hasn't caught wind of it."

"Thanks for getting back to me. I'll be in touch if anything pops up," Simm said.

He hung up, his mind a whirlwind. The sound of movement jolted him from his thoughts as Charlie peeked around the door. He waved her into the room.

"You look upset," she said as she slid into the chair opposite him.

"One way to put it. Stupefied would be another."

"Tell me."

Simm recited the phone call's content. "When Noah said they couldn't trace the funds, I expected human error or incompetence, not a technical snafu of this scale."

"Could Erik help?" Charlie asked. Erik was a tech wizard that Simm sometimes hired to tread through minefields of data.

Simm's lips tightened. "Maybe. But if the OPP's best can't find anything, I don't know how Erik will."

"Worth a try, isn't it?"

Simm nodded, a hollow feeling eating at his gut. He felt like a fly trapped against a window, desperately searching for a way out. Finding the money, the reason Noah hired them, appeared to be a dead end. Discovering Ethan's death was a murder threatened to put Charlie and Simm in over their heads. The investigating detective was stonewalling them, and the whole journal/key/underground tunnel quest seemed like an extravagant detour.

To top it off, his self-centered and power-hungry brother would be under his feet for a few days. Precious days needed to work on the case. His brain shifted to the shock he'd felt when they appeared on the doorstep.

"Why are they here?" Simm said, looking at Charlie. Her expression told him she knew exactly who he was referring to. "What would possess them to come here? Especially Walt."

"It's obvious he wishes he were anywhere else. I suspect it's entirely Clarisse's doing."

"Since when does he care what Clarisse wants? Or anyone, for that matter?" Simm shook his head in disgust.

"I know how you feel about Walter being here," Charlie said. "I'm sorry if I was hasty, but I thought..."

"Yeah. Another chance for us to reconcile. I get it, even if I don't share your optimism." Simm sighed. "Under normal circumstances, it might not bother me. But I don't want to talk about the case around him."

Charlie frowned. "You think he's involved? You have to admit that's a stretch."

His wife was right. His bitter feelings toward his brother sometimes blinded his sense of logic. Walter never met Ethan, and he had only an incidental link to Noah. "No. You're bang-on. It's crazy. I just don't like him sticking his nose in my business."

"Maybe he can help. He knows people in many circles."

Simm grimaced. "That's part of what I don't trust about him." Walter's circles included people just like him—people who twisted the rules and the laws to suit themselves.

"I suspect Walter's coming around," Charlie said. "Being here is a big step. Think about it. He's in the same house as Noah, the man whose family was killed, and Walter may have had a hand in it by helping Marcus Vaughn. Noah is none the wiser because we never told him our suspicions. As far as he's concerned, Walter's your brother; that's it. But Walt is aware of the connection and your feelings."

Simm considered Charlie's argument. It held merit. "You may be right. I'll think about it." He glanced at his notes. "I'll talk to Baxter about the disappearing files. Then I'll question the neighbors."

"The police did that but found nothing, right?"

"Right. Because I trust Baxter's investigation skills so much, I'll do my own legwork."

"All the more reason to accept help from Walter if it's offered."

Simm smiled. Charlie wouldn't stop chipping away with her pick and hammer. It annoyed him at times, but he loved her tenacity.

"I don't understand how Clarisse got him here," he said, amused, despite wishing it never happened.

Charlie chuckled. "Neither do I, but I'll find out."

$$\cdot \quad \cdot \quad \cdot$$

Simm left a message for Baxter, the voicemail a terse request to call him back. Pocketing his phone, he snuck into the entranceway. Harley snored contentedly in a patch of sunlight but perked up at Simm's approach.

"Hey, boy. Wanna go for a walk?" he whispered.

Harley's tail thumped on the tiled floor. Simm grabbed his leash from a hook, and they crept out the front door, the dog's low profile a testament to his espionage skills. Simm texted Charlie to let her know they'd left. As much as he appreciated Charlie's efforts to patch up his differences with Walter, Simm needed to get used to having him underfoot and didn't feel like running into him now.

Simm knew legwork wouldn't magically solve the case, but it was a start. He needed answers, and the neighbors, despite the slim odds, might unlock a hidden puzzle piece. Besides, a walk under the warm sun might be just the thing to clear his head and come up with a fresh approach.

Scanning his surroundings, Simm realized he couldn't expect much from the neighbors. Towering hedges, stone barriers, and expansive lawns separated the nearby mansions. The chances of anyone seeing something happen at the Wolfe house remained slim. Besides, the police already took this route.

Simm strolled three hundred meters before reaching the Wolfe's next-door neighbor. Turning and gazing back, he knew nothing would be visible from there, considering the distance and trees between the houses. But not asking questions got him nowhere.

He crossed the length of the stone-paved driveway to reach an immense house adorned with turrets and gargoyles that wouldn't have looked out of place on a gothic cathedral. A tall, thin, stiff-necked butler answered the knock, his nose aimed haughtily at the jeans-and-T-shirt-clad visitor with a pug sidekick.

A stuck-up butler didn't faze Simm, who was raised amongst the pretentious rich. He flashed his PI credentials, meeting the man's disbelief head-on and explained his need to speak with the owner. The butler, looking like he'd swallowed a lemon, ushered Simm into the foyer with a pointed reminder to control his "beast." Simm glanced down at Harley perched at his feet, his rolls making him look like an over-risen loaf of bread, and wondered how anyone could view him as a threat. A majestic grandfather clock ticked rhythmically in time with Harley's wagging tail.

An elderly woman approached, closely followed by the butler, and extended her hand, a brilliant smile lighting her thin, lined face. No doubt, she was once a tall, majestic woman. Now, a slightly rounded back and a cane revealed the passage of time on a body that had likely wandered the earth for over eighty years. Clad in a white-collared blouse, neat gray dress pants, and sensible black shoes, the woman held the title of mistress of the manor with pride.

"What a delightful surprise," she said. "Visitors are a rare treat. And what an adorable dog you have."

Her effusive greeting surprised Simm after the encounter with her employee. They exchanged pleasantries, then Mrs. McCollum, as she introduced herself, invited Simm into the drawing room.

The butler left them alone as Harley settled by Simm's feet and snored, exhausted from his walk. Simm hoped he wouldn't need to carry the dog home.

"I'm sorry to arrive here unannounced, Mrs. McCollum, but Ethan Wolfe's family hired me to investigate the circumstances around his death." Simm stretched the scope of his mandate, thinking a death generated more interest.

"The man next door?" the woman said, wide-eyed. "I heard about that. What a horrible way to die. In a fire. But wasn't it an accident?"

"They ruled it an accident, yes." Simm said. He added a touch of intrigue to his tone. "But it's tied to other matters. Financial matters."

"Oh, I see," the woman said, nodding her head. For her and most of her neighbors, money was a familiar language.

"I'm sure the police and fire officials already asked you these questions, and I don't mean to cause any inconvenience," Simm continued, "but sometimes repetition jogs the memory."

"Questions?" she said, her tone puzzled. "I haven't spoken to anyone."

Anger bubbled in Simm's chest. Baxter's story about questioning the neighbors didn't hold water. He struggled to push aside his outrage. No need to upset Mrs. McCollum. He'd direct it at the proper person.

"I realize there's a significant distance between your home and the Wolfe's, but did you see anything the night of the fire?" Simm asked.

"Oh, no. I was long in bed before it started. I believe it happened very late, didn't it?"

"Yes, around midnight."

"I'm afraid I can't be of help." Regret flickered in her eyes.

"Anyone else in the household awake and active?"

"No." A small smile appeared on her lips, and she leaned forward. "You see, I did my own little investigation. I'm too curious, I guess. Or too bored, one of the two. Only Wilfred and Anna live here, and neither witnessed nor heard anything that night."

"What about days before or after the fire? Did anybody see something suspicious? Strangers near the house, an unusual noise, things like that?"

"I didn't ask that question. It's a good one," she said, clearly excited at the opportunity to play detective. "Let's ask them." She reached to a side table and shook a tiny porcelain bell that rang more loudly than its size indicated.

CHAPTER 23

Wilfred, the stern-faced butler, a man Simm judged to be in his mid-fifties, stepped into the room.

"Fetch Anna, would you, Wilfred?"

He returned with a sturdy middle-aged woman, dressed neatly, but not in uniform. She grasped a pair of blue latex gloves in one hand, apparently disturbed while completing a household task.

When both employees faced Mrs. McCollum and Simm, the elderly woman undertook the questioning.

"Did you two see anything strange happening around the Wolfe place? Anything at all, besides the fire, of course," she said, her gaze as pointed as an arrow.

"Apart from the fire, no, madam," Anna said with a hint of an accent. From Newfoundland, if Simm had to guess.

He turned his gaze to Wilfred, who shook his head, his expression grave.

"Did you see the flames?" Simm asked, his attention moving from one to the other.

They answered in the negative.

"Can't see the Wolfe place from here, anyway," the butler grumbled, his voice low.

"Do either of you ever circulate on the street in front of the house?"

"Sometimes," Anna said. "I go to the store or run errands."

"And you witnessed nothing or anyone unusual?" Simm reiterated.

"Well," Anna said, "I saw Mr. Ethan a few times. Always polite, such a nice young man. But this one time, I saw him talking to a woman in the driveway. Looked serious, the way they were going at it."

This sparked Simm's interest. "Can you describe her?"

"Blonde and slim. I couldn't see her well. Eyesight's not good from a distance."

"Did you see a car?" Simm asked, feeling a tinge of hope.

Anna stared toward the window and squinted. "I don't remember one."

"You only saw her once?" Mrs. McCollum asked, taking the words out of Simm's mouth. He suppressed a smile at her eagerness.

At the housekeeper's nod, Simm asked if she recalled the date.

"Let me think. It was February, I believe. It was cold, with a wind that cuts right through you. I remember wondering why they were arguing in the driveway, when they could go inside to the warmth. I wondered the same for myself. Why did I walk to the store that day?"

"What made you think they were arguing?" the elderly woman asked, focusing the woman's attention.

Anna gestured dramatically, flinging her arms wide. "Like this! She was talking a mile a minute, waving her arms all over the place."

"Did you hear anything they said?" Simm asked.

"Not a word," Anna said, shaking her head. "Too far away, I'm afraid. Such a shame about Mr. Ethan. Seemed like a kind soul. Nobody deserves to go like that."

Simm questioned the stony-faced butler but found he had neither met Ethan nor seen anyone else near the Wolfe estate.

After Mrs. McCollum's dismissal, the two employees retreated, leaving Simm and the old woman alone. Her eyes, bright with desperate hope, met his. "Did they tell you anything helpful?" she asked, her voice trembling slightly.

"Definitely," Simm assured her.

"I promise you, if I hear anything more, I'll let you know."

"I appreciate your effort. I'll leave you my card. If you or anyone else remembers something, you'll have my contact information," Simm said as he rose from his seat. Harley, sensing a change in action, jumped to his feet, rested and eager to go.

"We will," Mrs. McCollum said. "I know it isn't proper to reap pleasure from someone's death, but I'm happy to have a visitor and a little excitement to brighten my day."

Simm smiled his understanding and said goodbye, nodding at the butler as he held the door open for him and Harley. He'd visit the woman again before they left Niagara-on-the-Lake.

Continuing eastward, he spotted a woman heading in his direction, walking a large dog. From a distance, it resembled a husky. It occurred to him a dog walker would be likely to spot action around the Wolfe dwelling. In a car, the glimpse was brief, but on foot, there was a better chance.

Simm pasted on his most charming smile as he neared the woman. Lucky for him, Harley possessed an uncanny ability to make friends with anyone.

"Cute dog," he said.

"Thank you. Yours is adorable." As the animals sniffed and explored each other, Simm snuck glances at the Husky owner. In her mid-forties, she wore casual but expensive clothing, and heavy gold and diamond rings weighed down her hands. She wore enough makeup for an evening out, although seemingly just walking the dog.

"I've never seen you here," she said, with a flirtatious smile. "New to the neighborhood?"

"Just visiting. My wife and I are at the Wolfe place." Simm waved his hand toward Noah's house.

"Oh, where that fire was. So tragic." Immediate sympathy flooded her expression. "Are you a relative?"

"A friend of the family," Simm said, keeping his answer vague. "Did you know Ethan?"

"We never met. I saw him while walking Fritz but nothing more than a glimpse."

"Did you ever see anyone else with him?" Hope bubbled in his chest again.

"A woman, once." She nodded.

"Can you describe her?"

The woman's eyes narrowed. "Why do you want to know?"

Simm hastened to allay suspicions, normal under the circumstances—a stranger meeting you in the street and asking questions about the neighbors. "We heard he had a girlfriend but hadn't met her yet. And then he died." Simm assumed a bereaved expression and let his words trail off. "We just thought she'd help us understand what his last months were like. I guess it's part of the grieving process."

Compassion replaced her concern. "Of course, I get it. Unfortunately, I didn't get a good look at her, and we never spoke. Blonde hair, that's all I can really remember. Not much to go on, I'm afraid."

"Did she have a car? Maybe that would help."

The woman seemed to strain her memory trying to recall specifics. "There was a car there. I think it was black or dark gray. Nothing special. Sorry."

"That's okay," Simm said, masking his disappointment. At least she backed up Anna's comments. "It was worth a try."

"Speak to Ray Brown." She turned and pointed behind her. "He lives across the street. The house with the fire hydrant in front."

"He knew Ethan?" Simm said, encouraged.

"It's possible. He's always out with his dog. Walks him often, sometimes late at night. And he talks to everybody. If he doesn't know, nobody does."

"That's very helpful. Thanks for your advice."

"Don't mention it," she said. She waved and continued on her way, Fritz at her side. Harley, with a mournful whine, watched his new best friend leave.

"C'mon, Harley. It's time to meet Mr. Brown."

Simm followed the woman's directions, turning onto a driveway paved with smooth, pale stones. The house that awaited him wasn't quite a mansion, dwarfed by its grander neighbors, but it held its own kind of loftiness. Red-brown brick, lush gardens, and a three-car garage hinted at a life of comfortable abundance.

Simm reached the dark oak door and knocked, the sound sharp in the afternoon quiet, as the soft and powdery scent of lilacs surrounded him. A deep bark resonated from within, and from the corner of his eye, he spied a curtain stir to his right. A moment later, the door swung open.

An older man in his late seventies or early eighties with wispy, uncombed hair glared at him with a frown. He was thin and wiry and wore beige trousers with a black cardigan. Plaid slippers completed the outfit. His right hand gripped the collar of a black labrador. The dog wagged his tail with eagerness, a stark contrast to his rigid master.

"Not buying anything," Mr. Brown said.

"That's good. I've got nothing to sell." Simm smiled. "I'm looking for someone who may have known Ethan Wolfe."

The man's face registered his surprise. "That poor young man that burned to death? I knew him a little. Terrible thing."

"Yes, it was tragic."

"Are you family?" The man squinted at Simm as if searching for a resemblance.

"A friend of the family. I'm here with his brother. We're trying to piece together his last few months. Noah didn't see Ethan lately."

"That's too bad." He shook his head then jerked as if someone pinched him. "Where are my manners? Come on in, and we'll chat."

Ray ushered Simm into his living room. The room seemed to serve as the man's main retreat. Comfortable and well-used furniture faced a wood fireplace blackened from years of service. A dirty mug and plate lay on a side table beside a best-selling thriller novel with a pizza flyer acting as a bookmark. A throw blanket was tossed across the arm of a chair and trailed onto the worn hardwood floor.

Mr. Brown settled into that chair and smiled as Simm sat opposite him on the sofa. The dogs, satisfied with their introduction, curled up at the feet of their respective masters.

"I hope I didn't disturb you," Simm said.

"Not at all. I'm just a lonely old coot who passes his time reading, walking his dog, and snooping." He chuckled, his manner much improved.

Simm smiled. "Another dog-walker sent me to you. She said you were often out and you might have met Ethan."

"Oh yes, we had a few chats. Not every day, mind you. Seems like he was always off somewhere. Pleasant fellow, polite and friendly."

Simm leaned forward, his interest piqued. "Anything unusual in the months before he died? Was he away more often? Seem upset or disturbed about something?"

Ray's eyes widened, and he leaned in. "Do you think his death wasn't an accident? You're not suggesting he did it on purpose, are you?"

"I'm not suggesting anything," Simm hastened to say. "His brother's grieving. They lost touch, and he's worried he wasn't there for Ethan when he may have needed him. Someone suggested he had a tough time. Just trying to piece together the puzzle."

The older man frowned and stroked his chin. "I can't say he was depressed, more like preoccupied. Never pried, though. Some folks think I'm a busybody, but I prefer 'observant.' Been living alone in this house for a decade, since the missus passed. Enjoy a good chat, you see. But I don't pry. If someone wants a listening ear, I'm here."

"I understand," Simm said. He felt sorry for the man but tried to refocus the conversation. "See anyone around the place? Visitors?"

"A woman a few times."

Again, the woman, Simm thought. "Did you speak to her?"

The man snorted. "Not exactly. Gave her a friendly wave once, but she wouldn't have it. Turned her back on me like a snob. Didn't seem like Ethan's type, that one. He was a good lad, deserved better." He paused then added grudgingly, "Though, I suppose I should give her the benefit of the doubt. Maybe just a bad day."

"Can you describe her?"

"Young, about his age, blonde, pretty, but I can't tell you much more than that."

The blonde woman—a recurring theme. "Did you notice a car?"

"One time she had a car. Can't remember what it was," he said. He gazed at the ceiling as if willing the memory to appear. "I saw her arrive by taxi, once. Other times, I just spotted her walking around outside the house."

This could be something. "Can you recall the taxi company's name? Maybe a logo or anything else you noticed on the car?"

The older man narrowed his eyes in concentration. "No, I didn't see a flashy company name or anything like that. Just one of those taxi lights on top with a phone number, I think." He shifted his gaze to Simm, a question forming in his cloudy blue eyes. "You looking to find this woman? What good would that do?"

"Another person mentioned a blonde woman, and yes, we'd like to locate her. With a girlfriend, we'd learn more about his life in the weeks leading up to the fire."

"I guess," he said, although his expression seemed doubtful. "Seems like hunting for a lost penny in a field."

"The day of the fire? Did you see her?"

Again, the squint. "Can't say I did."

Simm tried to hide his dismay. A promising lead that turned in circles. No description, little to follow up on. Simm stood, and Harley followed suit.

"I'll leave a card. If you think of anything, I'd appreciate a call."

Ray peered at the card. "You're a private investigator? I thought you were a family friend."

"Both. Someone with experience is the best help for a friend."

The elderly man nodded, seemingly satisfied with Simm's response. "I hope Ethan's brother makes it through this. There's nothing worse than losing someone close to you," Ray said as he escorted Simm and Harley to the door. "Even I was heartbroken when I heard Ethan was dead. When I saw those flames, I remember thinking, 'Thank God no one was in there,' but I was wrong."

CHAPTER 24

Simm whirled to face the man. "You witnessed the fire?"

"Sure did. I don't sleep much, so I walk late at night with Monty here." He patted the dog's head. "Saw the blaze and hightailed it over to see where it came from."

"Did you see anyone near the house?" Simm asked, his voice laced with anticipation.

"A fellow in a pickup truck parked by the house. Mike's his name. I ran over to him and asked if he called the fire department. He said he took care of everything and I should go home."

"Did you?"

"Not right away. I waited on the sidewalk for the fire department to arrive."

"And the police?"

"Yeah. That was strange."

Simm narrowed his eyes. "What do you mean?"

"I don't know." Ray shrugged. "I guess I expected them to show more urgency. After all, a man died." He waved a hand. "I realize they weren't aware of that at first but still... two or three police officers, standing around and watching. Someone chatted for a minute or two with the man in the pickup."

Simm mulled over this information but realized it didn't surprise him. "How long did you stay?"

"Maybe half an hour, tops. The sirens and commotion upset Monty, so we went home. The following day, I got the news about Ethan." He hung his head.

"Did the police or fire investigator question you?"

"Nope. Guess my late-night walk wasn't on their radar."

That response didn't surprise Simm either.

"Thank you for your help, Mr. Brown."

"Don't mention it. Pass my condolences on to Ethan's brother."

*   *   *

Each man dumped a reel of rope onto the ground beside the outside door.

"That should do it," Simm said as he straightened.

"If it doesn't, I'm going without it," Noah said.

"You know the women won't let that pass."

"Who said we had to tell them?"

"Don't go down there by yourself. Promise me that." A stern glare followed Simm's words.

"I won't. Believe it or not, I'm not that keen on small, dark spaces either."

"If the camera I ordered arrives today like it's supposed to, we'll have less to worry about."

"You think it'll do the job?" Noah asked.

"My buddy Erik claims it's the latest high-tech thing. Works under any conditions. It'll be a lot clearer than a phone camera, and it'll be hands free."

"We'll cross our fingers."

"Why are we crossing fingers?" Charlie said as she stepped onto the back porch.

Simm smiled at his wife. "A gadget I ordered. It's supposed to arrive today."

She nodded at the two reels of yellow rope. "Got everything you need?"

"The rope and two headlamps. Once the camera gets here, we're ready."

"This camera?" Sarah said from the doorway. She waved a small brown package.

"Perfect timing." Simm grinned as he opened the box and removed a rectangular gadget.

Noah grabbed the box and extracted a charger and data cable. They'd need it to download videos onto a computer.

Simm pressed a few buttons and sent Noah a victorious look. "It's charged. We're all set."

"Why don't we read the manual?" Charlie said.

"It's simple. Turn it on and go," Simm said. "We'll test it first. Make sure we can download the video."

Simm played with the various buttons on the gadget until he realized his audience had grown. Walter and Clarisse stood on the outskirts of the group. Simm stifled an inward groan. He didn't want his brother as an onlooker. In fact, he didn't want him anywhere near this investigation.

"This is the tunnel?" Clarisse said, her voice rising in surprise. "Where does it lead?"

Walter's frowning gaze shifted from the tunnel's open door to the two couples. "Are you going down there?" he asked.

"It looks dangerous," Clarisse added as she approached the hole and gazed downward. "No one should go down there."

Simm, determined to ease his sister-in-law's worry, offered a reassuring smile. "Actually, I've already been down. It's safe enough." He turned to Charlie. "Honey, could you grab my laptop? We need to sync them."

Minutes later, Simm set the computer on the patio table and adjusted it to avoid the sun's bright glare. Following Sarah's instructions, the camera synchronized with the laptop and a clear, colorful view of the defunct fountain appeared on the computer screen.

"It works," Noah said with a triumphant grin.

"I hope it works as well underground," Charlie said, biting her lip.

"Erik said it would," Simm assured her, as he strapped the device to his chest.

"I'll go with you," Noah said.

"Why don't you stay with Charlie this time, Simm? I'll go with Noah." Sarah said.

Simm wanted to argue until he spotted Charlie's hopeful expression. "Good idea. I'll go on the next run."

Charlie shot him a relieved smile and squeezed his hand.

The following minutes involved attaching the ropes around Noah and Sarah's waists, slipping the headlamps on their heads, and fastening the camera around Noah's torso.

"Charlie, don't let them go." Clarisse's gaze darted from them to the hole. "What if it collapses? They built that tunnel a century ago, maybe more."

"I've been down," Simm repeated, his tone gentle as he spoke to Clarisse. "There's no need to worry."

Despite his soothing words, Clarisse didn't seem comforted, and Charlie worked to calm her sister-in-law. Simm suppressed a chuckle at the role reversal. Clarisse's distress provided a helpful distraction for Charlie.

Everyone's attention focused on the cavity as Noah and Sarah lowered themselves down the ladder. Quick glances at the laptop reassured Simm that, so far at least, the camera was functioning.

Bosco crouched on the ground beside the hole, his nose hanging over the edge. Simm was sure he'd remain in that position until Noah reappeared.

Once their heads disappeared underground, everyone's focus shifted to the computer screen. The image, although clear, jiggled as Noah navigated the tunnel. The LED headlamps illuminated the shaft's walls and sides.

As expected, they turned left at the corner and proceeded down the tunnel. They hurried, the reels whirring as they unrolled aboveground. Within minutes, they encountered the second right-turn corner that Simm and Sarah had seen from a distance the day before.

As Noah rounded that curve, the group realized another long tunnel lay ahead of them.

"A door?" Charlie's surprised voice broke the tense silence as the image shifted.

Simm squinted at the screen, frustration rising with the shaky video feed. They needed walkie-talkies, some way to communicate with the explorers below. A thousand questions swirled in his mind.

The view swung to Sarah as Noah turned to face her. She nodded and, once again, Noah pivoted back to face the tunnel. Simm estimated another hundred feet would take them to the end and whatever waited there.

Anticipation built among the four remaining houseguests. Walter stood with his hands deep in his pockets and a customary frown on his face. Clarisse, despite Charlie's best efforts, still fidgeted and paced beside them, mumbling under her breath. Simm knew Charlie itched to do the same, but not if it would further unnerve Clarisse.

A mixture of excitement and disappointment coursed through Simm, wishing he was down there with them.

On screen, the couple reached the end of the tunnel. A large hand moved into view and pounded on a wooden door, sending the message he'd found something. Noah spent a moment filming the surrounding area and the door itself before focusing on the simple latch that held it closed. No lock to deal with, Simm thought with relief.

Drawing out the drama, Noah lifted the latch and tugged on the handle. Simm imagined the creaking of the hinges, but a cloud of dust obscured the camera's view.

"C'mon," Simm said impatiently, wanting the same perspective as his underground companions.

The dust cleared. Noah and Sarah waited a moment before moving.

"Stairs," Charlie said, her voice barely above a whisper.

Facing the couple, on the door's other side, were a set of stone steps, perhaps ten of them, leading upward, with another door at the top. It was dark, the headlamps providing the only light source. Noah stepped over the first threshold and came to an abrupt stop. Simm strained to see what hindered him. Why didn't they climb the stairs? Was it a noise? Were they in the basement of someone's house? Were they threatened?

A whimper from over his shoulder caught Simm's attention. He glanced at Bosco, who stared at the overturned reel. The rope had reached its end. Resistance stopped them.

Again, Simm cursed himself for not setting up communications. Returning his gaze to the screen, he saw the camera quiver. Noah was untying the rope. He then turned to Sarah and helped remove hers.

"Oh no," Charlie said, her head moving frantically. "They can't do that."

"It's okay. It was a precaution in case of a problem or collapse. They don't need it now. We have a visual," Simm said.

"Where are they?" Clarisse's voice held a frantic edge.

"They can't be far," Simm said. "It must be a structure, either on this land or somewhere nearby." He glanced around him. It was hard to judge what distance they'd gone, but he guessed they were underneath someone else's property.

"They should come back," Clarisse said, her words coming in a rush. "It could be dangerous. They don't know who's there."

Simm disagreed. If he was in that tunnel, he wouldn't hesitate to climb those stairs. He knew Noah would feel the same.

The big man ascended the steps. At the top, Noah's hand reached out and tried the second door's knob. Locked. He knocked, issuing his warning, and waited. Not surprisingly, there was no answer. Noah pivoted toward Sarah. She stepped back a few feet. The viewers watched as Noah turned to the door and a heavy boot shot up to kick it. Wood splintered but remained in place. Another shaky view of the boot making contact. A crack of light appeared through the partially open doorway.

With the quivering movements and dark perspective, it was difficult to discern what happened next, but eventually Noah stepped over the second threshold into a somber room with a single window. It was a small structure, perhaps twelve by twelve, from what Simm saw. An antique double bed, two chairs, and a wooden table furnished the room. The remnants of a cabinet lay on the floor. He presumed it toppled over under the force of Noah's boot against the door.

Simm stood and cast a sweeping glance around the backyard. No building fits that description. His gaze slid to the laptop on the table, and he watched Noah open the structure's outside door and step onto a green, manicured lawn. Noah turned left, and Simm realized where they were.

CHAPTER 25

"What motivates somebody to dig a massive underground tunnel only to reach their neighbor's property?"

Sarah and Charlie stared at Noah as if he'd spoken in tongues.

"Lovers met there," Sarah said, like she was explaining something to a child. "Someone from this house met another person from next door. And one or both were probably married."

"Really? Think of the challenges involved in building that," Noah said, his tone disbelieving.

"I guess it was true love." Sarah crossed her arms over her chest and glared at him.

"They may have used it for something else. Smuggling?" Charlie said.

"Whoever built it wanted it kept secret," Simm said. "You worked hard to find that ladder. And the door on the other end looked concealed. The only thing that hints at a connection between the neighbors is a small opening in the hedge."

Noah, his face sheepish, admitted they'd probably blown the whole "secret" thing. "The door's ruined, and the cabinet that hid it is in pieces."

"I doubt the neighbors go anywhere near that place. I haven't seen any sign of life over there. Maybe they're away, but when this is over, we'll confess and pay for damages," Simm said. "But for now, let's keep this under wraps until we find out if there's anything else down there that could interest us."

"What else could be in there?" Clarisse asked. "Didn't you solve that mystery? It was a lovers' meeting spot."

"Seems that way," Simm said. "But I'll keep my options open."

Noah raised his brows. "It was fun, but it didn't lead us any closer to Ethan's mystery. Should we focus on something else?"

"I don't want to dismiss it, but you're right, let's keep going," Simm said. "There's still work to do."

"Can I help?" Noah asked.

Simm realized keeping busy would bolster Noah's spirits.

"Why don't you contact your uncle?" Simm said. "See if he knows about the tunnel."

Noah answered with a grimace.

They hadn't heard from Eli since he left in a huff. Had he bounced back from his hard feelings? Simm hoped so. They could use his insight.

"I get it," Simm said. "But until we're certain there's no relation between the tunnel and Ethan, I don't want loose ends."

Noah nodded, grabbed his phone from the table, and headed to a private corner of the yard. Sarah clasped her hands together and announced she wanted to take notes. She bounded up the steps into the house.

"I'll go pick something up for tonight's meal," Charlie said. She turned to Clarisse. "Want to come along?"

The tension eased from Clarisse's face, the pinched lines disappearing. "Yes, of course," she said. "I'll grab my purse."

Simm, determined to squeeze every detail out of the tunnel exploration, retreated to the library with his laptop. Downloading the video footage, he scanned each frame, searching for anything they might have missed.

A movement caught his eye, and he lifted his head to find Walt on the threshold, standing as stiff as a funeral director. Simm transferred his gaze back to his computer, but his awareness centered on his brother as he marched into the room.

"You don't want me here," Walter said, his voice flat, his stare fixed on the desktop. "To tell you the truth, I don't know why I am."

"I guess Clarisse wasn't involved." Simm didn't hide the sarcasm in his tone.

Walter snorted a humorless laugh. "She and Charlie seem to have a few things in common." He shoved his hands into his pants pockets and sighed. "I don't know how to resolve our differences. You're hell-bent on believing the worst about me, and nothing I say or do can change your mind."

"You could prove you weren't associated with that accident."

"I can't prove something that doesn't exist," Walter said as his gaze swung to Simm. "Besides, what would I gain from a cover-up?"

Simm held his gaze. "We both know how this works, Walt. We grew up in the same house, remember? Favors owed, backs scratched. The more you have on Marcus, the more leverage it gives you."

Marcus Vaughn was a business tycoon in Montreal. Old money mixed with new. He was also a buddy of Walter's. Simm never proved his suspicions that both Walter and Marcus were involved in covering up the real perpetrator in the death of Noah's family, but he vowed he'd find it someday.

"I recommended a lawyer. Nothing else." Walter shook his head, his shoulders slumped. "It's no use. You'll never believe me. I'll talk to Clarisse, try to convince her to leave, but she's so excited about this," he said, waving his hand. "Mystery and intrigue. That's what she calls it. It's been years since I've seen her so animated."

Simm frowned. This was news to him. "Problems on the home front?" he asked, then mentally kicked himself for snooping. Charlie's curiosity was rubbing off on him.

Walter turned to the window again. He shrugged. "I guess you could say so. She gave me an ultimatum. Be more present, or she'll take off."

Despite his hard feelings toward his brother, Simm felt a sliver of sympathy. Memories of Walt as a child sped through his mind. He always had something to prove, mostly to his father. So had Simm, but he grew out of it when he realized the price his father demanded in return. Walt never gave up trying to gain Winston Simmons' approval, and he ended up as a copy of their patriarch: harsh, demanding, and self-involved.

Yet Simm glimpsed the sad, vulnerable Walter, the one who looked up to his brother and shared his problems and feelings with him. Simm felt an unexpected pang of loss for what used to be.

"If it helps your relationship, I have no problem with you staying," Simm said, his own words surprising him. "Clarisse seemed different, but I didn't realize it was because of the case."

Walter considered Simm's comments for several long seconds. "I'd appreciate a few more days, if you don't mind." Walter angled his face toward the window, his voice low. "I'll stay out of your way. I have business to take care of, anyway. I can do that from our room."

"Yeah, sure. No worries," Simm said.

His brother gave him a weak smile and a nod before leaving the library, his posture a touch less rigid.

Simm wondered when he turned into a softie. He'd make Charlie proud.

CHAPTER 26

Charlie parked the SUV in a public lot. Her compact car slipped into small spots in Montreal, but she was unaccustomed to handling a vehicle of this size and shied away from parallel parking.

Not only had Clarisse grabbed her purse, but she renewed her makeup and lipstick, and she changed into a peach silk blouse, gray capri pants, and high-heeled sandals. Charlie glanced at her own jean shorts, T-shirt, and sneakers. She rubbed at a stain on her shirt, courtesy of Harley's muddy paws.

"Don't you love this town?" Clarisse said as they strolled along the busy sidewalk. "I could spend hours here."

Charlie couldn't disagree. The warm weather drew people to the shops and outdoor patios. A pang of homesickness struck her, knowing Butler's patio would be open and bustling with people. For an instant, she wished she was there with Frank and the others, welcoming customers and serving drinks.

She jerked herself from her thoughts. They were in a lovely city, working on an important case that affected their friend Noah. Taking a week away from the pub was a small price to pay.

Besides, it offered Charlie the opportunity to connect with her sister-in-law, which could produce a ripple effect to include Simm and Walter.

"So, how are the kids?" Charlie asked, navigating the maze of a food market. Walter and Clarisse had two youngsters, Scott and Abby, aged seven and five. Though Charlie only met them at Simm's father's funeral, they seemed like good kids.

Clarisse gave a nonchalant shrug. "They're fine. Busy with school and activities."

The fact her sister-in-law didn't burst with pride and haul out her phone to show off photos struck Charlie as unusual.

"Who are they with this week?"

"We have a live-in nanny. She takes care of them most of the time."

Charlie searched for an appropriate response, but Clarisse blindsided her with a question.

"When will you and Simm have children?" she asked.

How to respond? Charlie wanted children, and it took nearly two years to sway Simm, but she couldn't explain why to her sister-in-law.

Charlie studied the bread selection as if it held the secret to eternal life.

Clarisse continued her line of questioning. "Aren't you having any?"

"We will," Charlie said. "It just hasn't happened yet."

Clarisse gave her a knowing smile. "I hope you have two just like ours. Carry on the Simmons tradition, you know?"

Charlie took a sudden interest in the cheese and tried to remember what she knew about Walter's children. How should she interpret Clarisse's words? And what exactly was the Simmons tradition?

She shook herself. One moment she looked down upon Clarisse for not showing pride in her kids, and the next she worried about the proud remarks she made.

"For the best cheese," Clarisse said, "there's a specialty shop nearby. Next to the bakery."

Charlie turned in Clarisse's direction, her eyes narrowed. "You know your way around this town. Have you been here before?"

Clarisse threw her head back and released her tinkling laugh. "Have you never heard of the internet, or this little thing called Google?"

Clarisse was right, Charlie thought. She was on edge, looking for villains in every corner.

She shrugged, at least thankful for a change of subject, and followed Clarisse from the store onto the packed sidewalk.

·   ·   ·

After returning with their purchases, Charlie found Simm and Noah in the library. Noah slumped in a chair, his expression glum. Simm paced beside him.

"What's wrong?" she asked.

"Nothing," Simm said. "Noah proposed we abandon the tunnel and focus on the money. We're discussing it."

"I'm the first to admit it's fascinating," Noah said. "But it's also a colossal waste of time."

"Don't forget we believe Ethan may have discovered the journal and hid the key behind the dishwasher," Simm said. "If we think the key and tunnel are connected, that's a point in favor of the tunnel. However, Ethan was not the only one with access to the house and dishwasher."

"You mean Mike?" Charlie asked as she settled on the corner of the desk.

"Mike and Eli. Maybe others," Simm said.

Charlie cast a glance at Noah to gauge his reaction to adding the caretaker and his uncle to the list of suspects. Mike claimed no knowledge of the key, journal, or tunnel. Eli had yet to be questioned.

"If it was Ethan, the laptop could be down there somewhere, making the tunnel crucial," Simm said.

A thoughtful silence descended. Noah tapped his fingers on the armrest, his gaze fixed on the window.

"There are other avenues to explore," Simm added. "Three people mentioned a mysterious blonde woman. I'll try to track her through the taxi companies. And I expect a call from Erik. He might shed light on the money trail."

"Simm's right," Charlie said. "We can't write it off."

"I realize you don't believe the Wolfe history is related, but I still want to reconstruct the family connections."

They swiveled to see Sarah standing in the doorway, her head raised and chin thrust forward. From her frosty tone of voice, Charlie knew she wasn't pleased. Whether because she felt excluded or that her interests were being maligned, Charlie wasn't sure, but she suspected ruffled feathers needed smoothing.

Simm raised a placating hand. "We're not dismissing anything, Sarah. If you unearth something in the family tree that clicks with the bigger picture, that's a win. We're not shutting down the idea."

Noah, straightening in his chair at Sarah's appearance, forced a smile. "Exactly. We're following all leads. If the Wolfe history somehow connects, fantastic."

"Sometimes even a little digging can surprise you. If nothing else, it intrigues me." Sarah smiled tightly.

"Maybe there's another way you can help," Noah said. "Isn't your ex a hacker? You're on good terms, aren't you? Could he give us a hand? It might go faster with two experts."

Sarah froze, her expression pinched. "Not a good idea." She swiveled and stalked from the room.

.   .   .

Charlie's plan was twofold. She needed help with meal prep, but she wanted to check Sarah's mood. She'd stocked the fridge with fruits and vegetables and chosen a variety of meat cuts. But she needed help to put it together into something appetizing. Under normal circumstances, she wouldn't stress over the chore. Simm ate anything set before him, even when she cooked it. Noah and Sarah were as laid-back about food as Charlie and Simm.

But Walter and Clarisse threw a new spice into the stew. A personal chef prepared their meals, or they dined in five-star restaurants. A confident person, Charlie still felt the weight of self-doubt on her shoulders.

She found Sarah in Ethan's bedroom. The scientist had commandeered the room and a small desk to use for her research mission. The journal, some blank paper, and note-covered pages littered the desktop. Sarah spun around, her hand flying to her mouth when Charlie knocked on the door jamb.

"Sorry. Didn't mean to scare you."

"That's okay," Sarah said, taking a sharp breath. "I become absorbed in my work."

"I get it." Charlie hated to tear Sarah away from her project, but she was the only one who could help her at this point.

Charlie still held hope for a romantic relationship between Noah and Sarah. She detected signs of affection between them, but Sarah seesawed from happy and positive to aggravated and defensive, and Charlie didn't know if it was part of her nature or if another reason lay behind it. Simm would scoff at her matchmaking attempts, but she saw nothing wrong with a little encouragement.

"Can I help you with something?" Sarah asked. "Dinner?"

Charlie released a breath and smiled. "You read my mind."

CHAPTER 27

In the kitchen, Sarah surveyed the contents of the fridge and nodded her head. She shot a side glance at Charlie. "Did you have any ideas?"

"None worth mentioning."

"I got this."

"I hoped you'd say that. I'll be your grateful assistant. Tell me what to do."

Sarah pulled ingredients from the fridge as methodically as a chess master. Charlie watched, half-amused, half-tempted to steer the conversation toward Noah. But the moment Sarah disappeared into the pantry, the kitchen door swung open, revealing Clarisse. A small bouquet of wildflowers filled her hand.

"These were just outside," she mumbled, offering the flowers to Charlie. "Thought they might brighten up the place a bit."

Charlie accepted the gift, a welcome splash of color in the tense atmosphere. "They're beautiful. Thank you." Maybe, just maybe, they could build a bridge between them after all.

She reached over and pulled a twig from the shoulder of Clarisse's shirt. "Looks like you went hunting for those." She chuckled, surprised her sister-in-law would risk getting dirty for her sake.

Clarisse's eyes widened as she inspected the rest of her clothing. Apparently satisfied, she turned to Sarah. "Can I help?" she asked.

Sarah didn't miss a beat. She instructed Clarisse to help Charlie chop vegetables as she pulled a bowl from a cupboard and tossed ingredients into it.

Sarah's no-nonsense, military approach to cooking amused Charlie and Clarisse, who exchanged coy smiles. The scientific brain approached food prep as another lab project.

Charlie, never one to pass up an opportunity, switched tacks and targeted her sister-in-law to learn more about her and Walter.

"Do you cook at home?" Charlie asked Clarisse.

"Not as much as I'd like. Walt thinks I have better things to do."

Charlie's gaze lifted from the chopping board. She caught the undertone of dissatisfaction. Her curiosity got the best of her. "What do you do?"

Clarisse emitted a humorless laugh. "Not enough." She rolled her eyes. "Transport the kids back and forth to school and activities, go to charity functions, shop, jog, go to the gym..." Her sentence ended with a shrug.

Charlie's hands stilled. It sounded like a 1950s story. She couldn't imagine not having a busy life, running a business, and interacting with people. Clarisse's tranquil life that she'd always pictured didn't hold any appeal. And what about the nanny? She didn't drive the kids back and forth?

Sarah also stopped her constant motion to stare at the other woman with sympathy.

"Not what you imagined, right? I envy you two so much," Clarisse said, although her tone seemed more lighthearted than brokenhearted. Charlie guessed floating in money balanced out the envy. "That's part of why I insisted we stay here. My home life is not as interesting."

Charlie couldn't let it pass. "How'd you convince Walter to come here?"

Clarisse squared her shoulders and pounded a fist on the countertop. "I put my foot down. Finally. After years of following his plans, I had some of my own." A grin split her face. "It feels great. I've thrown him off guard. I don't know how long it'll last, so I'll savor every moment."

Charlie laughed. This rebellious streak in Clarisse was unexpected yet strangely refreshing. Maybe there was more to her than meets the eye. Was it possible Walter also had appealing traits hidden somewhere?

Simm chose that moment to enter the room. "Wow. I've never seen Charlie so happy in a kitchen."

Charlie narrowed her eyes at him in fake anger. Simm wrapped his arms around her from behind and kissed her cheek.

"I hope you're taking notes. I'd love to have a home-cooked meal on the table every night," he said, exaggerating a grunt when she elbowed him gently in the ribs. "Spousal abuse. I have witnesses."

When Charlie raised her head, she glimpsed expressions of longing on her companions' faces. She presumed Clarisse yearned for something lost in her marriage and Sarah pined for a future yet to be discovered.

Charlie knew she was the fortunate one. Her relationship with Simm was strong, but they'd disagreed on a fundamental subject. Children. Charlie desperately wanted a child. However, Simm believed bad genes passed from one generation to the next, and he decided his father's mean-tempered ruthlessness would raise its ugly head in one of his children, as it had in Walter.

Intense discussions of nurture over nature followed, and Charlie prevailed, convincing Simm he'd be an excellent father. Together, they'd raise a child with morals and a conscience, unlike Winston Simmons Senior.

Would their relationship last, with or without a child? Charlie believed so, but as she snuck a glance at her sister-in-law, she wondered if Clarisse held the same optimism at the start of her marriage. Now, they were at the ultimatum stage.

"Do we have enough for one more?" Simm asked, breaking into Charlie's thoughts.

"Who?" she said, turning her head to meet his gaze.

"Eli. Noah invited him over. We'll grill him about the tunnels."

"Great idea," Sarah said. "I'll take whatever info I can get."

"No promises," Simm said. "God knows where this will lead. At the very least, it'll give Noah a chance to visit with his uncle and mend a few fences."

Charlie smiled at Simm's words. It was what she and Clarisse tried to do with him and Walter—mend fences.

The atmosphere changed after Simm left. Clarisse concentrated on her task, no longer taking part in the conversation. Did it sadden her to see the affection between her and Simm? Did it highlight something missing in her life?

While the boeuf bourguignon simmered, the women joined the others in the front living room. A ringing doorbell and the furious barking it unleashed interrupted their relaxed exchange. Noah quieted the dogs and answered the door, leading his smiling uncle into the room.

Eli, holding two bottles of wine, greeted everyone with easy warmth. "My finest vintage," he announced, handing them to Charlie. "Red and white, I wasn't sure what was on the menu."

Charlie thanked him as Simm introduced Eli to Walter and Clarisse. A flicker of unease crossed Walter's face, a subtle tightening of his jaw that Charlie made a mental note to ask Simm about later.

Eli had recovered his good humor since they'd last seen him. "I appreciate the invitation," he said to Noah. "I don't socialize much."

"You have a vineyard, don't you?" Charlie asked. "You must interact with people."

"True, but it's part of my work. I don't have time to go out." He took a deep swig of the whiskey Simm served him.

Charlie realized she might tread into dangerous territory but understood the family dynamic was part of why they were here. "Do you have any retirement plans?"

Eli's laugh held a trace of bitterness. "When they lower me into the ground."

He may have meant his remark as a joke, but Charlie wanted to dig deeper. "You must have a plan. Are you training someone to take over?"

His expression turned grave. "I am, but I can't say I'm satisfied with my choice. He's good, but he's not family. It's not part of him," he said, rapping his chest with a fist.

Charlie understood. She wasn't Jim O'Reilly's blood relative, but he'd treated her like a daughter, and she'd always considered the pub part of her, even before it became hers.

"It might grow with time," she said, her voice sympathetic.

"I'm seventy years old. I don't have that much time." He lifted his glass to honor his statement, but his smile didn't reach his eyes.

Charlie didn't venture into a discussion about family inheritances. It was a touchy subject in this crowd. She glanced at Walter. He didn't know the story about Noah rejecting his family's money. If he did, he'd offer a derisive comment. But Walter, who liked to be the first to contribute his two cents to business banter, remained quiet. Was he on his best behavior for Clarisse's benefit?

"We've made an interesting discovery," Simm said, changing the topic. "Were you aware there's a tunnel underneath the house leading to a neighbor's backyard?"

Eli's eyebrows lifted. "You found it?"

CHAPTER 28

Those three words caught everyone's attention.

"You knew of it?" Noah asked.

Eli shrugged, a sly grin tugging at his lips. "I heard rumors, but I didn't know where it was."

Charlie leaned forward. "What rumors?"

"The usual spooky stuff," Eli said, clearly enjoying the spotlight. He handed his empty glass to Simm and signaled for a refill. "A secret tunnel, a romantic hideaway, a ghost that roams the tunnel crying."

"A ghost?" Sarah said. Instead of fear, fascination filled her tone.

An amused snort came from Simm's direction. No doubt he thought this would pique Charlie's interest, but she focused on other people's reactions. A similar noise from Walter confirmed he shared his brother's belief that ghosts were hogwash.

Charlie glanced at Clarisse to gauge her reaction to a possibly haunted house. A gleam of something lit her eye. Amusement? Giddiness? The idea was a step up from taxiing kids, although Charlie would love that privilege.

"No one found the tunnel?" Noah asked. "You didn't look?"

"Oh, I did. I got into that dark little space under the house, sure I'd find it. No luck. I knocked on the walls and searched closets but never found it. Our parents told us stories about ghosts and hidden treasures, feeding my fanaticism. It kept me occupied and out of their hair." His mouth twisted into a grimace. "I suspect David and his friends knew more than me, but he didn't want to share with his little brother."

"You were warm when you mentioned the crawl space," Noah said, drawing Eli's thoughts away from the animosity between him and his brother.

Eli's eyes widened. "It's in there?"

Simm turned to Sarah. "Do we have time to show him before dinner?"

"Of course. It's simmering."

Eli bounded from his chair, dreary thoughts of retirement and succession forgotten. Everyone filed outside and gathered around the crawl space door. Noah heaved it open and stood back. Eli stared at it.

"It's how I remember. You go underneath?" He bent over and peered into the darkness under the house.

Noah kneeled beside the opening and flipped the lever underneath the steps. Eli gasped when they collapsed and revealed the hole and ladder.

"I don't believe it," he said. His wide-eyed gaze turned to Noah. "Did you go down?"

"We did. It leads to a small outbuilding." Noah nodded toward the neighboring property. "It has little more than a bed."

Eli gave a full-bodied laugh. "Someone had an affair with the neighbor's wife. It must've been old Percy. I heard he was a randy old guy. And I don't think he was the only one."

"It could have been a Wolfe wife," Clarisse speculated, her head tilted. "It works both ways, you know."

Eli grinned and bowed slightly. "I stand corrected."

"Nothing more than that?" Simm asked. "Do you think they used the tunnel for other things?"

Eli shrugged. "Possibly. Our ancestors were shrewd businessmen, always bending the rules a bit. They were in the food and wine business, but not only did they survive Prohibition, they flourished. Hiding illegal hooch was a priority, another rumor that circulated."

Charlie nodded, remembering Noah's remarks on the subject.

Eli's good humor, aided by the whiskey and wine, remained throughout the meal. The tender boeuf bourguignon with a velvety and full-bodied sauce evoked groans of appreciation from everyone.

"I almost forgot," Charlie said as she darted a glance in Sarah's direction. "We unearthed a treasure trove in the attic—a box of photo albums. I think there are some pictures of you as a child, Noah." With that, she disappeared into the kitchen, returning with the old box.

As they spread the albums across the dining room table, laughter and exclamations filled the room. Noah and Eli were lost in a world of memories, sharing stories and inside jokes. The rest of the group hung on their every word, their expressions a mix of amusement and curiosity. Except for Walter, who stewed in an armchair, nursing a glass of whiskey.

Bittersweet expressions crossed the faces of the two Wolfe men when they came across images of a young Ethan—a mischievous spark dancing in his eyes, a promise of trouble yet to come.

A pained expression appeared on Eli's face. "You two were like sons to me, I swear. I wish things could've been different..." He took a large gulp of his drink and seemed to shake himself out of his maudlin thoughts. "But let me tell you a story about my brother and Ethan." With a grin, he regaled them with a humorous tale of Ethan thinking the exquisitely manicured rose garden would make an excellent jungle gym. "David and I arrived and found him hanging upside down from the trellis. I thought my brother would explode. His face was as red as a fire engine."

More stories followed as they sifted through the albums.

Charlie noticed Sarah's jitters, certain she wanted to take notes but was too polite to leave for paper and pen.

"If you find the time, Eli, maybe you could help Sarah with her research," Charlie suggested. "She's piecing together the family history."

Eli's face lit up. "I'd be delighted. Truth be told, I've always wanted to map it out but never found the time. Now I have a personal historian at my disposal."

"Perfect." Charlie smiled. Even if nothing more happened, Eli's presence might help resolve his differences with Noah.

.   .   .

With his laptop open, Simm dialed another number. Despite his best efforts, the first taxi company's employee found no record of a passenger going to the Wolfe mansion.

On the second call, a woman answered. Her tone was efficient, ready to take the next request for a ride. Simm introduced himself as a private investigator and asked for someone to help him find information. Hesitant, she told him to wait on the line. A full five minutes later, a man picked up the call with another no-nonsense tone.

"What can I do for you?"

"I'm trying to trace a passenger that was driven to 357 Oakdale Drive."

"No date or time?"

"Nothing specific, but if you inputted that address..."

"Can't help you."

"It shouldn't take long."

"If the police produce a warrant, it's a different matter, but I can't hand out details to just anybody. Privacy, you know."

Simm suppressed a sigh. This wasn't unexpected. The guy had a point. Finding one helpful person doesn't guarantee it'll always work. He thanked him and disconnected the call.

He found two more obliging individuals, without results.

"Any luck?"

Simm glanced up at the sound of his wife's voice. "Three nothings and a privacy lecture."

"Did you try ride sharing?" Charlie said as she settled into the other chair.

"Ray said it was a taxi. He couldn't read the number on top of the car."

Simm's phone jangled. "Erik," he said.

Their conversations were usually short and to the point. Erik, the computer whiz, preferred the company of his keyboard to human interaction.

"Still need help with that money trace?" Erik asked.

Simm took that as a positive response to his request. "Yeah. What do you need?"

"Whatever you have. Name, address, date of birth, account numbers, anything and everything."

"I'll email it to you. You know the police got nowhere with this, don't you?"

"Yeah," Erik said. "I have a few channels they don't use."

Simm didn't ask for specifics. The less he knew the better, certain those channels weren't altogether legal.

"How long?" Simm asked.

"I'll try for tomorrow."

"Great. Appreciate it."

Simm looked at Charlie and read the despair on her face. Five days in, and they still spun their wheels. The tunnel probably wasn't linked to Ethan's death or the murder. The woman's identity remained a mystery. They hadn't found a lock for the key or Ethan's laptop. Among the documents in the house, none led them further than an interesting family history.

The only thing they'd achieved was to add spice to Walter and Clarisse's love life and to give Eli and Noah a chance to reconnect.

"Where do we go next?" Charlie asked.

"Too many things are still hanging." Simm ticked off a list on his fingers. "The cop is hiding something, that much is clear. The blonde woman is out there, with crucial information. The investment guy's death feels suspicious. The money trail has vanished, and all the important documents are gone. And of course, there's Ethan's missing laptop."

"Don't forget the tunnel," Charlie added.

Simm's lips twisted. "And the tunnel."

"How can I help?"

"I don't know how to help myself. Erik is working on one front. The ball's in his court. For the rest, I may need to pressure my detective friend a little." He focused on Charlie. "What are Sarah and Clarisse up to?"

In bed the night before, Charlie filled Simm in on her conversations with the other women during dinner preparations. Walter's staunch and outdated beliefs about Clarisse's role in the household irritated Simm, but they didn't surprise him. His father had been the same, insisting his mother fill the job of doting wife and occasional arm candy.

"Sarah's hard at work on the family research," Charlie said. "And Clarisse went jogging."

A knock on the door interrupted their conversation. With a grim smile, Walter ventured into the room.

CHAPTER 29

"Sorry to disturb you," Walter said. "I have something to discuss." He gazed at his half-full whiskey glass as if seeking permission from it.

"Do you have a complaint about the maid service?" Simm said.

Charlie sent her husband an exasperated glance. Normally diplomatic, the trait flew out the window when Walter was present. She'd hoped the brothers' small heart-to-heart talk the other day would make Simm more agreeable, but her revelations about Walter's attitude toward Clarisse erased the few warm and fuzzy feelings Simm had.

"Hilarious," Walter said, his tone sardonic. "I'm offering help, but if you don't want it, that's fine."

He turned to the door, but Charlie forestalled him. "Of course we'd appreciate your help. Please sit down."

Walter hesitated and glanced at Simm then accepted the offered chair. As usual, he was sharply dressed, while everyone else in the household chose casual attire. He straightened the creases on his dress pants before crossing his legs, setting his glass on a side table, and lacing his fingers together.

Not trusting Simm to contain his sarcasm, Charlie took control of the conversation. "What did you want to help with?"

"I need to share an observation. About Eli."

It clicked in Charlie's brain. Walter's unusually pensive behavior during dinner the previous night pertained to Eli. "What about him?"

"I know him. Or, rather, I know of him."

"You told us you knew the family," Charlie said.

"Eli's a wealthy person. You circulate in the same crowds," Simm added.

Walter ignored Simm's mocking tone. "I've never met Eli or seen him at a social function, but I've heard of him. Not in a good way, as I explained at dinner at your place."

His last remark intrigued Charlie. Apart from being a heavy drinker and holding a lifelong grudge about his ancestor's will, Charlie didn't find fault in Noah's uncle. He appeared to be a capable businessman, and he was friendly. His offer to help Sarah was a generous one. Walter had warned them about the Wolfe family's morals, but she'd witnessed nothing to justify the warning.

"What did you hear?" she asked, hoping to gain clarity.

"His business ethics are not aboveboard."

A derisive snort came from Simm's direction. Charlie hoped he'd keep his remarks about Walter's integrity to himself until after she got the information she wanted. Walter shifted his gaze to Simm, so Charlie leaned forward and spoke faster to grab his attention.

"Do you have an example?" she said.

Walter turned back to her. "As you know, he owns vineyards and two restaurants."

Charlie nodded.

"He also supplies wine to the casinos in Niagara," Walter said. "His exclusive contracts are worth gold."

Charlie raised her eyebrows. "I would imagine."

"Some speculate his only access was through a Mafia connection."

"The Mafia?" Charlie couldn't contain her alarm. She'd had personal experience with the Irish Mafia in Montreal and Ireland, an adventure she wasn't eager to repeat. From the corner of her eye, she saw Simm sit forward in his chair.

"How much weight do you give the speculation?" Simm asked, his attention captured and his tone agreeable.

Walter's gaze shifted to him, and for the first time, Charlie witnessed the brothers discuss a subject without their usual animosity.

"If I only heard it once, I wouldn't give it any weight. But I heard it multiple times, and I know how the mob insinuated itself into the casino business. Anyone who makes major inroads into the supply chain the way he has can usually thank organized crime for it."

Charlie caught Simm's meaningful glance before he turned back to Walter.

"Keep this between us, for now. I don't want it to get back to Eli or Noah. I'll dig and see if I can confirm anything."

Walter nodded and stood.

"Thank you, Walt," Charlie said, coming to her feet. "It may not be related to the case, but we can't ignore it if it's true."

"She's right," Simm said. "Thanks."

Walter gave his brother an awkward smile before leaving the room.

Charlie watched the door swing shut, the weight of Walter's words settling on her like a shroud. The case, already a tangled mess, had just taken another sharp turn. "The Mafia?" The words tasted like ash in her mouth. "Seriously?"

Simm ran a hand through his hair, his face etched with worry. "We can't dismiss it. Eli has the motive—a grudge against Noah, possibly desperate for funds. And with the Mafia's resources, the electronic transfer wouldn't be an issue."

"But wouldn't the police be all over that kind of connection?" Charlie said. Surely the authorities wouldn't miss something so obvious.

"Maybe, maybe not." A shoulder lifted in a shrug. "The police are playing their cards close to the vest. And the mob is notorious for being good at hiding their tracks."

. . .

Charlie felt at loose ends. She didn't have a specific task, an unusual condition for her. At the pub, she kept busy serving drinks, chatting with customers, or taking care of the general administration of the business. After five days in Niagara-on-the-Lake, she missed the bustle of home.

Charlie wandered into the garden, breathing in the fresh, spring air, the purity of it a sharp contrast to Montreal's urban aroma. She imagined it in its heyday with a groomed lawn and flowers, the fountains gurgling, the scent of roses, the chirping of birds.

A wrought-iron bench sat beside a fountain. It needed a good scrubbing, she thought, but it appeared safe to sit on. Lowering herself onto it, she leaned back and stretched her feet out. A woman likely sat here long ago, reading and soaking up the sun's warmth. Perhaps dreaming about an upcoming ball or an expected visit from a suitor.

On impulse, she grabbed her phone from her pocket and tapped speed-dial. Frank's deep voice at the other end cheered her spirit.

"Enjoying the sunshine and a glass of wine?"

Charlie laughed. "Sunshine, yes. Wine, not right now."

"How's it going?"

"Slow. We've hit walls, and we're waiting for people to respond about some stuff. How about you?"

"Great. Nothing to worry about," Frank said. If the pub collapsed around him, Frank wouldn't breathe a word. He'd handle it like he handled everything—with finesse. Pushing him for more information was pointless.

"I miss you," she said instead.

"Back at ya," Frank said, his voice mellowing. Despite his size and muscular bulk, Frank had a soft heart. They supported each other through good times and bad, and their bond ran deep. "When are you coming home?"

"We're giving it another couple of days. If nothing shakes loose, we'll hand it to the police."

"It sounds like Simm isn't sharing. That's not like him."

"We have issues with the cops at this point. Still need to settle that." Charlie heard chattering and the clink of glasses in the background. Getting set up for the lunch time crowd. She felt another pang of lonesomeness. "I'll let you work. Wanted to say hi and check in. I'll text you when to expect us."

Once the call disconnected, Charlie lowered her hands to her lap, unsure if she felt better or worse after talking to Frank. As Charlie's mind drifted, a creeping sensation overcame her, an impression of being watched. Wanting to avoid drawing attention to herself, she slowly pivoted to peer at the house. No one was outside. With the sun's glare, she couldn't tell if someone observed her from a window.

Charlie brushed aside her silliness. Walter and Clarisse's room overlooked the backyard. Perhaps one of them looked out and saw her. Or maybe Noah spotted her from the kitchen. Nothing sinister.

Yet, Charlie couldn't shake the feeling it was. She scanned her surroundings. She was alone. No houses were close, no one peered over the hedges.

Charlie inhaled a deep breath and released it. She shut her eyes and concentrated on the sun's warmth and the scent of flowers, no matter how unkempt they were.

She nearly jumped out of her skin when a heavy hand gripped her shoulder.

CHAPTER 30

Charlie shrieked and catapulted from the bench, swiveling in mid-air.

Stepping back, the man raised shaky hands to defend himself.

"Mike! You scared the life out of me," Charlie said.

"I'm sorry," he stammered, face flushed crimson. "I thought you heard me."

Charlie flattened her hand on her chest and struggled to regain her breath. "What are you doing here?" she asked.

"I wanted to mow the lawn, but if it's a bad time..."

"No, it's not. Go ahead. I'm going inside anyway," she said, her words tumbling out.

"Only if you're sure..."

Charlie's gaze passed over Mike's clothing. He wore a blue button-up shirt, khaki trousers, and nice shoes. She frowned. "You mow the lawn dressed like that?"

Mike glanced down as if he didn't realize he wore clothes. "Well... not usually. I drove by and thought the grass was a little long and figured I'd tackle it."

Charlie gazed at the overgrown lawn, thinking it had been like this for weeks. Why the sudden interest? "What about the flower gardens? Who takes care of them?"

"They used to have a real gardener, but I guess it's my job now. I'm not good at it." His nervous gaze darted around the yard.

Charlie thought that was an understatement. Despite her limited gardening knowledge, she recognized the dire need to weed and prune the flowers. "So, you cut the grass and take care of fixing things that are broken?"

"Yep, that's it." His thin fingers fiddled with the buttons on his shirt.

Charlie hoped the estate didn't pay him a big salary. The level of disrepair was unusual for a place with a caretaker. Mike seemed like a good guy, but did he take advantage of the situation or was he simply clueless? She leaned toward the latter. The more she saw of Mike, the less she imagined him as an architect of fraud and murder.

On her way to the house, she checked the windows once again. This time, she was certain a curtain moved in the upstairs bedroom, the one where Walter and Clarisse slept.

• • •

Charlie decided if she couldn't help Simm, she should keep busy. Plants needed love, even for a short period. From her perch inside the library, she heard a knock on the front door, setting off the automatic barking alarm system. Noah appeared from the kitchen just as Charlie stepped out of the library, a gardening book in her hand.

Following Noah's command, Bosco sat on his haunches and patiently waited for somebody to open the door. Harley, as usual, ignored Charlie's instructions. With the force of each bark, his hind legs lifted off the ground.

The tall, broad man at the door cast a cautious glance at Bosco and seemed reassured by Noah's firm grip on the mastiff's collar, showing much less concern about the tail-wagging pug.

"Can I help you?" Charlie asked. The man resembled a salesman with his suit and tie, albeit a salesman that earned little money. His gray suit and scuffed shoes showed wear and tear.

The stranger removed a badge from his pocket. Charlie leaned forward to examine it as Simm appeared by her side.

"Detective Baxter. Nice to see you," Simm said.

The detective may not have noticed, but Charlie picked up on her husband's sarcastic tone.

"A pleasure for me as well."

No, the cop noted it and tossed it back at Simm.

"I thought we saw the last of each other."

Baxter's smirk morphed into a condescending smile. "Just checking on your investigation."

Charlie fought back the urge to roll her eyes. This cop clearly relished needling Simm.

Her husband responded with a brittle smile. "Moving right along, Detective."

Baxter's gaze flickered to Noah, prompting introductions. The tension in the room thickened as Noah recognized the detective who investigated Ethan's death—the one who likely covered up a murder.

"Mind if I come in?" Baxter said as he gazed around the entranceway.

"Is there a purpose to your visit?" Simm dropped any pretense of politeness.

"I just wanted to know if you could add to the investigation."

"I thought you closed yours." Noah didn't pretend to be happy with the detective.

The cop focused his attention on Noah, his expression unreadable. "With new information, we can reopen it."

"Having second thoughts?" Simm asked, his brows raised.

"Not what I said. Just telling you how it works."

Charlie sensed a peak in testosterone levels. She remained curious if the detective would give away anything helpful.

"How about some coffee? Anyone?" Charlie offered.

"Love some," Baxter said, stepping around Simm and Noah to follow Charlie to the kitchen.

Charlie might not be a splendid cook, but serving beverages was her specialty. Soon everyone circled the table with steaming mugs in hand, and she wondered how to head off another squabble.

Clarisse interrupted them. Unaware of their visitor or the tense atmosphere, she sailed into the room and slid to a stop when she glimpsed the tall stranger. Dressed in her jogging clothes, she glistened with sweat, and strands of hair slipped from her topknot.

"I'm sorry," she said, her lips upturned in a shy smile. It was obvious she was uncomfortable being caught in a less-than-perfect state. "Didn't mean to interrupt."

Simm crushed her escape. "Clarisse, this is Detective Baxter. He investigated the fire and Ethan's death."

The former, timid version of her sister-in-law returned in full force when Charlie saw her take two steps back, easing out of the kitchen.

"This is my sister-in-law, Clarisse," Simm said. "She and my brother paid us an unexpected visit."

"How nice," the cop said, his disinterest clear. At Simm's words, a mask descended over his face, hiding his thoughts. "But, to correct you, Rick Clarke investigated the fire."

"Yes, of course. Any errors or omissions lie upon his shoulders."

Charlie tried to grab Simm's attention and send him a signal to lighten up on the sarcasm. If they wanted information, they needed to use a little honey.

"I'm sorry, you'll have to excuse me," Clarisse said. "My husband sent me to find his novel, but I don't see it here. It must be in the library." Clarisse turned and fled the room.

With a smile she hoped appeared unforced, Charlie turned her attention to the detective. "Have you been in this house before?" she asked.

The cop gave a slow nod. "We questioned a few people here."

"Who?" Noah asked, his body humming with tension. Charlie understood how much Noah distrusted the police and could only guess how difficult it was to sit beside an evasive cop.

"Your uncle and the caretaker." Baxter, unaffected by Noah's attitude, looked at Simm. "Any luck with the money trail?"

"Still working on it." Simm also did evasive well.

"I thought someone erased it."

"Something like that, but I haven't given up." Simm narrowed his eyes. "Speaking of the money, did you hear about Brent Holmes' death?"

The cop tilted his head. "The financial advisor?"

"Yeah. He died in Jamaica two weeks after the fire."

"I heard about it. I talked to Webber. They found nothing suspicious."

"That's what he told me," Simm said. "Doesn't strike you as fishy?"

The detective's gaze bore into Simm's. "If you want, look into it," he said. "Maybe the money trail starts there."

Simm didn't miss a beat. "Any hints where I should start?"

The cop pursed his lips. "Not my territory," he said. His gaze traveled over the room, not settling on anyone. "I'm surprised you're still here if nothing's shown up."

"Turned it into a brief holiday," Simm said. "We plan to visit wineries, check out the falls."

The cop stood, his chair scraping the floor. "I'll get going," he said. "Thanks for the coffee."

Since neither Simm nor Noah budged, Charlie led the detective to the door.

"Let me know if there's anything." He hesitated a moment. "Tell your husband I'll call him." She detected a trace of sympathy in his expression and wondered if he sent her a message. She puzzled over it as she watched him climb into his car and drive away.

CHAPTER 31

Angry voices emanated from the kitchen, and Charlie knew Noah was releasing his tension. A broad-shouldered storm cloud paced the room.

"What did he want? I don't understand," Noah thundered.

"Just feeling us out, that's all." Simm's usual levelheadedness replaced the sarcasm that prevailed during the cop's visit.

"Making sure we don't discover his cover-up." Noah said, trembling with rage. "But it's too late for that. I want to see him in jail."

"I don't think he's that bad," Charlie said, her tone thoughtful.

Noah turned on her, a finger pointed in her direction. "Don't defend him." His voice boomed.

Simm shot from his chair. "And don't talk to my wife that way," he said.

Noah's shoulders slumped as his temper deflated. He ran his hands through his hair. "I'm sorry. Being in the same room was unbearable. He's hiding something. He knows who killed Ethan. Dammit, maybe it was him."

Charlie clutched Noah's forearm. "You're angry. I understand. It's difficult for us, so I can only imagine how much worse it is for you. But we said we'd give it a week. If we find nothing, we'll go above Baxter's head and nail him to the wall."

Noah nodded before grabbing Charlie and pulling her in for a hug. She'd never known him to be demonstrative, so she recognized it as a heartfelt apology. He released her and turned to Simm, holding out his hand. "Sorry, man."

Sarah entered as the men clasped hands. "What did I miss?" she asked, her curious gaze flitting from person to person.

"Detective Baxter's visit. He generated some powerful emotions." Charlie wore a wry smile.

"The dogs made a racket, but I was neck-deep in research."

"Getting anywhere?" Charlie asked, changing the topic.

Sarah twisted her lips into a grimace. "I started, but I'm slogging through a pile of unrelated information. Eli just left. I dug into his memory bank." She laughed. "He's worn out. Gone home for a nap."

"More like a drink," Noah said, disapproval etched into his features. "He can knock 'em back."

Charlie agreed Eli enjoyed drinking, but she'd seen worse. Their Irish friend, Harry, visited them several months back and drank Guinness from noon to midnight with hardly any effect. Some people had a high tolerance.

She turned her attention back to Sarah. "I hope you're not doing all that work for nothing."

"It's possible, but I enjoy it. If something turns up, it'll be icing on the cake."

Charlie excused herself, grabbed her book, and retreated to their room. She needed to study up on gardening if she wanted to take a stab at the front yard's delinquent horticulture, and her bedroom seemed the perfect place to do so. Even if unsuccessful, it'd give her a much-needed distraction from the tension that pervaded the house. Perhaps Sarah's research served the same purpose for her.

A sense of desertion blanketed the upper floor. Even her faithful sidekick Harley remained downstairs, snoozing with Bosco in the sitting room.

A cool draft wrapped around Charlie as she opened the door to their bedroom. The curtain swayed slightly in the breeze from the window she didn't remember opening. As she walked toward it, she froze.

An eerie sound came from outside the room. It was faint at first but slowly grew in volume, a woman's voice filled with sadness. The words were indistinct, carried on the wind, but the raw emotion in the voice made Charlie's stomach clench.

Her heart pounded as she edged into the hallway, her desire to yell for help competing with the need to not scare away the mysterious person. Curiosity won out. She crept toward the sound that emanated from Ethan's bedroom. As she approached, the woman's wailing grew louder, but not clearer. Charlie couldn't make out the words, but the voice held a tone of pain and longing.

Who could it be? Sarah was downstairs. She didn't know where Walter and Clarisse had disappeared to.

Her hand wrapped around the doorknob, and she hesitated, questioning her decision. Taking a deep breath, she turned the knob and threw open the door.

CHAPTER 32

Cold air engulfed her. No wailing or crying. And no human presence. The curtains were almost horizontal. A strong wind howled through the open window, scattering papers and photographs across the floor like fallen leaves.

Charlie scrambled to close it and cut off the draft, wondering why Sarah would leave it open, other than trying to chase away the mustiness. As the drapes and papers settled, Charlie stood inert, her hands on the window sash, listening.

Where had the noise come from? She was convinced this room was the source, but it was empty, and the sound was gone.

"What's wrong?"

Charlie spun to face Clarisse, whose worried expression echoed Charlie's feelings.

"Did you hear something?" Charlie asked.

Clarisse's eyebrows descended. "Like what?"

"Like a woman crying and wailing."

"No," Clarisse said, her eyes wide. "Is it Sarah?" She cast a quick glance around the room as if looking for an aggrieved Sarah.

"I don't think so. She's downstairs, and it seemed to come from here. You heard nothing?"

"Heard what?"

The women turned toward Sarah, who stood on the threshold. Charlie doubted herself. Sarah's question said it all. She didn't hear anything either. Was stress sending her over the edge? Had she imagined the noise?

"Charlie thought the sound of a woman crying came from here," Clarisse said, her tone uncertain.

Charlie didn't think the comment registered in Sarah's mind. Her attention focused on the strewn papers and photos. Horror blossomed on her face.

"Who did this?"

Charlie forgot her uneasiness when faced with Sarah's fury. "The window was open when I came in. The wind…"

"I didn't open the window," Sarah said, her eyes wild as she scrambled to gather her treasured findings.

Charlie kneeled to help her, but Sarah brushed her hand aside. "Don't touch anything," Sarah said. Her tone veered from anger to sadness, as if a classroom bully had injured her child, and she needed to focus her attention on her offspring.

Charlie glanced at Clarisse. The scene seemed to both mystify and amuse her.

·   ·   ·

Charlie sat in the library's comfy armchair, the open gardening book in her lap, staring out the window at the untrimmed hedge and the disorderly hydrangea bushes. Harley snored at her feet while Simm concentrated on his laptop screen. Rapid key tapping complemented her thoughts—thoughts that had little to do with horticulture and everything to do with the cop's visit and the bizarre happenings in the room upstairs.

She'd explained the incident to Simm, expecting him to scoff at her guarded hint it may be related to a ghost. Scoff-less, he searched the entire top floor for anything suspicious and came up empty-handed. Despite wishing otherwise, Charlie didn't expect him to find physical proof of a crying woman. What would it have been? A dirty handkerchief? A sad novel left behind by a grief-stricken reader? The look she got upon his return told her he didn't want to discuss the other possibility.

Charlie wished she'd kept the episode to herself. Other issues weighed down Simm's shoulders, including the cop's visit. What had Baxter hoped to accomplish? He'd already alienated Simm. He had to realize he'd upset Noah. Was he so desperate to make sure his cover-up stuck he needed to question them? But what about his cryptic instruction to follow up on the financial advisor's death? And his intensity when he told her he'd call Simm? Something felt off.

Simm wrote it off as a distraction meant to make them chase their tails, the promise of a call as a warning that the cop was watching him.

A knock disturbed them.

Simm called out, "Come in."

Noah and Bosco entered the room, rousing Harley from his nap, but Charlie focused on Noah's expression. It didn't bode well.

"What is it?" she asked.

"Come," Noah gestured toward the door, his voice heavy.

Charlie's stomach lurched. What could it be now?

They followed Noah to the front door and watched in silence as he pulled it open. Charlie gazed outside but spotted nothing out of the ordinary, until she heard Simm's groan beside her and turned to see despair on his face. She tracked his gaze to the door. Her heart jolted in her chest.

CHAPTER 33

Once again, Charlie sought the bench in the garden. The house was so full of people she had trouble sorting through her thoughts. Unusual for someone accustomed to lively bars. It spoke to the gravity of her reflections.

Not wanting to be alone, Charlie had the dogs lying one on each side of her, making her feel protected. Harley might not fight an intruder as well as Bosco did, but he'd make noise.

She sensed a movement beside her, but it didn't startle or frighten her. She expected Simm. A muscular arm settled across her back as he lifted Harley aside and nestled close. Charlie let her head drop onto his shoulder.

The peaceful spot was just short of idyllic. But weed-filled gardens and the ominous presence of threats cast a dark shadow over it.

"We can go home," Simm said, his tone matter of fact. "It's not worth destroying our lives over it."

"I know."

"Noah will understand."

"He will."

"He's obviously worried about Sarah too."

"He is."

"Can you form a sentence longer than two words?"

"I could."

Simm squeezed her shoulder and gave it a little shake.

Her shock had dissipated since first seeing the door's defacement, but the implications continued to work their way through her system.

They'd stared at the black-painted door and read the message engraved in the wood. A knife likely made the simple carving, maybe even an ordinary kitchen knife, but the missive was clear.

GO AWAY OR SOMEONE DIES

Silence had lain over the group until Simm spoke.

"Somebody knows we're here and what we're doing," he said.

Noah's furious gaze lifted from the door to meet Simm's. "You can drop it. No hard feelings," Noah said. "I don't want anyone hurt."

Neither Simm nor Charlie had responded. Her thoughts frozen, Charlie suspected Simm's were all over the place.

Now, just a short time later in the garden, her feelings weren't any clearer. "I hate giving up," she said.

"I've heard that before."

Charlie snorted. "We've been down this road a few times."

This was the fourth case Charlie worked with Simm, including the one for which she'd hired him. Each time, they faced threats, as individuals or as a couple. It seemed to be par for the course, a job requirement.

But it didn't get easier to handle, not for Charlie. Involving more players made it worse. Six people now stayed in the house. Apart from her husband, she didn't know the others well.

She trusted Noah, and he'd hired them to be there, so that counted for something. Unless it was a smoke screen to throw off the investigators.

Sarah, her newfound friend, was a brilliant computer whiz, but her evasiveness and occasional outbursts made Charlie question her motives. Could she have the skills to manipulate an intricate financial system and steal from both Ethan and Noah?

Walter and Clarisse were her in-laws, but she'd rarely interacted with them. Strife and animosity between Walter and Simm crowded those few interactions. She'd never taken to her brother-in-law and only tried to reconcile the brothers because she wanted Simm to rid himself of angst.

Clarisse was a two-sided coin. She went from timid and skittish to strong and shrewd. Had she learned some tricks from her husband? Was her timid demeanor a mask, hiding a cunning personality?

Besides her housemates, she had to concern herself with Eli, who may or may not have Mafia ties, a possibly corrupt detective, and an intrusive and inept caretaker.

"There are a lot of moving parts," she said. "Can't decide which shoulder to look over."

"I'll say it again, we can drop it and go home."

What Simm implied was that he'd do whatever Charlie wanted. He'd abandon the case, help her pack up their things, and take her to the safety and routine of the pub. She loved him for it.

But what he didn't say, and she realized he felt, was that he hated to do it. Simm didn't like hanging threads. It ate at him, just like his unfinished business with his brother festered inside him. It was part of the reason she wanted that family dynamic resolved, even though it was not Simm's desired path. He needed to prove himself right, not wrong. His belief in Walter's guilt helped fuel his desire to support Noah, and leaving Niagara-on-the-Lake and the case behind would disturb his peace of mind.

Charlie shifted to the edge of the bench and faced her husband. "What if we didn't? What if we stayed and finished it? At least until the week is up. What can we do to move it along safely?"

Simm's smile reflected his relief, and his voice rang with conviction as he enumerated his plans. "We'll take precautions. Put up security cameras. We'll be vigilant. I'll check out Eli and pester someone in Jamaica about Holmes. I'll add Mike to the list. Erik will contact me soon regarding the money."

"Things'll move. I know it," Charlie said, feeling the same confidence. "Sarah will make headway with her research. Relevant or not, it's something."

Simm took her hand and rubbed her knuckles. "You want to see it through?"

Her gaze locked with his, and she saw the hope in his eyes. Yet he was offering her one last chance to pull the plug, letting the final answer be her call. But giving up wasn't in her nature. They were in this together, and she wouldn't abandon a friend in need. Her gut told her they were close to a breakthrough.

"I do," she said, feeling determination bubble up inside her. Maybe she was as stubborn as Simm, after all.

CHAPTER 34

"Do you need glasses?"

Simm didn't remove his intent gaze from the laptop to acknowledge his wife.

Charlie moved to his side, worried about what she'd see. The image filling the screen was a close-up of... mud? Black, gloopy mud. "What is that?"

"The fire scene. Look," he said, pointing at a close-up of the sludge.

Charlie shifted closer and squinted. She gazed at a swirl of muck. "I don't get it."

"I'll zoom out." Simm grabbed the mouse and displayed the entire image. "This is the scene as it was the day we arrived."

Charlie nodded. She remembered it. "Okay."

"This should be how it looked after the investigators finished their work. The ashes, combined with the water from fire hoses, created this mud. I have several pictures, but look at this one."

Again, he zoomed in on the swirls. "Once the scene is clear and safe, the investigators go in. Footprints everywhere."

Understanding dawned on Charlie. "And now they're gone?"

"Not all of them, but some. There's a path. Footprints wiped away from the door to the car. Hard to spot. I didn't catch it until now."

Charlie lowered herself into a chair, her thoughts spinning. "The footprints were distinctive, and they deliberately hid them."

"Someone took the trouble to conceal them while the ashes were damp," Simm said, his gaze fixed on Charlie's face.

"Detective Baxter was there," Charlie said.

"I've left him a message. If nothing else, I want original photos of the scene. Whether I get them is a big question."

"I doubt he'll hand them over."

"I'll hire a lawyer if I have to," Simm said, his voice firm.

"How do we find out if he's involved?" Charlie asked.

"I'll search for signs of newfound wealth."

"And if there's none?"

"I'll go to his superior," Simm said. "It's risky. The orders might come from there. Either that, or they'll close ranks."

"Let's say it wasn't him. Who else could it be?" Charlie asked.

Simm spread his hands. "The fire investigator, another cop, a firefighter... you name it. But whoever did it probably removed the device from the car after the fire, or tried to hide the fact somebody removed it."

"The killer or their accomplice." The words, even as they left her mouth, sent chills down Charlie's spine.

"Exactly."

"But cops guarded the place until the investigation ended. How'd they get past them?" Charlie asked.

"Either the guard was in on it, or someone paid him to turn the other way," Simm said, a muscle flexing in his jaw. He detested corrupt police officers.

"And the footsteps were obvious enough to distinguish themselves from those that were supposed to be there." Charlie stared at Simm with lowered brows. "So...what? Heels, sneakers? What could it be?"

"Not firefighter or cop boots. That's what you'd expect to see." Simm snatched up his phone. "I need the original photos."

.   .   .

Charlie found Sarah hunched over a desk, surrounded by dusty files. Relief washed over her—Sarah seemed to be in a better headspace now. Perfect timing.

"Mind if I pick your brain?" Charlie asked, knocking gently on the door.

Sarah glanced up, a smile lighting her face. "Of course, come in."

Charlie chose her words with care. "I need your objective opinion about something."

"Hit me with it." Sarah swiveled her chair toward her.

"I want your take on the noises," Charlie said, using her best casual tone.

"I didn't hear them." Sarah frowned.

"But I described them to you. Who or what do you think it was?"

Sarah glanced at her hands before moving her gaze back to Charlie. "I know you think it may have been a ghost."

"No one else was there. I thought it might be a possibility."

Sarah's eyes held sadness. "I'm sorry, Charlie, but I can't tell you what you want to hear. I'm skeptical of ghosts. There's a lack of evidence to support them. Rigorous scientific tests and controlled experiments are needed, and exploring the likelihood of natural phenomena is essential."

"How do you explain the noises I heard? The woman crying and wailing?"

Sarah gently took one of Charlie's hands in hers. "You've been stressed. Distress and grief can cause visual or auditory hallucinations. Account for the open window and the strong winds. They could have created a howling sound. And because of suggestions of ghosts and haunted houses, you already had it in your mind. The noise brought it to the forefront."

Sarah's analysis was valid and possible, but Charlie still felt deflated. Had she really hoped Sarah would confirm a ghost? Was a ghost better than the possibility she was losing her sanity? She knew what she'd heard, and it wasn't the wind.

CHAPTER 35

Consumed with questions, Charlie enlisted Harley to give her an excuse to take a walk to clear her head. She admired the estates along the street, having ample time to do so. Harley insisted on sniffing every tree, fire hydrant, and pole. Short of dragging him, nothing she said or did encouraged him to move faster.

It was another world from the streets of Montreal. The sounds of heavy traffic, horns, sirens, and construction were missing here or existed on a much smaller scale, even in the downtown area of Niagara-on-the-Lake. Peaceful, picturesque. A big contrast to Charlie's customary scenery.

She tried to imagine her and Simm living in one of these houses. She'd appreciate the extra room for their future family, although she saw no signs of children or backyard play structures. No bicycles lying on front lawns. Only older, established couples with their mansions, servants, and expensive cars.

Of course, to Simm, that was nothing unusual, raised in a mansion many times larger. But these houses were a major step up from their small apartment. Could she find happiness here? She doubted it. The novelty would fade, and she'd long for her place in a busy city, managing her own business and mingling with a kaleidoscope of people every day.

Something snagged Harley's eye, his ears popping up and his tail standing at attention. Charlie spotted an older man walking a senior black lab. As he approached, the man smiled.

"Well, who do we have here? A new boy in the neighborhood? We met one like him not long ago," the man said.

While the dogs sniffed each other, Charlie introduced herself. "You may have. This is Harley. Perhaps you spoke to my husband, Simm."

"Yes, I did. Hard to forget a strange name like that. And this good boy," he said, sending Harley a smile. "You're at Ethan Wolfe's place, aren't you?"

"Yes, we are."

"I'm Ray Brown. I live just down the street."

"Simm mentioned you. Apparently, you talked to Ethan."

A shadow crossed the older man's face. "Tragic business, that."

"I'm sure you know a few people in this area," Charlie said, fishing for information.

Ray's eyes twinkled. "Oh, yes. Been here since Noah's Ark landed, it seems. It's an old neighborhood. Most families, like the Wolfes, here for generations."

"Who lives behind the Wolfe's place?"

"That's the Donovans, also multi-generational. The original Arthur Donovan built the place in the 1800s, and it still belongs to one of his ancestors."

"Are they away? It looks deserted."

"They're snowbirds. Have a penthouse in Florida somewhere. To escape the winter. They'll be back before the end of the month. We have quite a few of those. I've never minded the cold weather. Like the change of season. Keeps things interesting. Of course, you're from Montreal. Your winters are harsher."

"Yes, but I'm like you. I'm a homebody, and I love each season." Charlie hesitated. "Any idea if Ethan had much interaction with the neighbors?"

"No, I don't. As I mentioned to your husband, I only ever saw a blonde woman. No one else."

The older dog strained on his leash, perhaps ready for his nap. Ray sent an anxious glance in his direction, and Charlie knew they were about to part ways.

"What about the Wolfes and the Donovans? Were there any relationships there?" she asked.

"Relationships?"

Charlie smiled. "I'm trying to think of a discreet term."

"Never mind discreet. I'm an old man. I've seen it all."

"All right. Do you know if, a few generations ago, a Wolfe and a Donovan had an affair?"

"Most definitely. It was a common story when I was growing up. It carried on for more than one generation. Lots of shenanigans, but they couldn't marry. The Donovans were Catholic, and the Wolfes were Protestant. The two weren't allowed to mix. It doesn't matter much now; back then it was a deal breaker."

"Anything about a secret tunnel connecting the houses?"

"Not that I'm aware of, but it wouldn't surprise me in the slightest. Even my house has concealed passageways."

Charlie clasped his cool hand and smiled. She had something to report to Simm. "Thank you, Mr. Brown. It was wonderful to meet you."

"Drop by for a coffee or a cup of tea whenever you like. Bring your husband and dog. I'd appreciate the company."

CHAPTER 36

"Any luck?" Charlie asked.

Simm raised his gaze from his computer screen. "Define 'luck.' I asked a lot of questions, and I'm waiting for a lot of answers." He sighed. "I looked at Baxter from every direction. No sign of an influx of cash, nothing out of the ordinary. I called Josh. The name rings a bell for him."

"In what way, good or bad?"

"I'm not sure. He said he'd call back."

Josh was one of Simm's connections and a good friend. A cop with the Ottawa Police Force, their relationship dated from Simm's days with the Montreal police team. They'd corroborated on a case, became friends, and the rest was history.

"Any news from Erik?"

Simm's expression turned grim. "He called. He's finding it tougher than usual. Apparently, the bad guys used a world-class hacker. And that hacker would charge a world-class rate for his work."

"A percentage of the pot."

"Yeah, and it's a big pot. Hundreds of millions."

The amount of money at stake shocked Charlie. No money justified murder, but she now understood the lengths this person went to. He or she could afford to hire the best and to bribe officials for a payoff that size. "Wow. I had no idea."

Simm raised his brows and nodded. "Exactly. It explains a lot."

"What about the guy who died in Jamaica?" Charlie asked.

"Holmes? I asked Josh if he had any connections for that one. I put Erik on it too. He'll tell me if Holmes came into a pile of money."

"That leaves Eli and Mike."

"Yeah." Simm drew out the word. "No sign huge chunks of cash came their way. Mike lives in a trailer park on the edge of town. Doesn't have much. No computer experience. Only odd jobs, the biggest being here. Nothing changed for Eli in the recent past. He's wealthy, seems to be acquainted with people within organized crime, but he has acquaintances in all walks of life. I have yet to find evidence he works with the mob, but I'll keep hunting."

A movement to Charlie's left caught her eye. Sarah stood there, and Charlie wondered how much she'd heard. They'd shared minimal case details, even with Noah. They had to keep the investigation contained and under control. A word in the wrong person's ear, and everything could spiral downward.

Sarah's expression worried Charlie. Her temperament varied from upbeat to biting, but this unusual, defeated look set off an alarm bell.

"What happened? Another threat?" Charlie asked, rising from her chair.

Sarah raised her hands, as if in defense. "No, nothing like that," she said. "I just hit a brick wall with my research."

Charlie relaxed. A threat to Sarah was a threat to all of them. A snag in her research project was minor in comparison. Despite its importance to Sarah, it might not have a major role in solving the mystery of Ethan's death or the lost money.

"Something's missing," Sarah said.

"Missing? From your room?" Charlie asked.

"From the journal. I'm close to the end. Daphne was meticulous. She wrote in it at least once a week, but now two months have vanished."

"Maybe she had nothing to write about," Simm said.

"I thought that might be it until I inspected the notebook. Pages are gone. Carefully extracted, almost impossible to detect."

"What's your theory?" Charlie said. "Who do you think removed them?"

"I don't know. Daphne, Percy, maybe even Ethan. But it had to be something important. Otherwise, why take them out? I need to find them." Sarah's over-bright gaze darted around the room.

It was an interesting development, but Charlie wasn't sure how to solve the dilemma. "We already did a full-scale search. We didn't come across any pages."

Sarah wrung her hands and bit her lip. "They might be in the tunnel."

Charlie's eyes widened. "What makes you think that?"

"I was there. I can't shake the feeling that I passed over something, maybe hiding places."

Charlie glanced at Simm to see if he bought into Sarah's theory, but his expression remained shuttered.

"You want to go back in?" Charlie asked Sarah, finding it hard to imagine being eager to descend into that dark pit. "You think someone hid the pages in there?"

"Yes, I do." Sarah said. "I can go by myself. I'm not afraid."

Sarah looked like a schoolgirl asked out on her first date, seeking her parents' permission.

"Absolutely not," Simm said, taking on the part of the disapproving father. "No one goes in alone. The same precautions apply."

Sarah opened her mouth to protest but closed it when Simm raised a warning finger.

"I'll go with you," he said. "It'll have to be tomorrow morning. This afternoon, Noah and I meet the lawyer."

Disappointment washed over Sarah's face. Waiting on someone else wasn't easy when you wanted to get something done. Charlie had been there many times. But she agreed with Simm. Going alone was too dangerous. How reliable was a tunnel built so long ago? The wooden beams might be rotten and unstable. And lack of communication remained a major problem.

Sarah pressed her lips together as if to hold back another protest, but she finally nodded and left the room, her head lowered.

Simm smiled and wrapped his arms around Charlie.

"She reminds me of you, always impatient," he said.

"I have the patience of a saint. I'm married to you, don't forget."

"Not something I'd fail to remember." He emphasized his words with an extra squeeze.

Charlie felt the vibration of Simm's phone in his pocket.

"Josh," he said, looking at the screen.

Charlie listened to the one-sided conversation but deduced nothing from the occasional "Yeah," "Uh-huh," and, "I see."

Her saintly patience reached its limit by the time Simm said goodbye to Josh.

"Interesting," Simm said.

"What?" she asked, eagerness bubbling beneath her calm façade.

"Glad I called Josh."

"Simm, I swear, if you don't tell me..."

Her husband grinned and lifted his hands. "He found something. Baxter had a corrupt partner who took bribes and looked the other way. They pinned nothing on Baxter, but they've had him under observation ever since. Prime candidate for blackmail, wouldn't you say?"

"Your theory is someone threatened to expose him on the other case if he didn't hide the evidence on this one," Charlie said.

"You got it."

Charlie considered it. "Makes sense. Can we prove it?"

"Perhaps not, but it'll explain why they ruled Ethan's death an accident."

Charlie nodded then remembered her encounter with Mr. Brown. She filled him in on the older man's revelations about the neighbors and his lack of surprise about the presence of secret passageways.

"That's good to know," Simm said, his expression thoughtful.

"Tell me why you're seeing a lawyer today?" Charlie asked.

"Noah needs to finalize things with the will. Even if the funds are gone, there are things to deal with. He wants me to be there. Not a bad idea. The lawyer might have insights on the money's whereabouts, or maybe he knows what the key belongs to."

"Good point," Charlie said. "I guess I'll tackle the gardens to keep busy."

"We shouldn't be long." Simm's look was sympathetic.

Charlie smiled at him, knowing he sensed her homesickness for the pub and Frank. Getting out of town and having a little adventure was fine, but she yearned for the vibe of her home base.

. . .

Charlie crouched beside a hydrangea bush, gloves protecting her hands from the thorny weeds as she yanked them out, reveling in the feeling of accomplishment. Though gardening wasn't her usual activity, the rhythmic motion and the fresh air soothed her nerves.

Simm and Noah left fifteen minutes earlier, Sarah was involved in her research, and Walter usurped the library to manage his business affairs, craving a bit more space. Clarisse went for her daily run. Everyone, including Charlie, had tasks to fulfill, and her newfound determination to conquer the weed battle fueled hers.

The late April sun heated Charlie's back, making her realize she needed a hat and a water bottle. Harley relished the heat as he stretched out beside her, snoring in the sunlight, but when she rose to her feet, so did he. Entering through the front, they bypassed the closed library door and headed to the kitchen. Bosco, who'd been snoozing in the entranceway, joined the procession, making Charlie feel like the Pied Piper. Filling her water bottle, she walked out the back to rest in the porch's shade.

As Charlie closed the door behind them, something caught her attention. A note, taped to the door.

CHAPTER 37

I've gone to explore the tunnel - S

Charlie's heart constricted. What? They told her not to go alone. Both Simm and Noah were away, and Sarah—reckless, stubborn Sarah—put herself in danger.

Swallowing panic, Charlie's gaze automatically searched for the door to the tunnel. It lay open, the stairs collapsed, exposing the ladder.

"Oh God," she breathed. She had no choice. Swiveling back to the house, she ran in to get a headlamp. Only one hung by the door. Sarah had the other.

Charlie returned to the tunnel's entrance and gazed into the dark depths. The dogs stood like sentinels beside her. She kneeled on the ground and yelled into the hole. "Sarah? Are you there?" Her voice echoed, unanswered. "Sarah!"

Charlie rose to her feet and ran her gaze over the gardens, searching for a makeshift weapon. She'd learned to never go into dark spots without one. Spotting a broken branch, she hurried to grab it. "I'll go in just close enough to convince her to come out."

Bosco's ears twitched as if he understood.

Charlie approached the hole, praying she'd see Sarah climbing the ladder. Instead, a movement caught her attention, and she jumped back in alarm, a shriek escaping her lips. A long, skinny snake slithered from the hole and headed toward the flower garden. Neither dog seemed to notice, their attention focused on Charlie, as if wondering what provoked her outburst.

She took a deep breath and told herself it was a harmless garden snake, not a rattlesnake or python. Still, it was one more thing to worry about within the dark depths.

Working up her courage, she patted each dog before she fixed the headlamp on her forehead, turned, and lowered her right foot onto the ladder. Mind over matter, she thought, as one by one she placed a foot onto a lower rung. Damp cold and mustiness encased her as her feet hit the hard-packed dirt of the tunnel floor. Turning, she switched on the headlamp.

"Sarah," she called, hoping to stop this before she was forced to continue. The silence terrified Charlie. Why didn't she answer her? Surely her voice carried down here. It echoed off the walls.

Charlie stepped forward on the uneven floor, tempted to put her arms out to steady herself, but the thought of spiders and slimy creatures kept them glued to her sides. As she reached the first corner, she realized she didn't tie a rope around her waist. In her panic, she forgot. Charlie hesitated. Should she go back? Deep down, she knew if she returned above ground, it'd be a hundred times harder to climb back down that ladder, perhaps impossible. She'd continue for a short distance. One step at a time, she turned the corner and viewed the tunnel, eerily familiar from the video. Except, in that case, there'd been two headlamps lighting the way. Now, she relied on hers. And still no sign of Sarah.

Regret twisted her gut. Why hadn't she gone into the neighbor's yard and searched the outbuilding at the end of the tunnel? Sarah was probably there, hunting for pages.

It was too late. Having come this far, she needed to reach the next curve. From there, a quick jaunt to the door and Sarah. With each step, her sense of unease increased. Fear crawled over her as Charlie craved an escape from this pit.

A scuffling noise came from behind her.

She spun halfway before a hand ripped the headlamp from her head. Agony shot through her scalp. She screamed in pain and shock, striking out with the branch. An "oomph" told her she hit her mark. The attacker recovered in an instant. A hand between her shoulder blades shoved her face-first against the dirt wall.

Charlie fought, desperation lending strength. She held the branch in a tight grip. Although long and awkward, she swung it and struck a body part. It loosened the attacker's grip. Charlie swung again, made contact, and shook off the grasping hands. She slipped away, racing to the next corner in the murkiness, where she knew she'd find a battered door at the end.

Footsteps pounded behind her. A hand reached out and caught the branch by mistake. Charlie surrendered it. She sped toward the room, Sarah, and safety. Her headlamp lay somewhere behind her, giving off a dim glow, barely lighting the way. Rounding the corner, pitch darkness enveloped her.

Panicked, she lost her sense of direction and rammed into the wall. Running her hands along it, Charlie took tentative steps ahead. The sound of distant scuffling propelled her faster, using the wall as her guide. She clung to the hope that her attacker faced the same black void.

Charlie cried out in pain when her foot encountered a chunk of wood and she fell forward, her shins connecting with the stairs. She scrambled up the steps and ran her hands over the door, searching for the latch. Splinters stabbed her fingers until she touched icy metal and lifted the latch. The door fell open on its broken hinges.

Bright sunshine blinded her as she scurried over the threshold. She glanced back at the tunnel. The shadows were thick and concealing. Charlie couldn't see her pursuer. She slammed the door, abandoning the pretense of quiet, and scanned the room for a barricade. The table might do the job. With loud gasps and groans, she shoved it across the room, hoisted it on its side, and rammed it against the door, her heart pounding.

Charlie levered her back against the table and braced for impact as she panted. Nothing happened. Calming her breathing, she strained to hear sounds from the tunnel. Silence.

Panic gave way to a fresh worry: Sarah. Where was she? Not in the room, not in the tunnel. Charlie's mind raced, searching for answers. Had Sarah escaped? Or had something far worse happened?

Charlie needed to return to the house. She'd trapped her attacker in the tunnel. Bosco prevented any escape from that end, and Charlie hoped her makeshift barricade did the trick here. If nothing else, it might slow him down.

Darting to the door, she peered outside to make sure the coast was clear. She hurtled for the small hedge opening, her gateway to the Wolfe property. The dogs stood guard, unmoved from the moment she descended the ladder. Bosco was the first to notice her presence, and the two animals rushed to greet her.

Charlie ran toward the house until a thought drew her to a halt. She swiveled and shouted, "Stay." Bosco responded to her tone, sitting back on his haunches. Harley appeared confused but stayed by his friend's side.

Charlie bounded up the steps and burst into the kitchen. She slid to a stop at the sight of Sarah standing with a coffee cup in her hand.

CHAPTER 38

Charlie's breaths came in ragged bursts as she confronted Sarah. "What are you doing here?" she said.

Sarah's brow furrowed. "What do you mean? Where should I be?"

"In the tunnel," Charlie said, the words rushing from her lips. "You left a note. Said you were inside. I went to find you."

Sarah's fingers flew to her mouth. Her gaze ran over Charlie in distress. "Oh no. Are you okay? Breathe."

Charlie clutched the kitchen counter, fighting dizziness. "I didn't imagine it," she insisted. "The note—it's right here." She pulled the crumpled paper from her pocket and thrust it at Sarah.

Sarah squinted at the note. "I didn't write this," she said. "It's signed 'S.' Simm, maybe?"

"No, he's not here. I went in, and someone attacked me."

Sarah reached for her. "Are you hurt? Is that dirt or a bruise on your face?"

"Maybe both," Charlie said. She looked down at herself and saw the black smudges on her clothing. Sweaty and dusty, she was a mess.

"What's this? Somebody attacked you?"

Walter stepped into the kitchen with a look of genuine concern.

"Yes, in the tunnel," Charlie said. "I'm not hurt. Just scared." With the immediate danger passed, and her adrenaline rush subsiding, tremors took over Charlie's body. With shaky hands, she grasped the kitchen counter to steady herself and sucked in huge gulps of air.

Walter grabbed his phone from his pocket. "I'll get the cops. Then we need to locate Simm and tell him. If he comes back and sees the police here, he'll have a heart attack."

Walter briefed the 9-1-1 operator on the emergency and disconnected the call. "They'll send someone."

He grabbed Charlie's elbow and led her to a chair. The novelty of seeing Walter so solicitous melted away part of Charlie's terror. Even Sarah stared at him like he was an exotic animal she'd never seen.

"What's going on?" Clarisse said as she entered the kitchen and saw her husband fussing over Charlie. Her spandex jogging suit clung to her like a second skin. Her unblemished face shone with a thin layer of sweat.

Walter turned to his wife. "Someone attacked Charlie in the tunnel. The police are on their way. No one leaves the house before then. Sarah, lock the doors."

Sarah rushed to each door and secured them as Clarisse stood as though paralyzed. Walter grabbed his phone again and walked to the other end of the kitchen. Charlie heard him relating a short form of the events and knew Simm would arrive soon.

•   •   •

Charlie tolerated Simm's scowl. The full-fledged lecture would come later. She braced herself for it.

Her husband and Noah arrived minutes before the police. She imagined the hair-raising drive Noah had, sitting in the passenger seat, his hands clenched on the dash.

Simm had time to reassure himself Charlie wasn't injured before Sarah ushered four uniformed police officers into the overcrowded room. Baxter wasn't with them. Charlie didn't know if that was a good thing or not.

Charlie recounted the events from the moment she read the note. She ignored Simm's eye roll and frustrated gasp when she described how she descended the ladder with a headlamp and a branch.

"We installed a camera," Noah said. "It'll tell us who left the note. Simm, where's your laptop?"

Charlie had forgotten about the camera. Now, the prospect of discovering the person behind the threats and the attack filled her with fear and anticipation. The same person was likely the fraudster and murderer.

Simm took up a position at the kitchen table, giving everyone a view of his screen. He booted up the computer and opened the camera software. Charlie sensed the group's tension.

Simm swore under his breath, his brows lowered in a frown.

"What's wrong?" Charlie asked. She tried to decipher the messages on the computer, but Simm opened one application after another in rapid-fire sequence, making it a blur of colors and images.

"It didn't work," Sarah said, her tone despondent. "The camera failed."

Charlie looked at her in confusion. "But we tested it."

"We did," Simm said through gritted teeth. "Something went wrong, either by accident or on purpose."

Deliberate sabotage, Charlie thought. It fit together too neatly.

"That's a dead end." A dismissive wave accented the cop's words. He turned his attention back to Simm after sweeping his gaze over the crowded room. "Who's staying in this house?"

Simm introduced everyone and summarized their reasons for being there.

Despite her efforts, Charlie couldn't provide a useful description of the attacker. The struggle in the dark rendered her headlamp useless, and the person hadn't made a sound. Two officers were dispatched to search the grounds, including the tunnel.

"You ran to the building at the other end." The police officer repeated her words.

"I tripped on the steps but got the door open and pushed a table against it."

"And the person didn't get in?"

"Not while I was there," she said. "But I didn't hang around. I ran back here."

"It's possible he escaped from this end," the cop said, nodding toward the backyard.

"The dogs were there all the time," Sarah said.

The cop's gaze locked on Bosco, still guarding the tunnel entrance, and nodded.

"He must've waited until after I left the other building and got away somehow." Charlie's voice trembled with the fear that still flowed through her veins.

"We'll search everywhere," the cop said. He turned his attention to the note lying on the table before addressing Sarah. "This isn't your handwriting?"

"No," she said, shaking her head.

"How many in the household with a name that starts with S other than Sarah?"

"Only Simm," Charlie said, pointing at the man beside her.

"I'd like to speak to you and your husband alone please." He turned to the others. "In the meantime, my partner will take your statements."

Simm guided them to the library, and as the door closed, the cop faced Charlie. "It's pretty obvious somebody enticed you into the tunnel. He also knew to deactivate the camera and sign the letter with an S. If it's not someone staying here, it's a person savvy enough about what's going on to work around it. It may have something to do with the case you're working on. I'd be careful who you trust."

Charlie realized those thoughts already ran through Simm's mind. The advice to be careful was unnecessary.

A knock on the library door signaled the other officers' return from their search.

"Nothing there," one of them said. "We saw signs of the attack, but nothing else."

"Did the attacker go through the other building?"

"The door was still barricaded. No one went through there."

"That's impossible. How did he escape?" Charlie said, dazed.

"He must have distracted the dogs somehow," Simm said. "Or there's another way out."

The cop glanced at the other two. "Did you spot another exit?"

"We didn't."

Charlie's mind raced. "The only way someone could get past Bosco is if the dog knew the person." She met Simm's gaze and knew he dreaded that possibility as much as she did.

The police officer gave them a skeptical look. "If that's the case, I suggest you leave the premises."

"We plan to," Simm said.

The cop nodded, taking his words at face value. Charlie knew better. Simm wouldn't scare away so easily.

As the door closed behind the police officers, Simm took Charlie by the elbow and steered her back into the library. Here it comes, she thought.

CHAPTER 39

"What in God's name were you thinking?" Simm said. His voice resonated with controlled anger.

"I was worried about Sarah."

"So, you ran into the tunnel with a branch?" Simm's eyes threatened to burst from their sockets. "What good was that?"

"It helped. I hit him twice. I got away."

"How many times did I say nobody goes in there alone? Didn't you hear me?"

"You weren't here, and neither was Noah."

"Walt was here." Simm stopped, contemplating his words "Never mind. You could've waited for us, called us."

"I thought Sarah was down there by herself. I couldn't wait."

Simm groaned and pulled Charlie into his arms. "You drive me crazy. As soon as I turn my back, you get yourself into a dangerous situation."

"I don't do it on purpose," she said, laying her head on his chest.

"Another few years and my hair'll turn gray."

"I'll still love you, even if you tear it all out."

A laugh rumbled in Simm's chest beside Charlie's ear. "That's another possibility," he said.

Arm in arm, they joined the others in the kitchen.

"And?" Sarah asked. "They find anything?"

"Nothing," Simm said. "We have to be extra vigilant."

.   .   .

Charlie woke in a sweat. Sitting up in bed, gasping for breath, it took a moment to realize where she was. Simm lay beside her in a deep slumber, undisturbed by her movements.

She eased herself back and wondered how she'd fall asleep again. But the alternative of going downstairs into a dark house where someone prowled around, possibly the person who attacked her, was worse than lying awake beside her husband.

She wouldn't even have Bosco for protection. He slept in Noah's room tonight.

A noise caught her attention. A scuffling sound from the first floor. Charlie glanced at Simm before moving her gaze to Harley, sprawled on his cushion alongside the bed. Neither of them roused from their sleep. Had she imagined it?

She held her breath as she concentrated, straining to hear.

There it was. A noise. Charlie's eyes widened, certain she heard footsteps on the stairs. Very slow and deliberate. But they'd locked the house up tight. It could be one of the houseguests, but the movements sounded stealthy. After all that had happened, she had to consider it was someone with bad intentions. But how did anyone get in?

"Simm," she hissed. When her husband didn't respond, she grabbed his arm and shook him. His eyes flew open, and he sprang to a sitting position.

"What?" His gaze swung around the room, scanning for danger.

Beside them, Harley sat up, yawned, and wagged his curly tail.

"Someone's coming up the stairs," Charlie whispered.

They froze and listened. The sound grew distinct as the person climbed higher. Simm snatched his jeans off the chair and yanked them on.

"Stay here," he said, as he crept to the door and pressed his ear against it.

Charlie scrambled from the bed and scooped Harley into her arms, both for his protection and to keep him out of Simm's path.

As the old wooden floor outside their bedroom creaked under the soft footfalls, Simm swung the door opened and pounced on the hunched figure in the hallway. A startled shout, a resounding crash, and a heavy thump preceded Bosco's deep and frantic bark and the rush of footsteps from the neighboring rooms.

A crowd of disheveled and barely awake people stared at the men. Simm, paralyzed with surprise, straddled a terrified older man who held his arms in front of his face. A metal box lay on its side beside him, various tools helter-skelter on the floor.

"Mike? Simm? What's going on?" Noah said. He stood like an odd mammoth with his fists clenched, wearing a T-shirt and boxer shorts, his feet bare. A confused-looking Sarah stood pressed against his side as if seeking protection.

If it wasn't for her acute anxiety, the incident might have amused Charlie. Certainly, the sight of Walter and Clarisse dressed in rumpled pajamas with their hair askew instead of their usual well-groomed and upscale looks made Charlie want to smile, but Mike's obvious distress seized the moment.

Simm rose and helped the caretaker to his feet. "Are you hurt?"

"No...no, I'm fine. Just surprised, that's all," he said, his gaze flitting toward everyone and everything.

He's also terrified, Charlie thought, as he backed as far from Simm as possible, trembling.

"I'm sorry," Simm said. "We heard someone on the stairs. I thought it was an intruder."

"I tried to be quiet," Mike said, wringing his hands. "I didn't want to wake anyone."

"Why are you here at this hour? It's six o'clock in the morning." Noah put into words everyone's thoughts.

Mike's already reddened face flushed even more. He dropped to the floor and scrambled to pick up his scattered tools. "There's a light fixture in the other room that needs fixing. I know Sarah works in there, and I wanted to do it before she started her day."

Charlie's mouth fell open. She didn't understand Mike's logic. Why was it so urgent to fix a light? No one noticed it was broken.

"Okay," Simm said, his tone bewildered. "No harm, no foul. Let's go back to bed."

Grumbles circulated among the group about being unable to sleep, and Charlie agreed. Her day was underway.

.   .   .

Mike nodded awkwardly as he left the house and climbed into his truck. Charlie assumed he'd repaired the light fixture.

Under Simm's skeptical gaze, they stood on the front lawn, and she explained her gardening plans. Ominous dark clouds coasted toward them while Simm studied the shrubs, plants, and weeds. "We're leaving in a matter of days," he said.

"I know." Charlie's shoulders slumped. "But I want to keep busy. You don't need me for anything. Besides missing the pub, I'm fighting to forget that tunnel ambush. Gardening helps fill my head with other thoughts."

Her husband draped his arm around her. "If that's what it takes, go for it. I won't stop..."

A door slammed, and Charlie and Simm turned toward the house. Noah barged down the steps like a mad bull. Charlie grabbed Simm's wrist and tried to tug him backward, terrified of this Noah, but Simm held his ground.

CHAPTER 40

Noah stopped a foot from Simm, his face flushed with fury, fists clenched. Charlie's muscles bunched, prepared to pounce if he attempted to hurt her husband.

"Why didn't you tell me?" Noah growled like a bear poked with a stick.

"Because I couldn't prove anything." Simm held his voice steady.

Like Charlie, Simm realized Noah had discovered what they feared he would.

"You suspected," Noah said.

"I lacked evidence."

Simm's conviction that his brother covered up a crime was a speculation only shared with Walter and Clarisse.

"How did you find out?" Charlie asked, her breath catching in her chest.

"I'm sorry. I thought he knew." A distressed Clarisse appeared by Noah's shoulder, her eyes tear-filled. "I never would've said anything."

"Thank God someone had the decency to tell me," Noah said, his rage-filled gaze fixed on Simm. "I've been hanging around with that monster all week, thinking he was a great guy because he's related to you. Turns out you're both the same."

Charlie felt Simm bristle beside her. His patience had its limits. So did hers. She stepped between the two men.

"If you think that, you're not a good judge of character." She threw an apologetic glance in Clarisse's direction before poking the tip of her index finger against Noah's breastbone. "Simm will turn himself inside out to help you. He sacrificed his relationship with his brother for you. Don't forget that." With each word, her voice deepened with anger.

Noah's glower shifted to her. Charlie recognized the contrast they presented. Noah's great hulk towered over her petite form. They engaged in a battle of enraged stares.

With a huff, the big man swiveled and stalked away to circle the house. Charlie released her breath and leaned back against Simm. His hands clasped her shoulders as her eyes met Clarisse's.

"I'm so sorry," the other woman repeated. She scraped her fingers through her hair. "For what it's worth, I know Walt has a terrible side to him, but he's my husband, and I still love him." She shrugged. "I thought Noah knew. I just mentioned I was sorry about his family and that I didn't agree with Simm's suspicions about Walt."

Clarisse buried her face in her palms and sobbed. Charlie stepped out of Simm's embrace and wrapped her arms around her sister-in-law, who reciprocated the hug.

"It's okay," Charlie said. "We're all human."

She pulled back, held Clarisse at arm's length, and made eye contact. "But, despite the size of this place, it's become overcrowded. We can't all stay here with the way Noah's feeling right now."

Clarisse's reddened eyes widened. "You want us to leave?"

"Don't you think it'd be best?" Charlie gave her a slight smile. "Walter will work better from his own office. And after the incident in the tunnel yesterday, it isn't safe here."

"You're staying. It isn't safe for you either," Clarisse said, moving her gaze from Charlie to Simm.

"No matter what, we intended to ask you to leave," Simm said. "For your safety. We've taken precautions, but the fewer people, the better."

Disappointment clouded Clarisse's face, but she forced a watery smile. Charlie realized their visit to Niagara was a welcome reprieve from boredom for her sister-in-law, but it wasn't necessary, and their presence, now more than ever, interfered with the investigation.

Clarisse turned and trudged to the house to tell her husband to pack their bags, the customary bounce to her step absent.

. . .

A haunting silence filled the house, broken only by the rain pounding on the roof and windows. The damp weather reflected the mood.

Simm huddled in the library, glued to his laptop. Sarah tried to plug the gaps in her research behind the closed door of Ethan's bedroom. Eli helped her for a while, but he'd since left. Noah barricaded himself in his room, probably pacing away his fury.

Charlie encountered Clarisse in the kitchen, helping herself to a cup of tea as Charlie poured a coffee, the gardening book tucked under her arm.

"I feel terrible," Clarisse said again.

"I know." Charlie waved off another apology. "Did you tell Walter what happened?"

Clarisse's face flushed. "Yes. He's not happy with me either."

This didn't surprise Charlie. The atmosphere in the house was as charged as the thunderstorm that raged outside, the tension only escalating after the tunnel attack. They didn't need more bad feelings circulating through a group of housebound people, even in a house this large. She wanted to ask how Walter reacted to her request to leave but decided not to rub salt in the wound.

The confrontation and the events of the previous day had taken their toll on Charlie. She envisioned the armchair in their bedroom, positioned beside the window. What better place to escape, drink her coffee, and watch the rain outside? She turned to exit the kitchen, but Clarisse forestalled her.

"You've really taken an interest in gardening, haven't you?" She nodded toward the book under Charlie's arm.

Charlie smiled weakly. "While I'm here, yes. No time or space for a garden at home."

Clarisse leaned against the counter and took a leisurely sip of her tea. "I should try a hobby like that. We have a magnificent garden, but we hire people to take care of it."

Internally, Charlie bristled. The clueless woman, with a team to cater to her every whim, contemplating gardening as a boredom cure—while Charlie longed to return to her twelve-hour workdays. Witnessing a new side of Clarisse had been interesting, but her patience wore thin. It was time for them to leave.

Instead of sharing her thoughts, Charlie smiled and said, "Sounds good."

Allowing no more interruptions, she headed for the entranceway and ascended the stairs.

A thrashing sound attracted her attention as she moved past Walter and Clarisse's room. Charlie froze and strained to listen. More thrashing, followed by a loud thump. Alarm swept through her, but she didn't want to barge in on a potentially embarrassing situation.

She stepped closer to the door. "Walt, is everything okay?"

A strangled cry erupted from the other side. Dropping her book and mug, uncaring about the mess, Charlie shoved open the door. Walter, dressed for a day at the office, writhed on the floor, hands clutching his throat. The room reeked of the vomit that covered his clothes. His terror-filled eyes pleaded for help.

CHAPTER 41

Walter's body suffered through a terrifying symphony of convulsions and choked gasps. Charlie raced to him, landing painfully on her knees, and tried to grab him under the shoulders to lift him upright. His weight and the violent tremors made it impossible. Her screams for help mobilized the house's other occupants, bringing a torrent of worried faces.

Noah reached them first. From opposite Charlie, his muscular arms lifted Walter to a sitting position.

"Call 9-1-1." Noah shouted, his voice barely rising above the guttural sounds escaping Walter.

"Got it," Sarah said from behind them.

"The Heimlich. He's choking," Charlie shouted.

Noah hoisted Walter off the floor, wrapped his arms around him from behind, and repeatedly thrust his joined fists into Walter's abdomen. All the while, Walter's body convulsed.

Simm and Clarisse raced into the room together. Simm stopped in his tracks as his sister-in-law cried in alarm. "Oh my God, what happened? Walter!"

Charlie cast a sweeping glance over the room, seeing it as they did. The bedspread lay halfway off the bed as if Walter grabbed it as he fell. His cell phone sat on the vomit-streaked floor; papers were strewn over a makeshift desk, a glass flopped on its side. Two suitcases stood in the corner.

Sarah's urgent voice spoke to the emergency operator and struggled to answer their questions. Most of her responses were, "I don't know."

Charlie prayed they'd hurry. Walter's eyes closed, and he slumped in Noah's arms as the spasms decreased in severity and number.

"I don't think he's choking," Noah said. "He's convulsing. It's something else."

Charlie pleaded silently with Simm, hoping for a solution despite knowing he wasn't a miracle worker. His look told her he wished he was. He may not hold loving feelings for his brother these days, but losing him would devastate Simm.

Charlie felt an overwhelming gratitude for the siren's wail. Sarah raced down the stairs to meet their saviors as Noah shouted an instruction to shut the dogs in the library. They didn't need Bosco to keep helpers at bay.

Seconds later, assistance appeared in the form of two paramedics, one male and one female. With Noah's help, they lowered Walter to the floor, then they instructed everyone to stand aside. The woman asked the observers questions as busy hands examined the now-unconscious Walter.

"Who found him?"

"I did," Charlie said, her voice sounding high-pitched and nervous to her ears.

"Was he conscious?" she asked, her gaze fixed on Charlie.

"Yes, but he couldn't speak. He held his throat and twisted on the floor."

"Had he already vomited?"

"Yes. We thought he was choking. Noah did the Heimlich, but he passed out." Charlie wrapped her arms around herself, trying to still her shaking hands. Had they done the right thing? Had they made it worse?

The paramedics leaned over Walter and checked his vital signs. Whispering, they exchanged words before the man retrieved a communication device from his belt and transmitted codes to someone else. The woman extracted a bottle of black liquid and a tube from her bag. Shaking the bottle, she dropped to her knees beside Walter's head.

As the medics inserted the tube into his nostril, Clarisse moaned and swayed on her feet. Simm caught her and held her to his side.

"Let's go to another room."

Simm's suggestion met with resistance. "No. I have to be here for him," Clarisse said, her voice filled with tears. She clasped both hands over her mouth.

Charlie knew she'd feel the same, but her sister-in-law was likely to become a patient herself if she fainted, and that wouldn't help Walter.

Having insinuated the tube into Walter's stomach, the paramedic removed the top of the container and inserted the tip into the end of the tube. The black liquid made its way into his stomach.

Charlie assumed the mixture was activated charcoal. Her first aid kit at the pub contained it in powder form. It helped absorb toxins. She prayed it wasn't too late for Walter.

The sound of barking reached their ears a moment before more feet thumped up the stairs.

As the medics lifted Walter onto the stretcher and secured him in place, two police officers appeared. One of them was Detective Baxter.

"No one touches anything, and no one leaves the house," he said.

· · ·

Clarisse paced the floor of the living room, alternating between sniffling into a tissue and fuming about the wait. "I belong at the hospital, not here."

Charlie repeated many times that it shouldn't be long, but even she didn't believe it anymore. The others waited in silence, tension blanketing their shoulders.

When the detective stepped into the room with his partner, the looks he received from the occupants wavered from relief to trepidation. His gaze drifted across the group and rested for a moment on Simm before he spoke.

"Could everyone take a seat, please?"

Clarisse ignored his request and hurried to his side. "I need to get to the hospital."

The cop's expression was not without sympathy. "I understand. We'll get this done as fast as we can, and someone will drive you there in record time."

Clarisse frowned and positioned herself on a chair, ready to eject herself at a moment's notice.

Baxter's partner removed a notepad and pen from his pocket as the detective cleared his throat. "We suspect somebody made an attempt on the victim's life," Baxter said. "That's why they called us here."

A collective gasp swept through the room. Clarisse's hand flew to her mouth as her eyes widened. Sarah, huddled on the couch beside Noah, grabbed his hand. He put a comforting arm around her shoulder.

Certain the idea had already crossed everyone's mind, Charlie still experienced a quake of alarm to hear the words aloud.

The detective raised a hand to ward off the barrage of questions and remarks. When everything subsided except for Clarisse's soft sobs, he continued. "His symptoms resemble poisoning, although the medical experts will confirm it. Our team is gathering evidence in case the results come back positive. In the meantime, we'll speak to each of you alone."

Simm sent a suspicious glare at the cop—a glare that Baxter met with a warning look.

They led Clarisse into the library for questioning, presumably to allow her to go to the hospital sooner. It was Charlie's turn to pace. She wanted to recall every detail she witnessed. As the person to find Walter, whatever she said was crucial to the investigation.

Twenty minutes later, Clarisse exited the room, grabbed her purse, and hurried from the house beside a police officer assigned as chauffeur.

As expected, Charlie was next in line.

CHAPTER 42

The detective's stern expression didn't encourage her, but a man had almost died, making his grimness appropriate for the occasion.

She started with her morning, walking him through all she'd done since waking. A sense of foreboding crept over Charlie. Clarisse had likely told the detective about the altercation between Simm and Noah.

Knowing her account didn't look good for either man, she tried to gloss over it, saying Simm and Noah had a discussion in the front yard before she spoke to Clarisse about them leaving. The detective's silence on the topic spoke volumes—he likely had a different account.

"Then everyone did their own thing," Charlie said. "Simm worked in the library, Noah went to his room, Sarah continued on her research upstairs, and I assume Walter conducted business from their room."

"Where was his wife?"

"I met her in the kitchen. I went to get a coffee, and she was drinking tea."

"Did you speak?" Baxter asked.

"Yes. We chatted for a few minutes about gardening." That wasn't a lie.

"Was she ever in the room with her husband?"

"I guess so. She said she told him they needed to leave, and she packed. I'm not sure of the timeline. I was in the library with Simm."

"Did you see anyone take food or a drink to Walter?"

"No."

"Did you see him come downstairs and help himself to anything?"

"No. Nothing."

"What did you do after leaving the kitchen?"

"I went upstairs. I wanted to sit in my room and look at a book."

"But you didn't. You went into their bedroom."

"As I walked past, I heard a strange sound."

"Like what?"

"Like someone choking." Charlie tried to imitate the noise.

"So, you went in?"

"Not right away. I called out to him. Asked if he was okay. It sounded like he fell or bumped into things. And he cried out, like a muffled scream."

"Then?"

"I dropped everything and opened the door." Charlie closed her eyes, trying to block out the image even as she understood she needed to recall every detail. "He was on the floor, squirming around. His hands held onto his throat. The pain... it must've been horrible."

Charlie couldn't stop the tears. Until now, she'd held them at bay, wanting to be strong for everyone else, but the horror of what Walter experienced crashed down upon her.

The detective allowed her a moment to compose herself. "What next?"

"I saw he'd thrown up. My first reflex was to lift him so he wouldn't choke. I screamed. I don't remember what I said, but everybody reacted and came running."

"Who arrived first?"

"Noah, I think. He was the first one I recall because he helped me sit him up. I couldn't do it alone."

"Did Noah say anything?"

"He said to call 9-1-1. That's how I knew Sarah was there. I heard her say she'd do it."

"And the others?"

"Simm and Clarisse got there soon after. They were both downstairs. It's hard to remember how much time passed. Walter was moaning and in pain. We tried to help him. It was chaos."

The cop nodded. "Did Walter speak? Say something?"

"No. Nothing clear, just groans of pain."

"Did anyone move around the room? Away from Walter?"

Charlie frowned in confusion. "I'm not sure what you mean, but I saw nothing else. We panicked. We didn't know what to do."

"What was your first reaction when you saw him? What did you think happened?"

"I thought he choked on something. I asked Noah to do the Heimlich, but it didn't help. He lost consciousness and kept convulsing. The ambulance people arrived then."

"What did everyone do while the techs worked on him?"

"Nothing. What could we do? We watched. We tried to calm Clarisse." Charlie ran her hands over her face. "It was terrible."

"How was the relationship between Walter and Clarisse?"

Charlie's eyes widened. "You think she wanted to kill him?"

"The spouse is the first person we check. Simple as that." He shrugged.

Charlie absorbed that information for a moment, thinking about all she'd learned about her in-laws over the past few days. "I think they care for each other. Walter came here for her, despite not wanting to. She told me her husband was far from perfect but that she loved him anyway." She held her hands to her sides, palms up. "I don't know them well. We haven't seen much of them over the years."

"Why is that?"

Charlie selected her words with care. "Simm chose a different life. He didn't want to be involved in the family business, and he didn't want to follow in his father's footsteps."

"Describe his relationship with his brother."

This was a minefield, and she had to tiptoe across it, or someone else would set off the bomb under her feet.

"It's strained."

The detective gave her a faint, knowing smile. "More detail, please."

"They're very different. Walter is a businessman who places money and power at the top of his list, and Simm, also a businessman, is happy to make a comfortable living. Of course, they clash over issues."

Baxter nodded. "How hard do they clash?"

"It's never become physical, if that's what you're asking, but yes, they've argued."

Charlie hated the direction this was taking, but she couldn't sugarcoat the brothers' relationship. Everyone knew they didn't get along. Clarisse had likely mentioned it.

"What about Noah?"

The quick change of subject took Charlie aback. "What about him?"

"Did he get along with Walter?"

"He did," Charlie said. She had to fess up. "Until today."

The cop leaned back and clasped his hands as if preparing for a long story. "Tell me about that."

Charlie sighed. She told him a condensed version of Noah's history and how Simm suspected Walter tied into it somehow. They'd never informed Noah because of the lack of evidence against Simm's brother. But Clarisse let it slip that day, and Noah was furious.

"He was angry with Simm," Charlie added. "For not telling him."

"He didn't have bad feelings toward Walter? Everything was rosy?"

"Of course it affected him," she said. "But don't forget Noah was the first person there to help me. He tried to save Walter's life."

"How hard did he try?" Baxter said, his lips twisted in a sardonic grimace.

Charlie's frustration with the turn of the interview veered into anger. "Very hard," she said. "I was there. I saw him, and trust me, if Walter was choking, Noah would've saved him."

Baxter leaned forward, his elbows on his knees. "And you, Charlie? How did you feel about your brother-in-law? No declarations of love?"

"To be honest, until this week, I shared Simm's opinion of him, although I didn't know Walter well. I was biased," she said, her chin dropping to her chest, the confession difficult to put into words. "I let Simm influence me, something I don't normally do. I tend to have a more positive outlook. But, since they've been here, I've witnessed a different side of Walter, giving me a glimmer of hope."

"Hope? In what way?"

"That he and Simm can patch things up between them. That Walt has a soft side. I think he genuinely cares for Clarisse. I also think this breach in his relationship with Simm bothers him more than he lets on. Yes, he's ruthless in business. Everyone agrees, but I think he misses his bond with his brother and perhaps with me."

"The big, bad wolf seeking redemption?"

"I hope so. Maybe they still have a chance."

Baxter took her off guard when he changed directions once again. "Was there anyone else here today besides the six of you?"

Charlie blinked. "Yes. Mike came by to fix something. He mentioned a problem with a light fixture in one of the spare rooms."

"Had someone asked him to fix it?"

Charlie snorted a laugh. "Mike has his own schedule. I think he takes care of things when he feels like it."

"What time was this? How long was he here?"

Charlie searched her memory for the details and related them as best she could.

"Anyone else?" the cop asked.

"Eli," Charlie said. "Noah's uncle. He's helping Sarah with her research, so he stopped by for a while." She narrowed her eyes at the detective. "You don't think...I mean, he doesn't even know Walter. Neither does Mike."

"I'm asking questions. It's my job to look at everyone who accessed the house."

Charlie shivered at the thought that someone snuck inside to kill Walter. She couldn't accept that it was someone she knew. Or that it was intentional. There must be another explanation.

"One last thing," the detective said. "Do you drink whiskey?"

"Not often." The reason for his question hit her. "The whiskey contained poison?"

He held up his hand to forestall her questions. "We have nothing conclusive. Found a whiskey glass in the room, nothing more. It made me wonder. Did he drink before noon?"

Charlie's thoughts jumped to the morning Walter joined them in the library to discuss Eli. He'd had a drink in his hand then. "He did," she said.

The detective thanked her and warned her not to leave the area. Charlie exited the room in a daze. It was incomprehensible. Several gazes zeroed in on her as she entered the sitting room. Simm approached and grabbed her hand, his face awash with worry.

"Are you okay?" he said.

Charlie wondered how bad she looked to warrant such concern. "Yes. It's just...crazy to think...do you have any news about Walter?"

"Not yet." He frowned. "I'd like to get over there, but he'll want to see me." He nodded toward the library.

"Be honest. He already knows a lot, and not just from me." Charlie didn't lower her voice. She wanted the others to know what to expect.

Baxter's partner arrived and asked Simm to follow him. Charlie gave her husband's hand a squeeze before he left her.

CHAPTER 43

Charlie's mind churned with the day's horrors.

The police questioned each person. While comparing notes afterward, the questions and answers followed the same lines. What did you witness? How was the relationship between Clarisse and Walter? Between Simm and Walter? And, of course, Noah and Walter.

When the cops left the house, Charlie assumed they'd visit both Mike and Eli and subject them to a similar interrogation.

Simm seemed unconcerned about the cop's interest in him as a suspect. "I'm innocent," he said when she shared her worries with him. "He won't find evidence that says otherwise."

Charlie realized dwelling on it would drive her crazy. Instead, she and Simm went to the hospital to check on Walter. They found Clarisse in a waiting room outside the emergency area. Sensing their presence, her gaze popped up from her phone. She dropped it into her purse and stood, her face creased with anxiety.

"Thank God you're here. I was about to text you," she said. "I don't know how much more I can handle."

"What's happening?" Simm asked with a frown. "No news yet?"

"Nothing. That's just it. If anything's happening, they're not sharing. I'm assuming no news is good news. It means they're working on him, doesn't it?" Her stricken look pleaded with him.

Charlie grabbed Clarisse's clammy hand. Her sister-in-law trembled like a frightened puppy. Simm narrowed his eyes and headed for the information desk. The women watched as he spoke to a nurse, applying his charm. The nurse's expression softened, and she nodded.

Simm returned to Charlie's side with the information that a doctor would see them soon. Relieved smiles rewarded him for his efforts.

As promised, twenty minutes later, a man emerged from behind the emergency ward doors with the required white smock. Thin, middle-aged, with dark, close-cropped hair and a hint of five o'clock shadow, his gaze roved the waiting room until it settled on them.

"Mrs. Simmons?" he asked, looking from Clarisse to Charlie.

Clarisse stood, her purse clutched in her fists. "That's me."

The doctor shook her hand before turning to Charlie and Simm. "And you are?"

They introduced themselves, and, satisfied with the relationships, the doctor led them to a small interview room furnished with a round table and four chairs.

Once settled, he placed his joined hands on the table and looked at Clarisse. "Mrs. Simmons, I'm aware you've met with the police. So, it should come as no surprise your husband suffered an intense reaction this morning to a poisonous substance."

Clarisse leaned forward, her knuckles white on her purse. "What was it?"

"The tests came back positive for arsenic."

The women gasped, their reactions identical. Tears surged to Clarisse's eyes.

"Is he okay?" she asked with a sob.

"We believe he'll recover with minimal adverse effects. The quick response of the medics helped. They administered activated charcoal, and it did its job. We pumped his stomach and are monitoring him."

Clarisse's eyes closed as she sagged back into the chair.

"Of course, we've given this information to the police," the doctor said. "This didn't happen by accident."

"Someone tried to kill him?" Clarisse's voice trembled.

"Yes. We can be thankful they didn't succeed." The doctor's grim gaze swept over them. "We'll keep him under observation, at least until tomorrow. Depending on his condition, he can return home after that."

"Can I see him?" Clarisse asked as she straightened, her bravado returning.

"He's resting now, but I don't mind if you sit in the room and wait. Only you," the doctor said, glancing at Simm and Charlie.

"Text us when you want a lift back. We'll come get you," Simm said to his sister-in-law as they stood.

Clarisse had already moved to leave the room. She turned and nodded at them before scurrying to the emergency ward.

.   .   .

Charlie leaned against the kitchen counter as Simm updated Noah and Sarah on Walter's condition. The events shook everyone, pushing Simm and Noah's spat to a back burner, hopefully never to boil again.

"Someone came into this house and poisoned him," Noah said, his voice soft and disbelieving. "How could that happen?"

"Things are intensifying," Simm said, his expression darkening. "The threat carved into the door, the attack in the tunnel. And now this. Somebody close to us is deadly serious. Walt could've died today. God knows what might have happened to Charlie in the tunnel if she didn't escape."

Charlie felt the weight of everyone's thoughts. Was it safe to stay? Should they drop everything and leave?

"I understand if you want to go," Noah said.

Simm's gaze bored into Noah's. "I'm not leaving if you're not."

"Ethan was my brother. I want to see it through."

"And Walt is mine, despite our differences," Simm said. "My wife was threatened. We all were."

"Why don't we stay here tonight?" Charlie said. "We need to be available for Walter and Clarisse. He's still under observation. We'll lock everything up tight, and we'll keep the dogs close. If we have to, we can take turns keeping watch."

"If we're staying, I want to go into the tunnel one last time," Sarah said, straightening her shoulders and lifting her chin.

Noah appeared baffled. "Why do you want to go back?"

"I'm missing part of the puzzle, and I think there's another hiding place."

"I may have an idea about that."

All eyes turned toward Charlie.

"What do you mean?" Simm said, his brows raised in surprise.

Charlie hastened to reassure him. "I remembered something. I guess, during the stress of the attack, it slipped my mind, but it came to me this morning."

"What?" Simm said.

"In the tunnel, I collided with a wall as I rounded the corner for the last part. It shifted a bit. I think there's a door there."

"A door?" Simm said.

"Or some sort of opening. I remember sensing the wall moving when I ran into it. It could be a door. Maybe another entry to the house." Her heart pounded at the thought of finding her attacker's escape route.

"It's worth checking out," Sarah said. Her eyes gleamed with excitement. "I want to get in there."

Simm grumbled under his breath, unconvinced.

"Why not?" Noah said. "I don't see the harm in it."

"I won't go with you," Charlie said. "But I can draw a map."

"Bosco and I'll go with you," Noah said, turning to Sarah. "We'll go in through the neighbor's place."

Charlie huddled on the back porch and watched Sarah, Noah, and Bosco walk across the expanse of lawn to creep through the hedge. She clung to a disappointed Harley. Charlie didn't want to be anywhere near them. She'd stay close to the house and Simm. Her view would be through the camera clamped to Noah's chest.

Simm lowered himself into the chair beside her and set his laptop on the table. Again, the constant motion shook the image, but they followed the couple's progress through the outbuilding toward the door that led to the tunnel. Charlie flinched when she saw the overturned table, remembering her panic when she held it against the door, waiting for someone to barge through and attack her.

Noah and Sarah activated their headlamps as they descended into the tunnel. A third one hung around Bosco's thick neck, helping to light the path before them.

Charlie had mapped out where she suspected an opening could be, but self-doubt plagued her. In fight-or-flight mode, what she sensed was a hidden passage could be a simple indent in the dirt wall. Under the table, she crossed her fingers, hoping she hadn't sent her friends on a fruitless mission. Another part of her feared they'd meet her attacker. But, she reasoned, Bosco would sense the danger and protect them. And Noah was big and imposing. It'd take more than one person to harm them.

They neared the spot where Charlie's directions sent them, and she watched as Noah ran his hand over the dusty wall. Her heart sank. Nothing there, she thought.

They stopped. Noah flattened his palm on the surface and shoved. Charlie gasped when it moved under his hand.

CHAPTER 44

The camera jerked then steadied as Noah turned to speak to Sarah. Powerful hands braced against the dirt wall, forcing it to yield. A cloud of dust rose and obscured Charlie and Simm's view. Several seconds later, once it settled, the headlamps lit up a small room.

"I was right," Charlie shouted, bouncing in her seat. Harley reacted with a bark, his bulging eyes scanning for danger.

Simm laughed. "I never doubted you, hon."

Charlie jabbed him with her elbow. "Yeah, right. You humored me."

Their attention returned to the screen and the two people who ventured into the hidden room that Charlie estimated measured about six-by-six feet, hardly bigger than a closet. Noah ducked to fit his frame inside the lower-ceilinged space.

Their arrival created a flurry of dust motes, making visibility difficult. But centered in the camera's view sat a small pile of cardboard boxes, the only items in the room. Sarah rushed forward and, with reverent hands, opened the first one. The contents remained hidden from view, but Sarah's broad smile when she turned confirmed her pleasure in the discovery.

Noah and Sarah moved the three boxes from the tunnel to the porch, the dogs sniffing each one before they removed the layers of dust and opened them. Two contained yellowed and worn documents. Old black and white photographs filled the other. Sarah clapped her hands with glee.

Charlie, Simm, and Noah exchanged baffled glances, none of them understanding Sarah's attraction to old and grimy things.

"Do you think Percy built that room into the tunnel?" Charlie asked the group.

"I would think so," Sarah said. "Daphne's inscription in the book hinted at it. 'He provided his own escape.' Remember? That must mean he built it."

"What did he use it for?" Charlie wondered.

Noah shrugged. "A hiding place of some sort. Illicit gains or bootlegged alcohol."

"And Ethan may have used it to store those boxes," Simm said. "There could be something in there he didn't want anyone to find."

"I can't wait to go through them," Sarah said as she grabbed a box and scurried to the house.

"I got the rest." Noah piled the other boxes on top of each other and followed her up the stairs.

"You were right about the door." Simm beamed a smile. "Maybe you have special powers."

"If I did, we'd know who was behind all this." Despite Sarah's joy, Charlie's shoulders slumped. "Who could've poisoned Walter?"

"Who said Walt was the target?"

Charlie remembered the detective's question. "You're right. Anyone could've drunk the whiskey."

"Exactly." He nodded.

"A limited amount of people have been in the house. That we know of, at least," Charlie said.

"You got it. And that's why I don't think we should trust anybody."

"But Noah and Sarah…"

"No one, Charlie. I mean it. You and I stick together."

· · ·

"Come in."

Charlie opened the door in response to Sarah's invitation. Following their new pact, she told Simm she wanted to check on Sarah's progress, and he agreed. She couldn't imagine Sarah represented a threat to them, even if her behavior sometimes took a few left turns. Who didn't have ups and downs?

Fresh air circulated in the room through a slightly open window. Sun streamed across the floor. Harley, after his initial investigation, chose a warm strip of light as the perfect napping spot.

Sarah's smile illuminated the space. In her element, documents and photographs covered every spare surface of the walls. Even Charlie's untrained eye detected the orderliness and the strict level of classification. She stood in the center of the room and gazed at the surrounding display. Although impressive, it didn't enrapture her like it did Sarah. Give her mayhem and unpredictability any day.

"Anything useful?" Charlie asked, waving her hand toward the boxes.

"Oh, yes. It's wonderful. A gold mine." Sarah tapped on the box of photos. "I'll sort them into chronological order. Many of them have names and dates on the back," she said. "I found some dated well over a hundred years ago."

"Amazing." Charlie tried to infuse her voice with interest, but the constant specter of a murderer in their midst dampened her enthusiasm. She wondered at Sarah's lack of fear. Charlie presumed she lived a sedate professor's life, unaccustomed to violence and crime. Yet, she had worked on archaeological sites in Egypt and perhaps elsewhere. She possessed enough courage to descend into the unknown depths of a dark hole. There was more to this woman than Charlie had initially thought.

"Did you find the missing pages?" Charlie asked. After all, that was the purpose of returning to the tunnel.

Sarah veered toward the opposite wall, adding notes to a document. She spoke to Charlie over her shoulder.

"I haven't gone through the paperwork yet, but I expect it'll fill the gaps." Without turning, Sarah waved a hand at her laptop. "I've set up a spreadsheet with links to these documents in .pdf form. I also incorporated links to genealogy websites that can send you down a rabbit hole of information."

Charlie shuddered at the thought.

She approached the wall of photos, thinking this fell into Noah's sphere of interest. The changing poses and improving quality of the photography over generations would fascinate him.

"You've identified these people and understand their place in the Wolfe family?" Charlie asked.

"Those, yes. Still plenty to go through."

Charlie leaned closer and squinted at a picture. A stern-faced man sat in a chair and an equally stern-faced woman stood beside and behind him, her hand resting on his shoulder, a classic pose for that period. The woman wore a dark dress, tight in the bodice with tiny buttons that reached her neck. Her skirt fell from her waist like a bell. A strict bun held back her dark hair. The man, bald and clean-shaven, wore a dark suit with a white shirt. Something about him attracted Charlie's attention, but she couldn't put her finger on it.

"Who is he? Do you know?" Charlie asked.

Beside the photo was a tiny round sticker with the number 38 on it. Sarah consulted her laptop and pulled up a document.

"Isaac Wolfe, married to Isabel."

"Children?"

"Yes, two sons. The oldest was Noah's great-grandfather," Sarah said, smiling.

"Did they live in this house?" Charlie asked.

"I don't know yet, but I expect to find out."

Charlie pulled her phone from her jeans pocket and snapped a shot of the photo.

"Why does it interest you?" Sarah asked.

Charlie chuckled. "I want to show it to Simm. Inside joke."

Pretending an interest in other photos, Charlie bided her time. Once given the chance, she hurried to the library.

Simm's head shot up when his wife came in. His brows lowered. "What's wrong?" he asked.

"I've got something." She raised her phone. "What do you see?"

"Two unhappy people."

"Look at the man. Add some hair to his head."

Simm concentrated on the photo for a few seconds until his eyes widened with sudden understanding.

CHAPTER 45

"Mike."

Charlie smiled, excited about her discovery. "They had two sons. One of them was Noah's great-grandfather. You want to bet Mike's an illegitimate descendent of this guy?"

"If he is, he may have been in line for the inheritance, except he was born on the wrong side of the blanket," Simm said.

"We wrote off Sarah's research too fast."

Simm nodded. "If it's true, two people missed out on the inheritance, Mike and Eli."

"There could be more," Charlie said. "How many other illegitimate people are running around? Conceived in that building." She gestured toward the house on the neighbor's property.

Simm rose from his chair and stood with his hands on his hips. "Who would benefit if Noah was out of the way?"

"Maybe either of those two men. Eli, for sure. With both brothers gone, who's left to inherit? You think Noah was the target and not Walter? The wrong person drank the whiskey?" Charlie asked.

Simm turned to the window. The warm spring sun had dried up all traces of the earlier downpour, and the greenery appreciated the dousing. "If you're targeting one person, why put poison in whiskey anyone could drink?"

"Walter starts in the morning and nurses one all day," Charlie said.

"True, but the timing could've been off. Both Noah and I drink whiskey. So do you, on occasion. I'm not sure about Sarah. Someone could slip it into the bottle, hoping one of us would drink it."

Charlie didn't like that theory. It meant whoever poisoned Walter didn't care who died in their quest, whatever it may be.

Simm hesitated. "Although, we're guessing it was in the whiskey bottle. It could've been in his glass, or something else. We haven't heard from Baxter."

Charlie's mind raced over all the times Mike appeared on random occasions. Eli also showed up unannounced to help Sarah, which could be a simple pretense. Both men were in the house that morning. "If Noah was the intended victim, and the culprit put the poison in the bottle, either he didn't think it through, or he hoped Noah would drink the whiskey and didn't care if he killed others along the way. Putting it in the glass would be a more direct approach, but that would mean Walter was the target. Why?"

Simm stared at her, frowning. "I don't see Mike being that reckless, and he has no motive for killing Walter."

Charlie sagged into a chair. "I agree. Same goes for Eli."

Simm ran his hand through his hair. "I'd like to know more about the family tree."

"It'd mean confiding in Sarah. Are you ready to do that?"

"I don't think we have a choice. She's the keeper of the documents, and she'd be a big help."

"How would we keep it from Noah? Ask her not to tell him? That'd be awkward."

"You're right," Simm said, his shoulders slumping. "But Walter and Clarisse will stay in the dark. They've got enough to handle."

Simm's phone dinged, and he glanced at the screen. "Speak of the devil. It's Clarisse."

As he opened his text, Charlie tried to read his expression. She hoped Walter's condition had improved over the past few hours.

"He's better," Simm said. "She's taking a taxi back."

"Good news," Charlie replied with a breath of relief. As much as she wanted Walt and Clarisse out of their hair, she didn't wish them harm. He was safe at the hospital, and when they released him, if he could travel, the sooner they left the better. Whether Walter was the intended victim or collateral damage, which seemed likely, he needed to leave this house.

Should they do the same? Pack their bags? It was obvious someone sinister had access to this place, and the stage may have been set several generations ago. Percy Wolfe dictated how each generation would survive, either with a bundle of cash, or by making their own way. In the house's structure, he integrated the means to cheat on his wife. How many women lived unhappy existences in this mansion?

Were the rumors of a ghost true? Did Daphne or one of her descendants seek revenge on the male inhabitants of the Wolfe estate?

. . .

"Slow down," Charlie said. "You've lost me."

Sarah grimaced. "Sorry. I get excited. To have someone who really cares, well..." She let the sentence dangle.

Sarah had constructed a makeshift family tree with dozens of sheets of paper that she taped to the bedroom wall. Documents were coded, cross-referenced, and stuck to walls or stacked on surfaces. She'd also coded and referenced corresponding photographs.

And she'd copied every morsel of data onto her computer. A jungle of research occupied the room.

"Did you go through everything?" Simm asked.

"No. Still a full box of papers and half a box of photos," she said. "But I think I found the missing pages." Her voice quivered with excitement.

"What did they say?" Charlie felt her own enthusiasm increase.

"She gave specifics about the illegitimate children Percy fathered."

"I understand why it'd be damaging if anyone got their hands on that. Numerous lawsuits could follow," Simm said. "Percy wanted to control the money."

"I wonder who removed them," Charlie asked.

Simm turned a thoughtful gaze on his wife. "Someone who wanted to eliminate others who stood in his path."

Charlie swallowed. There was a lot of that going around these days.

Sarah didn't seem to catch the undercurrent that passed between the couple. "I'll incorporate the illegitimate kids into the family tree and try to trace their offspring."

"Perfect. Can we help?" Charlie said. Without needing to divulge details to Sarah, she would likely come across a connection to Mike, if it existed.

"Sure." Sarah said without hesitation. "Why don't you work on these diaries?" She pointed to a stack of six journals. A couple were thin, resembling school notebooks. Thick leather covered others with at least a hundred pages. Some were yellowed and worn, while others appeared recent. "I haven't found anything more current than the early 2000s yet. Nothing from Noah's father's time, unless there aren't any. But see if you can find something useful," Sarah suggested.

Charlie hoped she recognized useful when she saw it. She selected two notebooks. "We'll look at them in the library. Get out of your hair."

Sarah gave them a distracted wave as she returned to her clipboard and annotations.

"She's intense when she gets into something, isn't she?" Simm said as they descended the stairs.

"That's what makes her an excellent scientist and researcher."

The front door opened as they arrived in the entranceway. Clarisse entered looking frazzled and tired. Charlie shoved the diaries into Simm's arms as she rushed to her sister-in-law.

"You're worn out," she said, wrapping the other woman in a hug.

"I've never had a day like today," Clarisse said, her voice weary.

"He's improving?" Simm asked.

"They say he is, but he's groggy. The police wanted to talk to him, but he wasn't up for it."

"They can wait until tomorrow," Charlie said, her annoyance with the police apparent. "Are you hungry? Can I get you something?"

"No, thank you. I couldn't eat if I tried." She tugged off her jacket. "What did the cops do?" Her gaze wandered over the entranceway as if police officers would appear.

"They took the bottles of alcohol," Simm said. "And other evidence from your room. They've taped it off. You'll have to sleep somewhere else tonight."

"We're lucky this place has so many rooms or we'd be sharing beds," Charlie said, aiming to lighten the mood.

"What are those?" Clarisse asked, her brow furrowed as she pointed at the old diaries in Simm's hands.

"Noah and Sarah went into the tunnel. There was a concealed storage room. They found more diaries and a box of old photos."

Clarisse's eyes widened. "What? I can't believe they went back in there after what happened." Her wild gaze moved from one to the other. "Weren't they afraid? Charlie, somebody attacked you down there, and then they poisoned Walter. Someone evil is in this house. None of us should be here."

Charlie knew she had a point. And that was why Clarisse and Walter needed to leave as soon as possible. They'd have a harder time convincing Noah and Sarah to do the same. They had too much invested in this.

"Simm and I decided we wouldn't give up, but we'll be very careful. I understand how you feel, especially after what happened today. Perhaps it's best if you stay at a hotel until they release Walter and you can go home."

Clarisse straightened her shoulders, seeming to regain confidence. "No. I'd rather be with all of you. I'll feel safer." She glanced up the stairway, maybe remembering the chilling events of the morning. "Did she find anything useful? To make the trip worthwhile?"

"She's sorting through everything," Charlie said, chuckling. "Sarah's in her glory with all that stuff to classify. Simm and I will read some of them to help her out and speed things along." Charlie took the diaries from Simm.

"I can do some, if you like," Clarisse said. "It'll help occupy my mind."

Charlie and Simm exchanged a glance. They'd rather work on this alone, but Clarisse seemed determined, and they couldn't deny her the chance to concentrate on something other than her husband's close call with murder. Besides, it'd go faster with three people. The clock was ticking.

In the library, Simm laid the two diaries on the desk. Using his computer, he noted the dates they covered and who had written them. One journal spanned from 1895 to 1904, while the other covered 1967 to 1975. Clarisse chose the more contemporary of the two, leaving the other for Charlie. They'd feed information to Simm, which he'd transfer to Sarah. If things worked out, they'd view another portion of the Wolfe family picture.

Quiet descended upon the room, punctuated by the tapping of computer keys. Charlie smiled, knowing Simm would spend his downtime following up on loose ends.

The cumbersome script wore Charlie down, but she stuck to it, searching for references to individuals, important dates, or events that might lead them to what Ethan was hiding. Amelia Wolfe, the author of that particular diary, led a boring life by all appearances. It included visits with neighbors, trite gossip about those very neighbors, details of parties and balls, along with more gossip about the partygoers. It was an endless episode of reality TV *à la* 1800s.

Charlie would mention names to Simm with whatever connection to the family she gleaned, but she suspected Amelia was clueless about how her husband spent his time or even how he earned the money that paid for her dresses and parties.

Clarisse had even less luck with her diary, written by Nora Wolfe. Although Nora chose her children over partying, she didn't find a lot to contribute to their investigation.

"Should we switch?" Charlie asked her. "Fresh eyes might find something new."

Clarisse sighed. "I think I'll go lie down for a bit. I'll take it with me and read it in bed. I can take notes."

"Good idea. Take the second room on the right. Sarah and I already washed the bedding and cleaned it up."

Clarisse smiled her thanks and left.

Charlie turned her attention to Simm. "A wild goose chase?"

"Maybe. But it's something to work on while I'm waiting for my other leads to bear fruit. I reached out to Baxter to ask about the poison's source. As expected, he told me to shove it."

"He said that?" Charlie asked with wide eyes. The cop didn't have a soft spot for Simm, but rudeness wasn't called for.

"He implied it. He suspects me of trying to kill my brother, and he hates me for snooping into his cases."

"The theory we worked with for Ethan's death was that he uncovered something dangerous that someone wanted to remain hidden," Charlie said.

"Right."

"If it's in those boxes, then Ethan either found it in the tunnel or hid it there. And the key will unlock it for us."

"Makes sense."

"Let's look at the latest video again," Charlie said. "I want to check something."

Simm pulled up the video while Charlie flattened her palms on the desk beside him. They fast-forwarded to when Noah shoved open the door.

"Plenty of dust, but it's normal. They're dirt walls," Simm said. Charlie agreed.

In the room, dust particles clouded Noah's camera. When it cleared, he and Sarah stepped closer and faced the boxes.

"Look," Charlie said, pointing at the screen. "Freeze it."

Simm clicked a key, and the video paused. They both leaned forward to squint at the image.

"Do you see it?" Charlie asked.

"Yes."

CHAPTER 46

Charlie spotted the detective's car in the driveway when she and Harley returned from their walk. Her heartbeat quickened as she hurried toward the house. What had happened now? She left just long enough to stretch their legs. How could things deteriorate so quickly?

Worried about a crime scene, she burst over the threshold to find no one in sight. Quiet murmurs emanated from the back of the house.

In the kitchen, Simm and Baxter faced each other. Their postures appeared relaxed as Charlie froze, her expression guarded and her hand gripping Harley's leash like a lifeline.

"You're back," Simm said as he turned to face her. His nonchalant tone helped to calm her heartbeat.

"Everything okay?" she asked, her smile forced and her tone a little too high-pitched.

"Of course. The good detective just wanted to chat."

"Chat?" Her confusion intensified. Simm made it sound as if the cop who hated him and thought him a criminal was now his new best buddy.

"He's curious about Sarah's research."

"Really?" This intrigued Charlie. She scrutinized the detective's face. What attracted him to the Wolfe family tree? Charlie slanted a meaningful glance at her husband.

"I told him we found documents in the tunnel, and we're going through them," Simm said.

"What did you want to know?" she asked, turning to the cop.

"Seems to me these latest events may tie to the family," Baxter said. His tone was indifferent, as if discussing the weather. "There could be something that'd help."

"Can you give us more of an indication?"

Simm emitted a low grunt. He liked her line of questioning.

The cop considered it for a moment. He sent an uncomfortable glance around the room and twisted his head to peer down the hallway. "Just wondering about recent history, that's all," he said in a low voice.

"How recent?" Simm shot back.

"I don't know. Past ten years, maybe."

"We've found nothing in that timeframe yet. Any idea what it is?"

"No. Look harder." Baxter gave them a tight-lipped smile. "I better get going. I'll see myself out." Taking two steps, he swung back to Simm. "Billy Martin. Montego Bay."

After the cop left the kitchen and the front door closed quietly behind him, Charlie sent Simm an intense stare.

"Were those hints or what?" she said in a whisper.

"More like billboard ads."

"He wants us to find something, both here and in Jamaica," Charlie said.

"Sarah said the most recent journal was from the early 2000s," Simm replied. "We'll have to keep looking. And I'll check out Billy Martin." Simm headed to the library.

"Where is everybody?" Charlie asked, following him.

"Clarisse went to the hospital. They're releasing Walt. Sarah and Noah took Bosco for a walk."

"How long ago did they leave?"

"Just before Baxter arrived, maybe fifteen minutes."

Charlie gave him a wide-eyed look. "Now's our chance."

They scurried up the staircase, Harley on their heels.

"I'll look at the diary Clarisse had. You look in Sarah's stuff. I'll meet you there," Charlie said.

With an uneasy feeling, Charlie stepped into the room Clarisse claimed. Her goal was to locate the diary, not invade personal things. Wanting to keep their interest secret, they needed to do it on the sly.

The untidiness of the room surprised Charlie. Clarisse always struck her as neat and organized. Yet, clothes were strewn across the bed, unmatched shoes lay on the floor, makeup containers spilled on the vanity. The room she shared with Walter had been tidy and clean. Even with the vomit and convulsions, Charlie saw how spotless and orderly it usually was. This room revealed the identity of the neat freak in the family.

The unmade bed held plenty of hiding spots for a diary. Charlie tossed the blankets and clothing and found the journal under a pillow. With a smile of success, she flipped through it, checking dates and hoping something would jump out at her. She slammed it shut and met Simm in Sarah's room.

"It's older than ten years."

"Nothing recent stuck in the pages?"

"No, but the room's a mess. If something fell out, we'd never find it," Charlie said. "What about you? Find anything?"

"Not yet. And we know from the video no one touched this one recently," Simm said, with a wave toward one of the document boxes. "The other journals have nothing shoved inside them. That leaves the photos."

"The almost dust-free box."

Charlie leaned over the box and groaned. Photographs were tossed into it, and despite the dozens that papered the bedroom wall, it was still three-quarters full.

"Let's classify them by date."

Charlie gave him a side-glance. "You sound like Sarah."

They dug into the box, pulled out handfuls of photos, and laid them on the bed in what they hoped was chronological order. Some had dates, but most required using the subjects' clothing style and background to guess the year.

About to toss one photo into a pile, something caught her eye, and she squinted at the picture. The sound of the door opening startled her.

"Oh," Sarah said, taking a step back. "I didn't realize you were here."

Charlie spun to face the other woman. "We wanted to help, so we started on these," she said as she slid the photo unnoticed into the back pocket of her shorts. "How was your walk?"

"Great. It really is a lovely town."

Sarah moved to inspect the photographs on the bed. "This is wonderful. Thanks for helping. I'll categorize them," she said, grabbing her clipboard.

"We'll leave you to it," Charlie said. She touched Simm's arm and motioned with her head for him to follow her.

They descended the stairs in silence, and Charlie headed toward the library.

"What's up?" Simm asked as he moved to the desk.

"You won't believe this," Charlie said.

CHAPTER 47

Simm started with the basics—social media. However, Billy Martin was a common name, even when narrowed down to Jamaica and using a search for William, Will, or Bill. He accessed other websites that proved fruitful in past cases but got nowhere this time. Simm blew out a breath of frustration. He had a solid lead from the detective and hit another dead end.

Simm preferred to let Erik concentrate on the money trail, but the tech wizard was still the most efficient information source. He sent him a quick text with the few details he had about Billy Martin and hoped for the best.

While he waited, he brainstormed the puzzle of Ethan's computer. They hadn't found it or a storage device yet. Ethan didn't have a bank safe deposit box or any other rental space they could find. During their visit to the hidden underground room, Noah searched and came up empty-handed. Short of covering the entire house, grounds, and tunnel again, Simm held little hope of finding anything. All they had was a key, but they didn't know what it opened.

Likely, the killer accessed the money through the stolen laptop.

A ping interrupted his thoughts. Simm smiled when he saw the email from Erik. His smile morphed to a grin when he spotted a file entitled "Billy Martin—Jamaica." Bingo. Erik had a knack for finding needles in digital haystacks. His services were costly, but at times like this, well worthwhile.

Simm's expression sobered as he scanned the information in the file. It contained photos of a middle-aged Jamaican man, with white teeth and bare chest displayed in most of them. He seemed to enjoy the high life of drinking and partying, often on a boat. But, more so, Martin wore a different hat—the police chief for Montego Bay. A man of contradictions, it seemed.

A brief newspaper article about Brent Holmes' accidental drowning didn't mention Martin's name, but his unsmiling face appeared alongside other Jamaicans standing on a beach with a fishing boat in the background.

Simm examined other images and found more of the same.

A document caught his eye. His "yes" was more like a hiss than a word.

Somehow Erik accessed Martin's bank account. Three days after the "accident" that took the financial advisor's life, a deposit of a hundred thousand U.S. dollars landed in Billy's account. For a Jamaican police officer, that was more than a windfall—it was a hurricane. Simm's pulse raced. Maybe other Jamaicans struck gold too.

But Baxter knew. The detective had nudged Simm in the right direction. Yet, the same rope that bound Baxter's hands tied Simm's. Unable to trust anyone, he couldn't use this information until he discovered the person in charge of the money.

He'd send Erik a fresh dossier.

. . .

The rainstorm swept in, cooling the bedroom. Charlie nestled closer to Simm, and his arm pulled her against his chest. The rhythm of raindrops on the windowpane provided a soothing backdrop to their conversation.

"Think we'll close this out by the weekend?" she asked.

"Two days? Doubt it."

"You'll hand it over to Baxter? What if he ignores it? You'll have to go higher."

"I'm not sure the problem isn't higher up. Why come here and drop hints? I think he wants us to solve this case to give him deniability. That way, he'll be free from blowback."

Charlie swiveled her head to look at him. "Blackmail?"

"Leaning that way."

"Somebody shut him down, that's obvious. How do we find out who?"

"I don't know. If Baxter won't talk, I may have more work for Erik. Another money trail," Simm said.

"Whoever is behind this has cash to burn. It rules out Mike."

"Not necessarily. He might get a cut. We can't rule out anyone yet." He squeezed her shoulder. "You want to go home?"

Charlie sighed. "I admit I envy Walter and Clarisse, knowing they'll be home tomorrow."

A weakened and shaky Walter had arrived back at the Wolfe mansion in the afternoon. Charlie felt a wave of pity for him. His usual cockiness absent, he leaned on Clarisse. Both Simm and Noah offered to help him upstairs to bed, but he wanted nothing to do with them. He made it clear he suspected at least one of them in the murder attempt. Charlie would wait until they found evidence to convince him otherwise. In the meantime, he'd wallow in his bitterness.

As Clarisse assisted him up the stairs, she spoke over her shoulder to the group in the entranceway. "We'll leave in the morning, once Walter's had a good night's sleep."

"We should leave right away." Walter may have meant his words for Clarisse's ears, but they carried downward to the others.

"Look at you. You're still weak. The morning will be time enough."

His mumblings grew indistinct, but Charlie heard "murdered in my sleep" as the couple progressed up the staircase. Clarisse's response must have comforted him somewhat.

Charlie admitted to herself it wasn't only envy she felt at the thought of her in-laws' departure. Without personal feuds and hostility, tensions would diminish, and they could focus on the case.

Now, lying in bed, she smiled at her husband. "You know me. Fun to escape, but I'm happier at the pub. And we've got other business to take care of." She wiggled her brows.

Simm caught her meaning and cleared his throat. "About that..."

Charlie stiffened. "What about it?"

"I've been thinking."

Charlie sat bolt upright, swinging to face him. "What? But you said...we decided."

Simm levered himself up to lean back against the headboard. "I'm not sure anymore."

"You were. You've been sure for months. It's too late to change your mind."

Charlie felt her heart cracking. She'd been over the moon when he agreed to have children. She was certain that as soon as she was pregnant, he'd fall in love with their child. Excitement and anticipation brightened her days. Now, once again, her dream-come-true resembled a never-to-be-dream.

Tears of loss, anger, and frustration rolled down her cheeks. "How could you?" she said, almost choking on the words. "How could you hurt me like this? You saw how happy I was."

Even through her feelings of pain and betrayal, Charlie witnessed the anguish in Simm's eyes. Deep down, she realized he felt her suffering and hated to inflict it on her, but it was another blow in a long battle.

"Why?" she said, gasping the word.

"Honey, it's the reason I've always worried about. Clarisse said her son is like a mini-Walt."

"What?" Charlie drew back and stared at him, flummoxed. He based their future on a remark from Clarisse. "What does that have to do with us?"

"The same thing could happen."

"You are not Walter. How many times can I repeat myself?" Her voice rose.

"We share the same genes."

"Maybe, but more of *your* genes would go into our baby." Charlie folded her arms across her chest. "Besides, Walter isn't looking as bad these days."

"I don't want a kid like him."

"You'd love that child no matter what, and you'd help to mold him into the best person possible."

"We've had this conversation a thousand times…"

"And we'll have it a million times more if that's what it takes to convince you." Charlie leaped from the bed, snatching her jeans and sweatshirt from a nearby chair. She swung the bedroom door open, and Simm's voice trailed after her as she stepped into the dimly lit hallway. She resisted the urge to slam the door—respecting the house's other occupants—but her emotions roared like a tempest.

The dogs sat at attention in the corridor. Perhaps they heard the angry words and wanted to be part of the discussion, but tails wagged when Charlie appeared. Her hand grazed the top of Bosco's head as she passed him, and eight paws padded behind her as she descended the stairs.

The house lay in darkness, and she welcomed it. With her thoughts and feelings in turmoil, she didn't want to see or talk to anyone else. The dogs were the only company she needed.

Moving through the kitchen, she unlocked and exited the door. Moonlight bathed the damp lawn in a silver sheen, and the air cooled her anger-heated skin. She clutched her clothing in her arms, knowing the cold would soon seep through the oversized T-shirt she slept in.

Charlie lowered herself onto the top step as the dogs assumed their positions as bookends beside her.

The door leading to the tunnel drew her gaze like a magnet. It seemed the pit caused trouble for many decades, from the man who built it for clandestine meetings with his lover, to the man who hid secrets from the person who ultimately killed him.

What had Ethan discovered? A major crime or a family secret that was dangerous enough for a person to kill to keep it hidden? And who tried to stop them from finding it? Someone sleeping in the house at this moment, or somebody with easy access to it?

Charlie's eyes narrowed. Access. That was the key. They'd found a hiding place inside the tunnel. Was there something else in there? Another way into the house? They'd already considered it. After all, her attacker had disappeared somehow, but Noah and Sarah hadn't found anything other than the storage room down there.

An eerie feeling passed over her. She grabbed her jeans and pulled them on in the nighttime darkness, followed by the sweatshirt. It gave her a level of comfort. So did knowing the dogs would alert her to strangers. She searched the gloom, looking for anyone or anything. Her arm tightened around Bosco's neck.

Harley reacted a split-second before Bosco, shooting to his feet, his little body trembling with excitement. Bosco followed suit. Charlie's heart pounded, her fearful gaze searching the blackness before her, intensely aware of the myriad places for people to hide amongst the trees and shrubs.

Both dogs raced to the tunnel door.

"Oh, no. I'm not going in there, guys. Not again." She jumped to her feet, turned toward the house and stifled a scream.

CHAPTER 48

Simm hurried down the steps. "What's going on?"

Charlie fought to catch her breath. His dark shape had scared the life out of her. Recovering, she pointed at the dogs.

"There's something or someone in there," she said, their earlier argument forgotten.

"The door's locked. No one went in that way."

Their gazes swung to the huge hedge in the back, the opening invisible in the darkness. Simm ran into the house and returned with a headlamp in his hand.

"You get inside with Harley. Lock the door. I'll take Bosco with me."

"You're not going in there alone, and you're not leaving me behind," Charlie said. The thought of Simm facing off against an unknown assailant in that tunnel struck fear in her heart.

"I brought a weapon," he said, pulling a carving knife wrapped in a towel out of his sleeve. "And I'll have the dog."

Charlie looked at the beautiful mastiff, who bristled with expectation. "We'll all go. No one can take on the four of us."

"Don't do this to me," Simm said, bending until his eyes met hers. "We've been through it before, and I won't do it again."

"I'll go to the outbuilding. I'll wait for you there," she said. As she spoke the words, she realized she wasn't likely to keep her promise.

Simm gave her a hard-eyed look and agreed with a nod.

The couple struck off across the lawn, sprinting to the hedge, the dogs following beside them. They squeezed through the opening and dashed toward the building. Simm eased the door open, the squeaking of the rusty hinges amplified by the quiet night air. As they stepped inside, Simm settled the headlamp on his head and flooded the room with light. Neither moved, until Simm whispered, "What the hell?"

· · ·

Charlie and Simm sat at the kitchen table, each holding a cup of coffee, not speaking. Exhausted from lack of sleep and overwhelmed by the jumble of thoughts whirling through their brains, they had nothing more to discuss.

Noah frowned when he found them there. Normally the earliest riser, he enjoyed his quiet coffee with only Bosco by his side. This morning, he'd adjust, the rule of the day.

As they exchanged mumbled greetings, a sudden shout and the clatter of footsteps echoed from the stairs. Sarah burst into the kitchen, breathless and distraught.

"It's a mess. It's ruined!"

"What happened?" Charlie asked, springing to her feet.

"My work. Someone went through it, destroyed it."

By now, everyone was on their feet and hurrying for the staircase. The sight that met them in the research room left them dumbfounded. Ripped papers strewn across the bed. Dumped boxes and shreds of the family tree scattered here and there. Hours of labor wiped out. Starting over was unimaginable. They didn't have time.

Charlie shared a grave look with Simm.

Hearing a gasp behind her, she turned to see Clarisse, a large travel bag hanging from her shoulder. "What happened?"

"Someone ruined my work," Sarah said in a tear-filled voice. "Who? They came in during the night. But the front door was locked. And how'd they get past the dogs?"

"Last night, I couldn't sleep and took the dogs outside," Charlie said. "It must've happened then."

"Let's get out of here," Walter, looking stronger but still pale, said from beside his wife. "I'm not spending another minute in this house. Come on, Clarisse."

As Walter grabbed the smallest of their three bags, Noah and Simm stepped forward to assume the role of bellboys. Having Walter lying in a heap at the bottom of the stairs wouldn't help the situation.

Charlie comforted a distraught Sarah, explaining that she'd have to note everything she recalled. The next day, they'd hand it to the police and return to Montreal.

Simm came back to the room, a smile on his face. "They're set to leave. Two out of harm's way," He turned to Noah. "You and Sarah should head back too."

Noah's brows drew together. "Absolutely not. Someone murdered my brother, and this is my house. I'll be the last person out the door." His expression softened. "But I agree Sarah should go."

The researcher's eyes widened. "After putting in so much work?" she said, pointing at the chaos surrounding them. "You don't think I'll see this through?"

"It's not safe," Simm pointed out. "There's ..."

"Somebody sabotaged our car." They pivoted toward the angry voice. A red-faced Clarisse stood there with her fists clenched.

"What?" Sarah asked, her brow scrunched in confusion.

"It won't start. It's a brand-new car. There's no reason for that."

"I'll look at it," Simm said, fighting for patience. "You guys continue with this mess."

Charlie watched her husband follow a raging Clarisse out the door and had the urge to go with them. They might need someone to douse fiery tempers.

"Let them go," a deep voice said by her side. "They have to iron things out."

She glanced at Noah and nodded. He was right. She couldn't micromanage everything. She joined him and Sarah in picking up the scattered documents and photos, attempting to restore some semblance of order.

Twenty minutes later, outraged voices rose up the staircase from the entranceway. Charlie froze, hoping no one resorted to violence. She moved to the top of the stairs and saw Clarisse and the brothers engaged in a heated argument.

"Don't look at me," Simm said. "I didn't do it. Why would I delay your departure? If anything, the opposite is true."

"Who the hell did it?" Walter demanded. "Somebody wants me to stay so they can try to kill me again."

"Don't be ridiculous, Walter. No one will do that," Clarisse said. She reverted to a mollifying tone.

Her husband turned his rage on her. "Don't say that! Someone already did. I was the one who almost died, remember? I was the one in the hospital." He whirled back toward Simm and poked a finger in his chest. "It was likely you or the hulk up there."

That was Charlie's signal to intervene. Simm didn't tolerate chest-poking, and if Noah overheard the accusation, he might act on it. She rushed to join the trio.

"Come to the kitchen, I'll make coffee and breakfast. We're all cranky before we've had a decent cup." She wedged between Walter and Clarisse, grabbed an elbow in each hand, and herded them to the back of the house. Over her shoulder, she spoke to Simm. "Honey, why don't you see about getting that car fixed? Even if it means calling a garage."

Clarisse threw herself into a chair as Walter paced in front of the window, the thickness of their anger almost suffocating. Apparently, their cease-fire interlude was over.

Charlie dispersed java and platitudes about how Simm would fix the car in no time. Neither of them paid attention to her, which suited Charlie. Her thoughts swirled in her fatigued brain.

"What did I hear before?" Walter said, finally noticing things happened that didn't concern him directly, an unusual event for him. "Someone messed with Sarah's research?"

"Yes, apparently," Charlie said, swiping her hand over her face.

"During the night? While we slept?" he asked.

Charlie nodded, aware of what would follow. It did.

Walter's voice rose several octaves as he turned an accusing glare on his wife. "What did I tell you? This place is crawling with criminals and people up to no good."

"It could be Charlie's ghost," Clarisse sneered, a look more common on her husband.

Simm entered the room and rushed to the coffeemaker. "I couldn't find the problem, so I took my lovely wife's advice and called a local garage. Someone'll be over in a while."

"How long is a while?" Walter asked, his tone hostile.

"He didn't say. But it should be quick." He took a deep, grateful sip of his coffee and glanced at Charlie. "We've got things to do, hon. Ready to go?"

"What about us?" Walter said, affronted.

Recent experiences had restored Walter's feelings of entitlement.

"I guess you'll have to amuse yourselves until your car is ready." Simm's smile was placating. "Charlie and I will walk Harley, and then we have work to do."

Charlie chuckled as Harley led them to the street. "Poor Walt."

"Poor Noah and Sarah. They're stuck dealing with his hissy fits."

"Tomorrow's the deadline," Charlie said, her expression serious as she delivered the reminder.

Simm's phone jangled. "This guy knows when we're talking about him." He tapped the screen and said, "Hello, Detective Baxter."

CHAPTER 49

He completed the call by the time Charlie reached her destination. She smiled at Simm before he turned and headed in a different direction, ready to take care of his own task.

She faced the long driveway.

"Come on, Harley. Let's do this."

Charlie rang the doorbell and waited. When the door opened, she met the man's surprised gaze.

. . .

They heard the arguments as they set foot inside the house. Harley scurried to greet Bosco, leading him into the quiet library and curling up on the rug beside him.

Charlie envied them. She'd love to curl up and block out the voices. She pitied Noah and Sarah. Upon their arrival in the kitchen, they observed the couple staring into their coffee mugs with pained expressions as Walter and Clarisse argued.

"There you are," Walt shouted. "Nice of you to wander around, taking in the fresh air, while we're waiting for our car. You could've left us the garage name. No one's shown up yet."

Simm frowned. "That's strange. I'll call him."

"Be sure to complain about the service."

"I'll pass that on," Simm said, his smile sarcastic.

A rap on the door followed by the cacophony of barking interrupted Simm's intended phone call.

"That's them." Walter moved toward the entranceway, his usual vigor returning, with Clarisse close behind. Noah and Sarah emerged to calm Bosco and open the door.

The sight of the couple on the doorstep brought Walter and Clarisse to an abrupt halt.

The petite woman wore a long, black skirt and sensible shoes topped with a floral-patterned blouse and a thin, black cardigan. Her short, gray curls formed a cloud around her head, and a warm smile lit her lined face. The slender man beside her stood straight and formal, wearing navy blue dress pants and a long-sleeved blue striped shirt, buttoned to the neck. A tweed Irish cap covered his wispy gray hair.

Charlie stepped forward with a wide smile. "Mr. Brown, how delightful to see you. And this must be your friend, Mrs. McCollum. We haven't had the pleasure of meeting. I'm Charlie. Welcome," she said, leading them into the sitting room. Everyone else, including the dogs, followed, consumed by curiosity.

"Let me introduce you to the others. You both know my husband." The couple beamed at Simm. "This is Noah Wolfe, the house's owner."

"Oh, my goodness, yes," said Mrs. McCollum. "You look just like your father, David, when he was a boy. I'm so sorry about your brother," she added with a tragic look.

Noah nodded as Charlie took up the introductions again. "This is Sarah Heaton, Noah's sister-in-law."

"Heaton?" Mr. Brown said. "I knew a Heaton years ago. He was a smart fella, probably too smart. That's what got him into trouble." He chuckled and turned to his companion. "Do you remember that story, Elsa?"

She pointed a shaky finger at him. "Yes, I do, now that you mention it. Wasn't he arrested for stealing a secret formula from a vineyard?"

"That was it. And I believe it was Eli Wolfe's vineyard."

Noah swiveled to Sarah, brows raised. Her face bloomed a deep red as she spoke to him in a whisper. "I can explain. It's not what you think."

Simm took over for Charlie, leaving a stunned Noah staring at a sputtering Sarah.

"Over here, is my brother Walt and his wife Clarisse Bowan-Simmons."

"Bowan?" Mrs. McCollum said. "Are you related to Ian Bowan? I see the family resemblance as clear as day."

"Yes, of course," Clarisse said, the blood draining from her face. "He's my father." Her smile was polite, but Charlie sensed she wanted to go outside and fix the car herself, just to escape.

Mrs. McCollum clapped her hands with delight. "This is wonderful, meeting all of you. And you're so closely tied together. Ian and David were the best of friends."

Noah pivoted to Clarisse, his expression astonished. Shocking revelations bounced at him from every direction.

"You're Ian's daughter?" he said. "I know him."

Clarisse's hand went to her throat. "I didn't realize he was close to your family. The subject never came up."

"I'm surprised he never mentioned it," the older woman said. "He spent so much time here as a youngster playing with David. I remember your grandmother so well, Noah. She called them 'scallywags.' She'd say, 'Those young scallywags found the secret passageway in the upstairs room.' She'd laugh, of course. And when they came across the tunnel." She chuckled and rolled her eyes. "That was another story."

Clarisse laughed, a hollow sound. "They knew about those things? How funny."

"Your father never mentioned it to you?" Charlie said.

"No, not at all." Her gaze flitted around her, not meeting Charlie's.

Walter turned to his wife, annoyance flashing in his eyes. "What? Your father tells you everything. You share every detail of your days with each other. We can't move an inch without him knowing about it. He said nothing when you told him we were coming here?"

"I don't tell him everything," Clarisse said, crimson splotches blossoming on her cheeks. "I didn't even mention coming here."

Walter's annoyance morphed into anger. "You were on the phone with him, saying we're going to Niagara-on-the-Lake. Why are you lying?"

"Don't feel bad, Walt," Simm said. "She's adept at lying."

"Excuse me," Clarisse said, putting on her best offended look. "You can't talk to me like that. Walter, it's time to go."

"You're not leaving yet," Charlie said. "We found some things you forgot to pack." In one hand, she held up a journal with a plain brown leather cover. A small, black USB key was in the other.

Clarisse's eyes widened, her frantic gaze leaping from the diary to the USB key. It was clear her mind searched for an explanation.

"You're crazy," she stammered, trying and failing to come up with something stronger. Clarisse grabbed Walter's arm, but he tugged it out of her grip, his gaze darting from her to Charlie. As did everyone else, he waited for details.

Charlie waved the book in the air. "The last diary. Filled with incriminating facts. Was this what you were looking for?"

"I don't know what you're talking about," Clarisse declared, but her voice, shimmering with fear, lacked conviction.

"And a USB key," Charlie continued. "You never found it, but Simm did. Inside a concealed passageway between the tunnel and Ethan's room. It was hard to find, but you know where it might have been, right? You must've passed by it several times." Charlie shook her head. "Evidence was in there, hidden by Ethan. In a small antique chest."

"He documented everything, Clarisse," Simm said, taking the device from Charlie. "It's all on here. I made a copy and sent it to the police early this morning."

Clarisse wavered on her feet. Charlie felt no pity.

"Something bothered me when you came upon us at the door to the tunnel that first day," Charlie said. "I forgot about it, but it came back to me last night."

All eyes veered toward Charlie, but her gaze never left Clarisse's face.

"You said, 'This is the tunnel?' I don't understand why I didn't realize it sooner. Too much on my mind, I guess."

"What are they talking about, Clarisse?" Walter's confusion was apparent. "What did they find? What did you do?" His voice trembled as the gravity of the situation sank in.

"I don't know. This is ridiculous." Clarisse turned to her husband. "We'll leave the car here and rent another one. These people are crazy."

"We hadn't mentioned a tunnel to you at that point," Charlie said. "Only the four of us knew, yet you spoke as if you were aware of it, perhaps looking for it."

"Clarisse?" Walter said, his gaze pained and confused.

"And you seemed overly familiar with Niagara-on-the-Lake. You knew where to find the best cheese and bread," Charlie continued. "I fell for your Google excuse, and you threw me off with your questions about children. But it was all a little too pat."

Clarisse stalked to the door.

"And what about Marcus?" Simm's voice cut through the room. "We can't forget about the man in Gatineau, can we? The one who had a dubious implication in the accident that took Noah's family from him?"

Noah and Walter turned in unison, their eyes fixed on Simm. Clarisse faltered, her steps coming to a sudden stop.

"Walter, we're leaving. It's dangerous here, remember?" Clarisse spun and waved her arm at Simm and Charlie. "And now they're making up conspiracy theories. They want something to satisfy Noah so he'll pay them."

"Charlie found a photo in a box," Simm said. "And we discovered plenty more. We recognized Marcus. There are some interesting ones of Clarisse as well. But most interesting is a file that Ethan found. It was created by his father, David. I guess it was a kind of insurance, something to hold over Marcus and Ian's heads if they double-crossed him."

Clarisse's wild-eyed gaze swung across the room, as if searching for a means of escape. Simm continued while Charlie attempted to ignore the man who quietly entered the room and stood behind Clarisse.

"Fortunately, Ethan's neighbors have excellent memories and recalled the family connections. We went to see them this morning. Mr. Brown also remembered seeing you outside this house on a couple of occasions. It seems you're the mystery woman we searched for."

Walter sank into a chair, his legs seemingly unable to hold him any longer.

Noah and Sarah stood and stared, uncomprehending. Sarah reached over and clutched Noah's hand in hers.

Clarisse's eyes flashed. "You're insane," she repeated, as she turned toward the door, only to collide with Detective Baxter.

"You'll need to come to the station with me," he said. "And call a criminal defense lawyer."

Clarisse leaned in, fists clenched, face twisted into an ugly grimace. "You can't do anything. I hold the cards here."

"Not anymore. They removed my boss from his position this morning. An anonymous tip about him accepting bribes. We'll add that to the charges against you."

Clarisse whirled toward her husband. "Walt, help me."

Walter stared at her as if she was a stranger. "You did all this?" he said. "You tried to kill me?"

"Don't be ludicrous. This is a trap to frame me. I need your help."

Simm laid a hand on his brother's shoulder.

CHAPTER 50

"I should call a lawyer."

Charlie frowned at Walter. "For her? Let her make her own calls. The only lawyer you need is a divorce lawyer." She caught Simm's admonishing look and softened her tone. "I'm sorry. I know this is terrible for you, but I'm furious. She murdered Noah's brother, stole his money, tried to kill you, and perhaps more." She slid a quick sidelong glance at Simm.

The elderly couple on the sofa watched, riveted. Their quiet lives had suddenly become a gripping drama.

Her sympathy for Walter warred with her fury. He appeared to age ten years before her eyes, but she'd seen the evidence, felt the weight of it. Clarisse was no innocent victim; she was a predator. And Noah, poor Noah, faced the truth about his brother's killer. His eyes blazed with rage, pointing toward the door as if Clarisse still lingered there, a phantom of evil, but she'd been handcuffed and stuffed into a police car. "I want an explanation. That's my brother's killer," he said.

Walter sagged in the chair, shoulders curled inward, eyes glazed over. He shook his head. "I don't understand. How? Why?"

Charlie understood how hard this was for both men. She and Simm had time to let it sink in, and they still struggled with the shock.

"Let's start with coffee or something stronger," Charlie said.

Ray Brown's eyes lit up. "I wouldn't mind a dab of whiskey in mine."

"I'll have the same," Walter said. "But hold the coffee."

Sarah helped with the drink orders as Charlie imagined the drama at the police station. Her sister-in-law would've contacted a lawyer and gone through the process. Detective Baxter had enough information to get the ball rolling. He'd be back to gather more evidence later.

Once served and settled, Charlie looked at Simm to start the conversation.

"It's hard to know where to begin," he said. "We knew someone inside the house, or a frequent visitor, searched for something, likely incriminating evidence, and they'd kill to find it. We thought a journal had vanished."

No one moved. They barely breathed, not wanting to miss any detail or nuance.

"The suspects included Mike and Eli. Both had a motive since they were cut off from the family fortune. My radar led me in their direction first."

Noah held up a hand. "Wait. Mike was cut off? What are you talking about?"

"I forgot," Charlie said, dismayed. "You never heard that story."

"You and Mike are related," Simm said. "We discovered he's the illegitimate child of Ronald Wolfe, your grandfather's brother. Actually, Mike is his only child. We found it with the rest of the evidence Ethan hid. If his father had acknowledged him, he would've inherited the fortune, and neither you nor Ethan would've been in line."

"I didn't know." Astonishment filled Noah's voice. "Is Mike aware of this?"

"We're not sure," Simm said. "But if he was, it gave him a motive for revenge. Eli faced a similar situation. If you were removed, he'd be next in line to inherit, making him our top choice."

"We couldn't imagine anyone else having the motive or the inclination," Charlie said.

Simm's gaze slid to the canines lying with Harley's back nestled against Bosco's stomach. "The dogs pointed us in the right direction," he said.

Bosco sensed his moment of glory. His ears twitching, he raised his head to look at a confused Noah. Harley's snores continued uninterrupted. Realizing treats were not being handed out, Bosco resumed his position and fell asleep.

"Charlie and I were outside late last night." Simm didn't explain their argument and the reason they were in the backyard. "The dogs reacted to something or someone in the tunnel. With a locked door on this end, we went to the other side." He nodded in that direction. "The table still blocked the entrance."

Simm allowed that information to sink in. Noah was the first to respond.

"Another access to the tunnel."

"There had to be," Simm said. "Ray mentioned hidden passageways in his home. Last night, we assumed there was one we hadn't found."

Charlie cleared her throat. "When somebody attacked me in the tunnel, the dogs didn't react to anyone entering or leaving from this end. It had to be someone free to circulate within the house undisturbed, known by the dogs, and unafraid of Bosco."

Another ear twitched, and the mastiff opened an eye.

"Since the doors were kept locked, we narrowed it down to the house's occupants," Simm said. "We eliminated Walt. It was risky for him to stage his own attempted murder."

Walter's eyes widened at the statement. He might be many things, but he wasn't dumb enough to take that chance.

"Noah hired us, and since he wouldn't hire ace detectives expecting us to fail, we removed him from the list of suspects," Simm said with a slight smile. "That left the women."

Sarah straightened. "Me?"

"It was possible," Charlie said. "You're intelligent and computer-savvy. Your ex-husband is a hacker who could've helped you. And you desperately wanted to study all the documents from the tunnel."

"Blonde, fitting everyone's description, and aware of the family's wealth," Simm added. "Maybe you stole Ethan's money and needed to get into this house to hide your tracks. A possibility."

A dark red flush climbed Sarah's cheeks as she averted her gaze.

"We went into the research room last night. Unfortunately, Clarisse had already destroyed your work." Simm gave Sarah a sympathetic look. "We left everything as it was. I found the secret door in the back of the closet, and Charlie had a great idea," Simm said, looking at his wife to take the lead.

"I thought of the poem Sarah deciphered and remembered Ethan's penchant for puzzles. We took a chance and applied the same directions. Down the steps, left, then right." Charlie beamed a smile. "It was there. A small hiding place built into the wall. It looked like a recent addition, something Ethan probably made, placing it in a spot that used the same directions."

"A small chest was in there, and the antique key opened it. It contained a USB storage device, along with a journal implicating Clarisse's father and Marcus in various illegal activities, written by David Wolfe," Simm said. "I assume Clarisse took Ethan's laptop after he died and worried about him making a copy, rightly so."

"The dogs heard someone last night," Charlie said. "Clarisse must've descended into the room within the tunnel to make a final sweep before they left. Then, she went into the research room and destroyed it, looking for the journal and the digital copies."

"We still needed to prove who the culprit was beyond a doubt. We had access to two fountains of information." Simm said and nodded toward the couple on the sofa. Proud smiles lit their faces. "As we learned, this is an older, affluent area. Most estates passed from generation to generation, staying in the same families. Mr. Brown and Mrs. McCollum lived among them all their lives and knew the connections. They recognized your name, Sarah, and filled us in on the gossip about the stolen wine formula."

Sarah squirmed, her confession tumbling out. "It's true someone in my family stole the formula, but I didn't suspect it until after we came here. I was too shocked and embarrassed to say anything. And I knew Eli would be furious if he found out." She studied her hands in her lap before lifting her head and sweeping her gaze over the group, bringing it to rest on Noah. "My mission was twofold. The family history and connections fascinated me, and I hoped they'd help to find Ethan's killer and the money. But I also wanted to discover the truth about the formula theft. And I did. I'm sorry."

Noah reached over and wrapped a hand around one of hers. "How did you think I'd react? It happened decades ago. You weren't involved." Bewilderment filled his expression and his tone.

"I didn't know what to think, needing to see the proof for myself before showing it to you. I intended to tell you about it." Her tone pleaded for forgiveness.

Noah squeezed her hand and smiled. "We'll discuss it later." He nodded at Charlie and Simm to resume their explanation.

Charlie replied with a relieved smile. The stress resulting from the wine formula theft explained much of Sarah's fluctuating behavior, and Noah's reaction demonstrated his feelings toward her.

"Luckily, Charlie had come across a photo in the box that caught her attention," Simm said. "Why don't you explain, honey?"

"It was Marcus. He was with two other men. One was your father," Charlie said, glancing at Noah. "The other one was familiar. I saw him somewhere before. When we realized Clarisse might be our suspect, I remembered seeing him at Winston Simmons' funeral. Clarisse's father. The three men were connected. It was enough to put Clarisse on the top of our list."

"It brought back into focus the mystery woman," Simm said. "Mr. Brown saw her, so we visited him and showed him pictures of Sarah and Clarisse. You can guess his answer."

"I recognized her right away," said Ray Brown. "That arrogant look she gave me was unforgettable."

It was a look Clarisse didn't display often, preferring to assume the persona of innocent, loving, and submissive wife. But Charlie snapped a photo that morning during her tirade about the car. She'd never caught the same expression on Sarah, but she had several of her concentrated face. Regardless, Mr. Brown eliminated the researcher from the start.

"We didn't understand the exact connection between Marcus Vaughn, Ian Bowan, and David Wolfe," Simm said. "But our friends helped us." He nodded toward the older couple. "They remembered Ian as a close friend of David's."

Noah settled on a chair, his hands clenched. "How did Ethan get tangled in this mess?"

Simm leaned forward, ready to unravel the web. "We only have assumptions, but here's our theory. Ethan discovered the diary and stored information from it on his computer—all of it dangerous for Clarisse's father and Marcus. We think Clarisse, egged on by one of them, got close to Ethan. The goal? Find those implicating documents. But Ethan caught on, hid the journal, and planned to turn her in. Clarisse rigged the fire to silence him."

"That's impossible," Walter said, rousing himself from his daze. "Clarisse couldn't kill anyone. She's my wife, a mother..." Pain filled his eyes, and his voice faltered.

Charlie hated to add to Walter's agony, but someone needed to tell him, and it was better to be them. "Simm studied the photos of the aftermath of the fire," Charlie said. "Somebody swept away traces of footprints. I can think of only one reason to do so. They were distinctive, perhaps a woman's shoes. Baxter confirmed no women worked on the site. Not conclusive, but it's another piece of evidence."

Charlie's heart went out to the two men, one whose wife betrayed and almost killed him, and the other who lost his brother.

"I called Albert, your family butler. He told me Clarisse was absent the night of the fire," Simm said. "Albert keeps a strict timetable of the comings and goings in the house. He said Clarisse was often away when Walter traveled on business trips. She claimed girl-getaways."

"She had an affair with Ethan." Devastation colored Walter's features. "I didn't know."

Charlie suspected Walter's business kept him blind to his wife's activities.

"Little things became clearer," Charlie said. "Clarisse persuaded Walt to come and insisted on staying until she found the evidence. She came up empty-handed, but I guess she realized she had to leave and find another plan. She didn't know about the photo I found or the USB." Charlie glanced at her husband. "She said things to Simm, trying to distract us from our mandate. The message on the door, the attack in the tunnel, the research destruction, and the poisoning were all distractions. She was blowing smoke, hoping we wouldn't see through it, and we'd decide to leave."

"Blowing smoke? I could've died!" Walter said, his eyes filled with distress.

"We don't know if you were targeted specifically, or if she slipped it into the bottle, but as the most frequent drinker of whiskey among us, you were the likely intended victim. I don't think she cared, as long as someone provided a diversion and scared us away," Simm said. His expression turned sheepish. "I rigged your car so it wouldn't start. Needed time to meet with our co-conspirators." He nodded toward the elderly couple. "And I briefed Detective Baxter."

"What about the money?" Sarah asked. "Wasn't that the motive for killing Ethan?"

"It could've been," Charlie said. "But we think it was a bonus. Clarisse and/or her father had the means to hire a professional hacker to move the funds. The opportunity was there for her to feather her nest. We suspect Brent Holmes, the finance guy, either caught on or helped, and they eliminated him too. The police chief in Jamaica got rich overnight."

A horrified silence fell over the group. The depths Clarisse and her accomplices sank to for the sake of money shocked everyone, but none so much as the two men most affected.

"What else?" Noah asked, his eyes narrowed. "What are you not saying? You implied she's involved in something other than this."

Charlie wrung her fingers and glanced at Simm. She needed to preface the answer to Noah's question. "We don't know. It's just a faint suspicion. Marcus Vaughn had close family ties..." She let the sentence hang. Noah didn't need any further explanation. Marcus had a connection to his family's deaths, and Clarisse had a connection to Marcus. Could it be? Had they blamed Walter for something Clarisse orchestrated?

"It was through Ian and Clarisse that I met Marcus," Walter said, raising his head in a daze. "The two families were friends forever. Ian and Marcus did business together."

Walter's gaze connected with Noah's, and his eyes widened in alarm, realizing what everyone suspected. "Do you think...?"

"Let's not think anything until we meet with Baxter," Simm said. "Within the next few hours, I expect answers."

CHAPTER 51

Charlie was the first to spot the detective circling the house. She signaled him to join their small group in the backyard while Noah hunted for an extra chair.

Charlie had invited Mr. Brown and Mrs. McCollum to have a late lunch with them, an invitation they accepted with delight. Sarah helped Charlie throw together a light meal, and they ate outside to take advantage of the beautiful day. A day marred by painful revelations of betrayal, greed, and murder.

Simm and Noah set up a table, and even Walter helped gather chairs. When asked, Baxter admitted he hadn't eaten yet, so Charlie scurried to prepare another plate.

Her stomach fluttered as she waited to hear about Clarisse's questioning. She watched the others fidget and play with their food. Only Ray and Elsa seemed relaxed, reminiscing about the Wolfe family and the neighborhood during their youth. Walter scowled, his world unraveling. They all wanted answers, and the detective's mealtime briefing was their lifeline.

Finally, he set down his utensils, took a last sip of water, and cleared his throat. "You're curious, so I'll fill you in. We interrogated and arrested Mrs. Simmons this morning."

Charlie's stomach churned. Hearing it aloud shook her. Walter flinched beside her.

"Simm provided us with the basics of our case against her." The detective nodded in her husband's direction. "Many questions and assumptions remained, as you surely realize."

"She talked?" Simm asked. Charlie shared his fear that Clarisse would hold her peace and refuse to cooperate.

"Not at first, but once she realized what we knew and how we intended to go about finding the rest, she caved." He sighed. "It's long and complicated, but the gist of it is that Clarisse's father, Ian Bowen, had shady dealings with Noah's father, David Wolfe. They brought Marcus Vaughn onboard. At that time, Clarisse had an affair with him."

Walter groaned and fell back in his seat. Charlie squeezed his hand, her heart aching.

"It's still unclear if her involvement with Vaughn was voluntary or forced," Baxter said. "She seems to have a complicated relationship with her father. It lies somewhere between devotion and fear. I have yet to meet him, but he must be quite a guy." His lips twisted into a grimace.

"There's a diary that documented everything," the detective continued. "They tasked her with the job of finding it."

"And that task involved having an affair with Ethan?" Noah asked.

"Yes. She needed to get into the house. The secret passageways and the tunnel. She couldn't find the underground room with the documents, nor the hiding place in the passageway. Ethan caught on and confronted her." The detective's voice lowered. "With her father's guidance, Clarisse arranged the fire. They eliminated Ethan, and while they were at it, they hijacked the money. We had Simm's photos of the device and how it was set up. Apparently, she lost the remote control that night and she'd been sifting through the hedges looking for it."

Charlie recalled the day Clarisse gave her flowers and how she'd noticed the twigs and leaves on her clothing. She shuddered.

Sarah, appearing confused, spoke. "But I thought you covered up the fire." A flush climbed her cheeks when she realized what she'd said, and she looked to Simm for help.

"That's okay," the detective said. "I didn't come across as a boy scout. I get that. But my hands were tied. I figured out I needed Simm and Charlie to untie them for me." He grimaced. "Clarisse's father paid off my boss, Matt Lynch, to cover up the fire. And the cop posted to protect the scene got a chunk of change. Matt instructed me not to investigate any further. He wanted it declared a clear-cut accident."

Baxter turned his gaze to Noah. "It went against the grain. It was wrong. Lynch was corrupt, but I had no proof. It wasn't just losing my job. That would've been one thing. But they threatened to build a fake case against me, and I'd have done jail time. I needed to find a way out."

Charlie looked at the circle of people. All except Walter leaned forward, entranced by the detective's account, like a group of children listening to campfire stories.

But her brother-in-law slouched in his chair, his eyes glazed and his mouth slack.

Baxter continued. "I suspected they paid Matt to cover-up the fire. I also think he influenced his Jamaican counterpart to declare Brent Holmes' death an accident. Still need to build that case. It was no accident. The question is whether Holmes was involved in the money theft or became suspicious. Either way, Ian Bowan made sure he died."

Charlie felt a heaviness in her chest. Two people lost their lives because of someone else's greed. Charlie couldn't understand how anyone thought human lives held no value compared to their own desires.

"I couldn't look into it without my boss finding out, but Simm took care of it. He found enough proof to create a suspicion, and they arrested Lynch this morning," Baxter said.

Charlie had never seen the man so relaxed, the lines of tension in his face erased.

"I'll give credit where it's due. My hacker friend did the grunt work and it lead to Matt Lynch," Simm said.

"What about the money?" Charlie asked the cop. "Do you know where it is?"

"Detective Webber and his experts are working on it. With what we got from Clarisse, we're confident we'll trace it." The detective looked at Noah. "Give it a few days, and it'll be yours."

Noah gave him a small nod, but Charlie saw the cop's revelations take their toll on him, as did the events of the past week. He'd lost touch with his brother and didn't help him through the crisis that took his life. If he'd seen the signs of trouble and noticed the changes in Ethan, he may have prevented the tragedy. Instead, his brother dealt with Clarisse's betrayal alone. Had he been in love with her? Why go to such lengths to hide the evidence? Was he trying to protect her, or was he aware her father had far-reaching tentacles? And what of Daphne's hidden pages? Did he know what secrets they held? Had he discovered Mike's true identity? Did he try to hide it or was he waiting for the right moment? They'd probably never know his reasoning, but Noah would always live with his guilt.

Baxter swiveled toward Simm. "I did what you asked. Questioned her about Marcus and the incident in Gatineau." He slid a quick glance at Noah. "I didn't get a confession, but I've got several leads to follow up. The Montreal fire investigator told me about the device used to set the fire in your pub. I think history repeated itself."

Charlie felt a stab of pain. When they were in Gatineau the previous year, someone had tried to burn down their pub, probably to make them abandon the case and run back to Montreal. Fortunately, they didn't succeed. The pub was saved, and Frank handled everything for them. The arsonist was never caught. Now, another arrow pointed to Clarisse, taking them full circle back to Gatineau and the tragic accident that changed Noah's life forever. The queen of distraction at work again.

Charlie's gaze roamed over the group. Trust had been twisted into a weapon—sharp, unforgiving, and wielded by hands that knew only betrayal and evil.

"It's a terrible thing, what people do for money," said Mr. Brown. "I came from a rich family and lived a good life, but I'm still alone and lonely. I'd rather be poor and have a happy life."

Mrs. McCollum reached over and squeezed his hand. "I know what you mean, Ray. I feel the same."

CHAPTER 52

"Glad to be back?" Frank asked.

"Ecstatic." Her smile radiated her feelings. "No place like home."

"Another great experience." His tone was sarcastic. "You guys know how to pick 'em."

"This one was the least scary for me, I think."

"Someone attacked you in a dark tunnel," Frank reminded her, his brows raised.

"In hindsight, Clarisse attacked me. I could've taken her on. I didn't realize who it was. I assumed it was a man."

"The house was haunted," Frank added with a smirk.

Charlie rolled her eyes. "Funny. Clarisse was smart and knew how to get to me. Planting that recording in the passageway was a stroke of genius." She poked a finger into Frank's ribs. "But she didn't succeed. I didn't run away screaming."

"You're a tough one. But Walter almost died."

"I agree. That was scary." She set down her towel. "The best thing is the change in Simm and Walter's relationship. They're spending time together, getting to know each other again."

"Yeah, I can picture them hanging out on the couch, drinking beer, watching sports."

Charlie laughed. "Not going to happen. They're too different. And neither one of those leopards will change their spots. But at least they don't hate each other." She sighed. "Walter's having a rough time. How do you explain to your kids that mommy's gone to jail?" She couldn't prevent the tears from clogging her throat.

Charlie and Simm had spent time with Walter and the kids. Walt grappled with the enormity of Clarisse's betrayal. He met with her to work through his feelings and make sense of it all. Although he'd been aware of his wife's devotion to her father, he didn't realize the hold Ian Bowen had on her. Her father's promise to share the proceeds of their scheme helped to motivate Clarisse, allowing her the means to remain wealthy after a divorce she intended to seek. However, being a rich widow took on its own importance when she poisoned her husband. And Baxter confirmed the poison was only in Walter's glass, not in the bottle everyone had access to.

The betrayal cut deeper than any physical wound, leaving scars on Walter's soul that would take time to heal.

Charlie found Scott and Abby to be lovely, well-behaved children, with no resemblance to their parents. If anything, Scott reminded her of Simm. He chuckled when she told him so.

Both she and Simm had deep regrets about the years lost with Walt. It wasn't only time lost; it was time filled with hostility and suspicion. A suspected betrayal from someone close blinded them. The wound created a curtain of pain through which they couldn't see the person's good side, only their treachery.

Strong arms enveloped her and pulled her close, drawing her out of her deep thoughts. "They'll make it through. They have you and Simm to help."

"Hey, what are you doing with my wife?"

Charlie turned to see her smiling husband arrive, Noah and Sarah trailing behind him.

"How'd it go?" she asked, eager for news.

"Good," Noah said. "The easiest part is my place in Gatineau. There's not much there. Sarah's is more complicated."

"Including our house plans, we'll have a lot to handle," Sarah said, but her expression said she didn't mind the extra load.

Charlie was certain several lists existed and were cross-referenced on spreadsheets with diagrams and presentations attached.

Noah's arm slid across Sarah's shoulders, and he hugged her against him. "It'll be fine. We're not in a rush."

Sarah's bright smile reflected her new unburdened outlook. The strain of worrying about Noah and Eli's reaction to the formula theft was lifted from her shoulders. The admission that her ex-husband was serving time in prison because of his illicit computer expertise had been another embarrassment for the ethical professional and had added to her testiness.

The past few weeks had flown by as they dealt with police interrogations and the recovery of the money. The authorities arrested Ian Bowan and Marcus Vaughn on charges of murder, conspiracy to murder, and fraud. Other charges would likely follow once they sifted through the details in the journal.

With Clarisse's cooperation, they found and arrested the hacker she hired to bypass the system. In exchange for a lighter sentence, he told them where the funds rested. They were transferred to their rightful owner, Noah. A sizeable chunk went to Mike whose illegitimacy robbed him of his rights. Now, he lived a comfortable life in a neighboring mansion. Another significant portion went to Eli as payment for his business.

Taking over the vineyard was a simple decision. Noah could never live in the city. Being a hermit in the bush made him value the outdoors and hands-on work. Sarah's compulsion for research and organization was transferable to a vineyard for the study and creation of wine.

Eli, content with the outcome, agreed to stay on until they flew on their own. He also put to rest any rumors of past or present associations with organized crime. He admitted to bending a few rules in his lifetime, but he drew the line at criminal activity.

The way things turned out for Noah and Sarah delighted Charlie. They made a terrific couple with Noah's stoic strength balancing Sarah's intense activity.

Most of all, Sarah restored Noah's faith in love. The pain of his losses wouldn't disappear. Knowing Noah, they would always fester, but he'd have someone who understood and would help him through the worst of it.

Meanwhile, Charlie kept in touch with Mr. Brown and Mrs. McCollum. They resumed a friendship that had faded over the years. Having grown up together in Niagara-on-the-Lake, Ray's boyhood crush ended when Elsa married his best friend. He soon found his own true love and raised a family. Now, their friendship revived old memories and staved off loneliness. Charlie smiled at the thought that they had a small part in making it happen.

Noah and Sarah joined Charlie and Simm for dinner that evening. They planned to leave for Niagara early in the morning. They had business with the lawyers to transfer ownership from Eli to his nephew, and they'd scheduled meetings with contractors to renovate the old homestead. Preserving the house's historic state was a priority, but it was important it didn't collapse on top of them.

Charlie and Simm had an open invitation to visit whenever they desired. Charlie was certain they'd take them up on it, perhaps within the next few months. After that, they'd have a newborn baby on their hands.

Charlie smiled at her husband, and his hand squeezed her knee. Things were on track.

THE END

ACKNOWLEDGEMENTS

As I like to do, I took Charlie & Simm to a new location, giving them a chance to explore different areas of the country. Unfortunately, they didn't have time to take full advantage of lovely Niagara-on-the-Lake this time around.

For the residents and other people familiar with the region, please forgive my alterations to the city. The streets, the mansions, and the businesses were created in my imagination to fit the storyline, as was the fictional Butler's Pub in downtown Montreal.

I hope you enjoyed this fourth novel featuring Charlie & Simm. I would like to thank my beta readers, Timothy Gene Sojka, Cam Torrens, and Rachel McCarthy for their thoughtful advice and encouragement. Mary Ellen Bramwell deserves a huge round of applause for her extraordinary editing skills. And a big thank you to Reagan Rothe and the staff at Black Rose Writing for giving me another chance to share a story with my readers.

ABOUT THE AUTHOR

The award-winning author of mystery suspense novels, A.J. McCarthy is always on the lookout for new ideas. Her friends and family are cautious, concerned they may become a victim in her next novel. Those who are more adventurous offer up ideas and are willing to sacrifice certain family members for the cause. A.J. bides her time, waiting for the right moment and the perfect victim. She hides behind a quiet façade, and few know what she's really thinking.

A.J. grew up reading Agatha Christie, Sidney Sheldon, and many other masters of mystery and suspense, developing a lifelong love of the genre. She's a member of Crime Writers of Canada, Sisters in Crime, and International Thriller Writers. When she isn't writing, chances are she's reading.

NOTE FROM A.J. MCCARTHY

Word-of-mouth is crucial for any author to succeed. If you enjoyed *Smoke and Secrets*, please leave a review online—anywhere you are able. Even if it's just a sentence or two. It would make all the difference and would be very much appreciated.

Thanks!
A.J. McCarthy

We hope you enjoyed reading this title from:

BLACK ROSE
writing™

www.blackrosewriting.com

Subscribe to our mailing list – *The Rosevine* – and receive **FREE** books, daily
deals, and stay current with news about upcoming
releases and our hottest authors.
Scan the QR code below to sign up.

Already a subscriber? Please accept a sincere thank you for being a fan of
Black Rose Writing authors.

View other Black Rose Writing titles at
www.blackrosewriting.com/books and use promo code
PRINT to receive a **20% discount** when purchasing.